PENGUIN BOOKS

# Baby It's Cold Outside

### Readers Have Fallen in Love with
### *Baby It's Cold Outside*

'If you only read one Christmas book, make it this one'

'I read this in a day and loved every single page.
A wonderful, heart-warming, festive tale of love,
loss and finding what really matters'

'A refreshing romance filled with holiday spirit and second
chances. The perfect read for the holiday season'

'This is ADORABLE. The Christmas setting is perfect
and Dublin is lovely – it's just like a big hug. If you like
those Christmas movie channels, you'll adore this'

'Loved it! Feel good, heart-warming story that
pulls you in and doesn't let you go'

'A flipping fantastic five-star read.
Norah Jones you are my hero'

'I did not have the opportunity to devour this book – it
devoured me. I loved the descriptions of Dublin
and the festive decorations; I felt like
I could have been there myself'

'A beautiful, atmospheric read that has stolen my heart.
If you want a book that will take you away from
all your troubles then look no further!'

'Left me ⬚⬚⬚⬚⬚⬚⬚⬚⬚⬚⬚⬚ my arms and a smile

## ABOUT THE AUTHOR

Emily Bell grew up in Dublin and moved to London after university. She has had various jobs including tour guide, bookseller and pub singer, and now writes full time. She lives in north London with her husband and daughter.

# Baby It's Cold Outside

## EMILY BELL

PENGUIN BOOKS

PENGUIN BOOKS

UK | USA | Canada | Ireland | Australia
India | New Zealand | South Africa

Penguin Books is part of the Penguin Random House group of companies
whose addresses can be found at global.penguinrandomhouse.com

First published 2021
002

Copyright © Emily Bell, 2021

The moral right of the author has been asserted

Set in 12.5/14.75 pt Garamond MT Std
Typeset by Jouve (UK), Milton Keynes
Printed and bound in Great Britain by Clays Ltd, Elcograf S.p.A.

The authorized representative in the EEA is Penguin Random House Ireland,
Morrison Chambers, 32 Nassau Street, Dublin D02 YH68

A CIP catalogue record for this book is available from the British Library

ISBN: 978–1–405–95030–5

www.greenpenguin.co.uk

*To Stella*
*I love you to the moon and back.*

# 1. I've Got My Love to Keep Me Warm

## *Saturday, 14 December 2019*

There aren't many rules of singlehood, but I have made a few for myself in the two (if anyone asks, but really it's four) years in which I've been single. One: make sure you have somewhere to go for Christmas *at least* two months in advance. Two: make an effort with your family, even if they drive you mad. Oh, and three: never dump your female friends for a better offer. Unfortunately, all these rules seem to be news to my mum, who dumps me for Christmas a week and a half before I'm due round hers.

It's five o'clock on a chilly, sleety day, looking almost as if it might snow, though, typically for London, it won't commit. I've braved the West End to do some last-minute shopping and I'm in Fortnum & Mason buying some of their special lemon biscuits for my mum. She'll complain about how overpriced they are, but I know she loves them really – which I think sums up our relationship. I'm wondering whether to add some Lady Grey tea when I hear my phone and see that it's her. I hate talking in shops so I'm tempted to ignore it, but I don't ever do that because you never know when it might be your last chance to speak to someone.

'Hi, Mum,' I say, edging to the least busy corner and lowering my voice. The place is packed with Christmas shoppers going nuts over the festive treats: boxes of Turkish delight, turquoise tins of biscuits and macaroons, and gleaming rows of champagne and sparkling wine. With its deep red carpets, swags of greenery hung on all the mantels and its central staircase sparkling with giant gold baubles, it's like a Victorian Christmas card come to life. Choral music is mingling with the hum of conversation, and there's a scent of tea and gingerbread from the café downstairs. I'm feeling pretty festive – or I am until I hear her next words.

'Hi, darling, can you talk? It's about Wednesday week.'

'Wednesday week. As in Christmas?'

'Yes. Christmas. Here's the thing . . .' There's a clatter in the background; I can picture her wiping down her kitchen counter and making a cup of tea while talking on her headphones, still in her tracksuit bottoms from a long muddy walk. My mum believes in keeping busy and rarely calls me without taking care of some other task at the same time. 'I was wondering if we could actually rethink our plans? Something's come up. I know it's a pity, but we could always do something the week after?'

'You mean the week after Christmas? Really? What's come up?' I teach music at a secondary school, and I'm crawling towards the end of term next Friday.

'Well, I know you're going to think it's ridiculous. But you know that incredible woman whose book I read, who travelled around South America and had the visions . . .'

2

'And did all the drugs?'

'Not drugs, just *ayahuasca*, which is very different. It's more of a spiritual experience. Anyway, you'll never believe it, but she's here in the UK, and she's running a Yule retreat – a four-day self-healing immersion experience! In Herefordshire, fully catered.'

'With drugs?'

'There will be *ayahuasca*, but it's much more than that. Darling, I am really sorry to renege on our plans. But I feel this is exactly what I need – after this year.'

With those words, I know she's got me. I can't object to anything she does after this year. She got made redundant from her job as a PA in a travel company, aged fifty-nine: replaced by a twenty-two-year-old intern who can also explain the difference between Instagram reels and stories, for half the wages. She was understandably very cut up. So I want to be supportive. But I really, really wish she could have decided this sooner and given me and my brother time to form a plan B. Unless he already has one, of course.

'What about Miles?' I ask.

'Oh, he's going to his girlfriend's. It was no problem, so you don't have to worry about him. I called him just now.'

'That's a relief,' I say, sarcastically.

'You don't have to be like that, darling – I had to call him first; he is the youngest. You know, a trip like this could be just the thing you need, too.'

Now I'm confused; is she offering for me to come with her? It sounds all kinds of awful but maybe it

3

could be a bonding experience of some sort. 'Do you mean you'd like me to come too? What's the accommodation like?' I ask, wondering if there's any conceivable way I could come with her and hide in my room with a book.

'I'm afraid not, darling. I got the absolute last space – it was a freebie from the lady herself, and I feel I can't turn it down.'

'OK.' Well, at least I don't have to weigh up the pros and cons of taking *ayahuasca*. I take a minute instead to absorb the fact that my mum would rather spend Christmas with a bunch of strangers than with me. Is it me? Is it something I've done – have I not called her enough, or been around to visit as often as I should? And then the worst thought of all: this wouldn't be so bad if only my dad were still around. I can remember Christmas time with him and how special it was, even when we weren't together on Christmas Day itself after my parents split. He decided early on that, rather than a second sad turkey dinner with me and Miles, the best approach was for our Christmas celebration with him to feel grown-up and sophisticated. A stroll along the South Bank and a hot chocolate at the BFI café before watching a matinee showing of *It's a Wonderful Life*. Or dim sum in Chinatown, followed by an afternoon browsing in Foyles bookshop, and going home with a stack of new paperbacks. I hope he knew how much I loved those non-Christmas Christmases. He died six years ago when I was twenty-six, and my parents split up when I was twenty, so there weren't very many of them: three, to be precise.

'Well, I hope you have a nice time, if this is what you want to do,' I say to Mum. 'I'll stay at home. I'll be fine,' I add, in case she wondered.

'Darling . . . thank you for understanding. I do feel awful about it, though. So here's what I'd like to do. I'm going to share my air miles with you, for your Christmas present – you can fly anywhere in the world that you like. My treat.'

What a heartwarming gift from mother to daughter: you can go anywhere in the world you like – except my house. But I can't be too angry with her. She's not really a textbook narcissist, as my friend Kiran once claimed after too many red wines: she's just busy with her own life. And it's made me resilient. This is disappointing, but I will cope. I'm thirty-two, not twelve: I can spend a Christmas alone.

'That's nice of you, Mum, but I don't need to get on a plane. I'll hang out here.'

'What about . . .' Mum's voice pauses as we skip over the missing option, the one we never mention: Dad. 'What about your friends? I bet you can do something with them. What's Caroline doing? You've always wanted to do Christmas with friends, haven't you – it could be really great fun!'

Now I'm annoyed. I can accept her changing the plans. But I'm not prepared to be told that she's doing *me* a favour by cancelling our Christmas.

'It's fine. Look, I'm next in the queue. I'll call you later.' I hang up and put the biscuits back – I won't be able to get to the post office in time to send them – and start walking towards the door. Ella Fitzgerald is playing now, singing that she has her love to keep her warm. There's a German couple in front of me, wearing matching parkas, having a debate over different boxes of macaroons. A young mum with a baby in a sling is standing in front of the hamper selection, gazing at different options while she rests her chin on the baby's head. I push my way outside towards the exit and start walking towards the tube.

And then it happens; a wash of sadness descending over me from nowhere. Like in the early scenes of *The Wizard of Oz*, the angel lights and festive colours of Piccadilly drain away, and everything is grey and cold. The ground seems to be slipping away from under my feet. Christmas is the least of my worries, really. I could stay home and watch *Doctor Who*, or volunteer somewhere, or maybe go to Javier and Paul's. But I can't help thinking; when will it be my time? When will I be at the centre of my own life instead of on the fringes of everyone else's? A lump grows in my throat, and I'm terrified that I'm going to cry. I hate crying and never, ever let myself do it. I'm about to go down the steps of the tube, when I realize what I've been listening to – what the busker beside the entrance has been singing for the past few minutes.

It's 'River' by Joni Mitchell. I haven't heard this song

or thought about it in years. I stopped listening to it because it made me think of *him*: the only person I knew who loved it as much as I did. The busker's voice sounds Irish, and for a mad second I wonder: could it be him? I push through the crowd on the edge of Regent Street to see – but of course it's not him. This guy is blond and tanned, not dark-haired and pale. I don't know where in the world he is now, but wherever he is I am pretty sure he's no longer busking. And anyway, he never sang. He played the guitar, while I sang.

I stand, listening to the music with the crowds passing around me, until I can't listen any more. I throw a few pound coins in the busker's hat, without meeting his eye, and start walking again. I don't feel like going home to my empty flat yet; I'm sad and restless and troubled by old memories that should be long forgotten. So I turn away from the tube and I find myself drifting along Rupert Street and through Soho, looking at all the strangers laughing and chatting through the steamy windows, stepping over the puddles, lit up by neon lights and filament bulbs. A *Big Issue* seller offers me a copy of the Christmas edition. I buy it, looking at the date. December 2019. I remember sitting opposite him at that café in Italy, when he said: *If you come to Dublin, in ten years' time, I'll be there to meet you . . . I'll see you at six o'clock outside Bewley's Café on Grafton Street, on Christmas Eve.*

That was ten years ago, hard though it is to believe. The year 2019 seemed so far off, almost futuristic, when he first suggested it a decade ago, but the years flew by, and now it's here. Not that I'd expect him to remember. I had almost forgotten myself, until I realized, back in January, that it had finally rolled around. But I had other things on my mind, and my days were all full – until now.

I take out my phone, wondering who I could talk to for a boost. I am lucky: I know I can call Caroline or Kiran at any time. We've been friends since we were fifteen. If I had a body to hide, I know that Kiran would be there with a shovel. And Caroline would supply a blanket, a flask of tea and probably a podcast that would validate my feelings about it. But I don't want to talk about the memories that the song's brought flooding back. Or about my mum's decision to cancel on me. I don't want them to think that I'm inviting myself to spend Christmas with either of them – both of them have plans already, made with their husband and boyfriend, respectively. And I know they wouldn't like me to feel alone, but I'd rather talk to someone who understands what it's like to make all your own decisions all the time, and be responsible for yourself and no one else.

It's starting to rain again – a cold, thick rain, almost sleet. I've ended up in Bloomsbury Square, near the bowling alley. Coming out of my reverie, I see that I've walked all the way to my friend Joe's place, following a familiar path like a car on a GPS route. This route – from Soho to his flat – is one I must have taken several hundred times, either just with Joe or more often with our group of friends. No wonder I wandered here without thinking. His light is on; thank God. He's the person I most want to talk to right now, and how much nicer to see him in person than have to call or text. I take out my phone and dial his number.

## 2. Baby, It's Cold Outside

For most people in London, to drop in on someone at such short notice is an antisocial act on a level with spitting or littering, maybe even vandalism, depending on the time of day and the level of acquaintance. But Joe and I are like family – in fact we're obviously an upgrade from family, given what my mum has done this evening. All our group is close – we've all known each other since schooldays – but it's different with the others. Caroline is having a romantic evening with her boyfriend Stefan, from whom she's expecting a proposal at any minute. Kiran will be putting her twins to bed, and Javier and Paul are away having a romantic weekend in Bath. Joe and I are the single ones, though he's much more successful at it than me. In fact, I half expect him to be getting ready to go out on a Saturday-night date – or finishing a Friday one.

Evidently not; he answers the door in his 'soft clothes', as he calls them – a soft red flannel shirt, tracksuit bottoms and thick grey wool socks. His dark hair is standing on end, and he looks as though he's recently woken from a nap. 'Hey, stranger,' he says. 'You're freezing – come in!' He leans down to give me a quick hug.

He's got music on – probably a Spotify Christmas

mix – and it's playing one of my favourite duets: Frank Sinatra and Dorothy Kirsten singing 'Baby, It's Cold Outside.'

'You know, you can't play that song any more,' I tell him, taking off my coat. 'The lyrics are all kinds of wrong. It's basically about a guy trapping a woman in his flat while she begs to be released.'

'Oh, come on . . . Really? It's from another time. Isn't that overthinking it?'

'Mmm,' I say. 'It was so harmless when Mickey Rooney played that Japanese guy in *Breakfast at Tiffany's*, wasn't it? From another time.'

'Point taken,' Joe says. 'Hey – hold on. Hold it right there. No, over your head like it's a shawl . . .'

I freeze, on the point of unwinding my scarf. He grabs a sketchbook and pencil and executes a few quick strokes while I roll my eyes. 'Joe, seriously . . . give me a chance to get inside. Can I see?' He shows me. My reddish-brown curls are windblown, and my eyes are wild; he's even done my freckles.

'I just wanted to catch it in case we do a troll film . . .' I swipe him with the boot I've taken off before putting both of them in his specially designated shoe rack, as I've been trained. I peer at the mirror and try to smooth down my hair, but it's a law unto itself; a curly weather system that coils up at the first sign of moisture in the atmosphere.

'Sorry, Norah,' he says. 'It wasn't really for work. I just couldn't resist.'

Joe is an animator or, to be more precise, a 3D character modeller. He sketches a lot for practice, though at work I know he mainly uses programs called things like Python and Z-brush. He works for a studio based in Soho, mostly making video games, until they did an *Avatar*-style feature film last year that was a surprise megahit. I remember how worried his parents were when he gave up his engineering job to work in animation. My job as a teacher seemed so stable in comparison. But now Joe can afford the rent on a studio flat in Bloomsbury – albeit one with a dodgy landlord who can't put up the rent because of his own visa issues – and his company are moving to a new £10-million building in Brentford with a 200-seat private cinema for screenings. So you could say that it's worked out OK for him.

'Fortnums! Are we celebrating?' Joe says, looking at my bags.

'No, we're not. But you're welcome to some truffles.' I take them out of the bag and put them on his kitchen counter. I love Joe's flat. It's just one big room plus a tiny bathroom, but it's got high ceilings, bookshelves, plants that he keeps alive somehow and tall windows overlooking the street. And art everywhere – sketches hung up on nylon lines with mini clothes pegs, and original art in frames, on all the walls and over the fireplace which he's filled with pillar candles. Also a bar cart, which has been responsible for more of my hangovers than I care to remember.

'I made gingerbread, would you like some?' he asks.

'You didn't!'

'I did.' Joe puts out cake, plates and paper napkins with reindeers on them, while I curl up in my favourite chair beside his fireplace; a beaten-up leather one that's like Frasier's dad's. I see he's put up Christmas decorations; he even has a mini Christmas tree, which I haven't bothered with. Joe is really unusual in this respect, I think. Most (hashtag not all!) single men I know don't care about their surroundings, as if they're waiting for a woman to come along and 'curate their space' or at least put shades on the lamps. Joe is different; he has it all just how he likes it.

'So what's up?' he asks.

'You know I was meant to be going to my mum's for Christmas?'

'What's happened? Don't tell me she's met a guy.'

'No. It's actually quite funny, she's going on a sort of druggy retreat – a New Age thing. Anyway. I just . . .' I draw up my knees and curl my arms around them. 'I feel a bit crap, generally . . .' My voice breaks, and I'm horribly afraid I'm going to cry, again.

'OK, forget cake. Let me make you a drink. Do you want a boulevardier?'

'A boulewhat? Sure.' I take a deep ragged breath. 'Has it got whisky in it?'

'Yeah, whisky – and sweet vermouth, and campari. On ice, with orange peel.' He starts mixing and shaking, using his special cocktail-making kit that we all bought him for his thirtieth. A gift with benefits if ever there was. 'Here, light some candles.' He throws me a box of matches.

I catch it and kneel to light the candles, grateful for the task: Joe knows I always find action to be the best antidote to any sad feelings. As I strike the match and light the fat pillar candles, I start to feel a little calmer. I watch Joe pour the amber liquid over the ice, into the cut-glass tumblers that we bought at the stall in Camden Passage last summer. Whisky. Irish whisky. Dublin. Andrew.

*Come to Dublin . . . six o'clock outside Bewley's Café on Grafton Street, on Christmas Eve.*

But of course he won't show up. It's – I make a quick calculation – six years since we were last in touch. He won't remember, and even if he does there's no way that he'll be there. He will have somewhere to be and someone to be with for Christmas – unlike me. I always thought that I would, too. I never imagined that, when Christmas 2019 finally rolled around, I would be single *and* have no plans to boot.

'Norah? You OK?' Joe asks.

'Oh – yeah! I'm fine. Honestly.' I give myself a shake, trying to stay present. 'So, no date tonight? How was it last week with Kristy – Misty?'

'Felicity. Fliss. Yeah, it was good! She's nice.'

'Will you see her again?'

'Sure.' He shrugs, and I feel a pang for poor Fliss. I hope she's not waiting for his text.

As I watch him shake the cocktails, I consider how different the power balance is for Joe in his dating life than for me. For me to be single is an everyday London single girl tragedy, but for Joe it's an inexplicable mystery that nobody can account for. Personally, I think the transition from teenage geek to hot, well-paid single man happened so quickly it went to his head, and now he's having too much fun to give it up. He is boringly discreet about his dating, though, and never tells me anything interesting.

'What are you doing for Christmas, Joe? Going to your parents'?'

'No . . . as it happens, I'm a Christmas orphan also. Didn't I say? My parents are jetting off together on a no-kids-invited trip.'

'To Hong Kong?' I ask, as that's where Joe's father is from.

'No, skiing, in Austria. A thirty-fifth wedding anniversary thing.' He grins. 'So I'm not invited. And my sister's spending it with her new husband. I might do something with people from work. Some Australians have clubbed together and got a turkey – that sounds like the beginning of a joke, I know.'

It's really good to know that I have a plan B. But while he's been talking, my mind has been wandering again until I'm miles away. Four hundred miles, to be exact. Of course, it would be crazy to go to Dublin – but what if I did? There's nothing actually stopping me.

'Norah, what is it? You're obviously brooding over

something.' He hands me my drink, and I take a grateful sip.

'Nothing. It's silly. I was just thinking . . . do you remember that Irish guy I met in Italy?'

He throws himself into the armchair opposite me, clinking his ice, and sticks his feet up on a footstool. 'Yes – I think so. In Rome? Cheers, by the way.'

'Cheers.' I take a sip, feeling the whisky and sweet vermouth thaw me from the inside. 'No, it was in Verona. This is delicious, by the way.'

'Ah yes. On your Girls Gone Wild trip. What was his name again?'

I ignore that. 'Andrew.' I haven't spoken that name in years, and a shiver goes down my spine. 'It was . . . special. We kept in touch for a couple of years but we never managed to meet up again. He went to America, and I was over here. It just never worked out. But I remember he said: if you don't meet anyone, let's meet again in Dublin in ten years' time. Christmas Eve, 2019. We agreed the time and place and everything.'

Joe raises his eyebrows. 'And you're thinking of going?'

'No . . . of course not.' I add a second later: 'Though, it's not like I have anywhere else to be.'

'Yes you do,' Joe says instantly. 'You can hang out with me. I'm sure I could bring someone to the Australian turkey feast.'

I'm touched at this. 'Thanks, Joe. That's good to know.' But my thoughts keep circling back to Andrew.

'Except . . . Do you really think it would be so crazy, to go?'

Joe runs his fingers through his hair, which is thick and wavy yet enviably obedient. 'Well, of course it would. I mean, why haven't the two of you met or been in touch before now? Why this cutesy drama of writing your number on a paper plane and seeing if it floats down the stream to your house or whatever? Surely he could have suggested a trip or a visit at some point in the past ten years . . .'

'He did,' I say. 'But I was with someone by then – Matt, remember? Andrew was in London for a concert and he asked me to meet, and I said no.'

'Oh.' Joe's face changes. 'That does make a difference.'

'And we did keep in touch . . . we emailed. But then – not long after that concert – we lost touch. And I changed my email address, and I think he changed his – I didn't get a reply to my last message anyway.'

'Have you googled him?'

'Of course I have – not for a while now, but there was nothing last time I looked. There was maybe *one* entry that could be him, but no picture, so I don't even know if it was him. He never did any social media or anything, so he disappeared.'

'Give me twenty seconds. I'll find him,' says Joe.

But Joe doesn't have any more luck than me; he finds an Andrew Power who's a flautist, but nobody who looks like the person I knew.

'You know, he could have googled you if he wanted to,' Joe says.

I point to my chest. 'Have we met? Norah. Jones.'

Joe grins. My parents couldn't believe it when a woman who shared my fusty, old-fashioned name had a giant pop hit. Then, as I got older, there were so many jokes about me inviting everyone to the Grammys, so many times my friends told me to 'Come away with me', so many attempts to change my ringtone to a Norah song while my back was turned. It was also not helpful to my own fledgling singing career – like trying to be a model when your name was Naomi Campbell. Even if you changed it, it was like a sign from God: don't bother.

'Try harder, mate. Norah. Jones. Teacher. North London. There you go.' He shows me his phone. 'Found you. Nice photo.'

'He doesn't know I went into teaching,' I say triumphantly. 'It was after we lost touch. When we met I was still trying to be a singer.'

Joe shakes his head. 'You weren't trying; you were a singer. *Are* a singer.'

'You're too kind,' I say, trying to hide the wobble in my voice. 'Anyway. I'm sure he could find me if he wanted to, but maybe he's just moved on.'

'Yes, and so have you! Haven't you?'

'Evidently not, because here I am.' I shrug, trying not to think about everything that's gone wrong. My mum. My dad. This Christmas. Being single at thirty-two and

19

not loving it the way I'm supposed to: a double failure. 'Look, believe me, I know how nuts it is. But what have I got to lose?'

'Nothing, but I hate to think of you being disappointed. If you go and he's not there. Which he won't be, I'm afraid. He'll be married with kids or living with someone, or even if he's not he won't show up. Because men – yes, I'm generalizing – men don't tend to think about the past in the same way that women do. I never think about my exes, let alone girls I met on holiday. He won't remember this arrangement.'

'I know that! But thanks for mansplaining the situation to me.'

'I don't think it can be called mansplaining when I'm explaining . . . what it's like to *be a man*,' he protests.

'Whatever. Look, I do realize he most likely won't show up. But he might, you know. And I'll never know if I don't go.'

'Are you seriously going to do this?'

I've finished my cocktail by now. 'Actually, yes. I think I am. I mean, why not? What have I got to lose? Except ten minutes waiting on Grafton Street.' I sigh. 'It would be pretty grim, though. To go all the way there by myself and wait in the cold for someone who probably won't show up.'

'Well, yeah.' Joe gets up and starts to make another round of drinks. As I watch him, I think about the fact that he's said he's at a loose end for Christmas. And an idea begins to form in my mind.

'I don't suppose . . . you would come with me?' I ask.

'With you? To Dublin?'

'Yes. Why not? It could be fun,' I say hopefully. 'I mean, we could have fun. Pints . . . see some art . . . stay somewhere nice . . . Maybe?'

He shakes the cocktail shaker, not saying a word. 'You wouldn't have to, um, wait around on the street with me,' I add. 'Christmas Eve, you could do your thing. You could wait back in the hotel, with a whisky and a book.'

'Thanks. That sounds like a riot.'

'Well, the rest of the trip would be fun! And it would mean so much to me. Joe? Would you . . . consider it?'

He pours the drinks wordlessly and hands me mine. 'Maybe. But no traditional music. And no jazz, either. I'd consider it – on those conditions. Oh, and we'd have to have somewhere nice to stay. And at least one really good dinner out.'

'Really?' I stare at him, starting to smile for what feels like the first time all day. Having him come along would make it feel less pathetic and terrifying. If it's a trip with a friend, and I happen to drop by somewhere at 6 p.m. – that's so, so much less pressure than if I fly four hundred miles purely to see a guy I last saw ten years ago.

'Would you really come with me, Joe? Seriously?'

'I mean, I think it's a terrible idea. But OK. I will come with you.'

'That would be great! Thank you!' I pause. 'What will the others say?'

21

'How do you mean?' But he knows what I mean. We have all been away together before, loads of times. And I've done trips with just the girls. But for me and Joe to go away, just the two of us, for *Christmas* – that will definitely be seen as odd. Remarks will be passed, and explanations will be wanted. Side chats will be created, and jokes about us two – the last singletons standing – will be made.

'We could just not tell them,' he offers, just as I expected him to. Joe's great quality is that he knows how to make life good and to make the people around him happy. His less good quality is that he will do almost anything to keep them happy, including going to absurd lengths to avoid confrontation. Like when he didn't actually tell his parents he had given up his engineering job until his first video game had a release date – a whole year later.

'Of course we'll tell them. Why shouldn't we? We'll just tell them that . . .' But here I'm stuck, because I don't particularly want to tell everyone that I'm flying to Ireland in search of my long-lost crush from a decade ago. It's stupid enough without having to provide hourly updates on the group WhatsApp. Though I will tell Caroline. She is one of my best friends, and she might find it odd if I don't say anything; not least because it also happens that she once went out with Joe. It was a long time ago, and it was only for six months, but still. As we've established, women remember these things.

'Well, let's worry about that later,' says Joe, in one of his favourite phrases. 'Let's finish our drinks and then we'll look at flights.' Another favourite phrase.

'Great. Let's do it on your computer.' I stand up, my heart hammering. Christmas 2019. It's here. It's happening. And Joe's coming with me. 'Oh, wow, look outside. Is that actually snow?' I go to the window and look out. It's the same as earlier; it's slush, sleet. But it's not snow, not yet.

'Close, but not quite,' Joe says, standing beside me.

'The story of my life,' I crack back. But excitement builds as I think: maybe not for much longer.

# 3. Remember Me

After I leave Joe's, I head for the tube and squeeze myself on to a Piccadilly Line train towards Turnpike Lane. As I sway with the crowd of festive shoppers, my mind drifts back ten years ago, to a different train. Instead of the bags of Christmas gifts, I see backpacks piled on each other in the corner of a train carriage where we're sitting in second class. Instead of the steamy fug of the London tube, I can feel the sun beating through the window where I've leaned my tanned arm. I can hear the rattle and hiss of the train taking us from Florence to Verona, all those years ago.

Caroline, Kiran and I had all decided to take two weeks' holiday together and backpack around Italy. We had originally intended to do this in the months after uni, but we were too terrified that we wouldn't land jobs unless we got straight into it. I was temping by day and trekking around doing gigs by night, singing in every pub or restaurant in London that would have me and my Casio keyboard. Mum and Dad having split up during my second year at university, I was now living with Dad in his flat in Ealing, to save on rent. Caroline had managed to land a job at *Industrial Metals*, a trade magazine that did what it said on the tin; we made that joke, a lot, but we were in awe of her for actually working in journalism. And Kiran, lucky Kiran, was working at a sort of headhunter firm – it seemed to specialize more in cutting heads than hunting them, but we didn't press her too hard on the specifics. She was very open and upfront about the fact that she wasn't prepared to live on rice and fishfingers a second longer, recession or no recession.

It was 2009, which in retrospect seems like another era. Caroline and I still had Nokia bricks, and we navigated our way around with a much-thumbed *Lonely Planet*, while Kiran had the far more swanky *Rough Guide*. She also had a smartphone, but it only worked when it connected to Wi-Fi, which not all of the hostels had. So we divided and conquered. Kiran was our tech support, and Caroline was our art history guide, telling us what we were supposed to be looking at as we trailed around various churches and squares prior to stopping for a beer or coffee. And I was the sensible one, who had an extra phone charger and adapter (Caroline had forgotten hers), a month's supply of paracetamol and a printout of all the hostels which we had managed to pre-book, ordered by date with their addresses.

In Italy, though, the system had fallen apart. We had managed to get on the wrong train in Florence – making a classic mistake by mixing up *arrivi* and *partenze* – and found ourselves heading to Venice instead of Rome. We had hopped off at the first stop, Verona, where we found the tourist office closed. After spending a fruitless half hour at a payphone trying to find accommodation, we had given up and sat down to regroup at a café.

The scene couldn't have been more idyllic. We were in Verona, home of Romeo and Juliet, a town of beautiful mellowed brown and gold buildings and medieval alleys where balconies almost kissed under a heavenly blue sky. Our café was in a square overlooking the famous Roman amphitheatre, where the opera would be held later. A fountain nearby trickled in three tiers, sparkling in the sun. But it was six o'clock in the evening, and we had nowhere to sleep. We had to decide whether to try and catch an overnight train back to Rome or to actually pay for – horrors – a hotel room as opposed to a bunk bed in a hostel, like we usually did. Kiran was in favour of the hotel idea, while Caroline and I were against it.

'It would blow our budget for the entire week, Kiran,' Caroline was saying, when we were interrupted by a new voice.

'Sorry, guys …' A young guy around our age approached and half-raised a hand. He sounded Irish. 'I don't want to interrupt. But we just heard you saying you're stuck for somewhere to stay?'

We all stared at him, making split-second assessments. Kiran and I also looked instinctively at Caroline, to see if she had somehow attracted him to our table. As well as being our art historian, Caroline was also the boy magnet. She had always been pretty, but somehow this week, with her tan and her long legs and her big brown eyes, she was emanating or exuding something that Kiran and I weren't. She had already caused an older French man in Siena to offer to move to London; had got us invited to an amazing house party at Genoa; and we had actually left Florence at dawn to escape one of her admirers, who had told her he would 'follow her through her dreams' in a genuinely quite worrying way. It was so obviously out of her control we couldn't even be jealous; she was just having *that* moment. Mine would come soon, hopefully.

'It must be something to do with your break-up with Dan,' Kiran declared, referring to her horrible university boyfriend. 'Your light is *on*.'

Incredibly, though, this guy didn't seem to have noticed Caroline. He was looking directly at me. He wasn't obviously gorgeous, but with his dark hair ruffled over his brow and his grey eyes squinting in the sun, he was attractive in a way that was even more unsettling.

'Yeah – we arrived this afternoon, and everywhere's booked up,' I said.

'We weren't even supposed to come to Verona,' said Kiran. 'We got on the wrong train.'

I winced; I hadn't wanted to admit that, as it made us sound like such novices – helpless girls unable to navigate basic public transport *or* read a map.

'That's what they call a happy accident, then,' said our new friend. He smiled, and I got a shock – a feeling like déjà vu, a certainty that we had been here before, that this had already happened or that I had met him somewhere, some time.

'Anyway,' he continued. 'It was just to let you know that there is definitely room in the hostel where we're staying. It's up in the hills above town, about twenty minutes' walk. It's a beautiful old place ... a whole crowd of German folks just moved on, and the girl on the desk was saying to me today that they have vacancies. It's pretty good value too. Sixty for a triple, which is what we've got. Are there just the three of you?' he asked, still addressing me.

My heart sped up slightly at the question as the two others were busy telling him that, yes, it was the three of us and it sounded great. 'If you give me the number, I'll call them?' Kiran asked, bringing out her phone.

He produced a flip notebook from his hip pocket, and Kiran keyed in the number while I tried not to stare at his tanned forearms or handsome profile. Instead of the ubiquitous slogan T-shirt, shorts and sandals uniform sported by most backpackers, he wore a white shirt and dark blue cotton trousers, with scuffed white tennis shoes. I noticed his two friends at a nearby table. One of them had a cello case propped up beside his table, and I also noticed two other cases – violins? This guy seemed too at home here to be another backpacker but he didn't seem like a busker either.

'Booked us a triple!' Kiran said triumphantly after a brief conversation. 'We can arrive any time, reception's open 'til nine.' We all shrieked with genuine relief and euphoria.

'Thank you,' I said awkwardly, forcing myself to

meet his eyes. They were even more attractive than I'd thought; a strange pale grey, almost silver.

'Great. Enjoy,' he said, and paused before he added, 'Ah – myself and my friends are having a drink at the table over there if you wanted to join us? Depending on your plans.'

'Great. We'll come join you in a minute,' Caroline beamed. This was our standard move; it gave us time to strategize and agree our level of commitment in advance, rather than trying to decide awkwardly in front of them.

'So . . . that's your evening sorted, Norah,' Kiran said, as soon as he moved away.

'Don't be ridiculous. I barely spoke two words to him.'

'The looks, though,' said Caroline. 'I got a bit burned there – from all the sparks flying.'

'Ha, ha,' I said, feeling my face engulf in flames. 'What's our plan? Quick drink and then back to the hostel to shower and dump bags?'

'Yes please. I'm on day three with these shorts. They're starting to stand up by themselves,' said Caroline.

'That's why you need smart wool. I'm on day five of this T-shirt,' Kiran said proudly. She was obsessed with packing light and had a micro-wardrobe of strange sports fabrics that allegedly didn't need washing.

'We know,' said Caroline. I joined in the laugh, though I felt completely distracted and irrationally worried that we were taking too long and that the guy – I didn't even know his name – would think we weren't coming and leave with his friends. Or, more realistically, that he would notice Caroline this time around and ignore me.

'OK, let's go,' Caroline said. 'Make sure you sit beside him, though, Norah! Let's not have another Tom catastrophe.' She was referring to the time when I had invited my university crush over for a 'dinner party' and then spent all evening in the kitchen pounding spices for a totally forgettable 'Thai curry' which tasted worse than a packet.

'Never again,' I agreed. We stood up and started walking over to their table.

'So what's with the instruments? Are you guys playing in the opera?' Kiran asked, once we were all sitting around together – with me beside Andrew, as he turned out to be called.

'Ha! No, we are not playing in the opera,' said Conor, Andrew's friend – a smiley, slightly toothy guy with a balding forehead and a charming manner. The third Musketeer, Niall, was small, dark and shy, and predictably entranced by Caroline. They had all just graduated from Trinity College, Dublin, where they had been studying music.

'We are actually – oh God, this is embarrassing. Do you want to tell them?' Andrew asked Conor.

'We're on a small concert tour of chamber music, plus two weddings. We were *supposed* to be a sextet. Yes, well may you laugh,' Conor said, as the girls cackled.

'I didn't even know a sextet was a thing,' Kiran said.

That was something I envied about her; she was never embarrassed to admit she didn't know something, which conversely made her seem much more confident and intelligent than those of us who prevaricated and tried to cover up our doubts – i.e., me.

'It's a thing. Two cellos, two violas and two violins. Except when three of them go to a water park and spend the day running around in the thirty-degree heat without reapplying sunscreen ... and then get heat-stroke and have to drop out in the interval of our concert last night,' said Andrew. 'We left them steeping in cold baths, back at the hostel. So now we're a trio. Thank God we didn't lose both violins, really.'

'God knows what will happen tomorrow,' said Niall. 'We're supposed to be flying home. We'll have to scrape them out of the bed, maybe Medivac them to the airport.'

'It does make you wonder, like,' said Conor. 'How did white people manage to invade everywhere when we can't even last a day outside without frazzling to a crisp?'

Everyone laughed, but I said, 'Actually, there's a book that explains exactly that. It's called *Guns*, um ...' I trailed off, worried that I'd misjudged the mood or that I sounded like I was lecturing everyone or ruining the joke. But Kiran and Caroline were looking proudly at me, the same way we gazed proudly at Caroline when she knew the difference between a Doric and an Ionic column, or at Kiran when she explained how the

Facebook algorithm worked. We were lifting each other up, long before the phrase was even invented. '*Guns, Germs and Steel*,' I finished.

'*Guns, Germs and Steel*,' Andrew repeated. He took out his notebook. 'I'll make a note of it.'

This seemed to be the signal for the other boys to start hooting. 'The notebook! It's going in the notebook! Watch out, Norah. Once it goes in the notebook, there's no going back.'

'This whole trip has gone in the notebook,' said Conor. 'Italian phrases, *churches* he wants to visit, books to read, little notes on how his fellow musicians can improve . . . it's all there in black and white.'

'We're hoping he will donate the notebook to the Trinity archives, when he's a famous composer,' said Niall.

They cackled while Andrew grinned good-natured curses. It was obviously a running joke of the trip, like the ones we had, and equally unfunny to anyone else.

But I saw Caroline and Kiran widen their eyes at me, because what the boys didn't know was that I also had a notebook. I, too, was writing down my Italian phrases and lists of things to see. *It's just a notebook*, I told myself. *It's not a sign, it doesn't mean we're soulmates*. But I also loved that Andrew was someone who was willing to write down the name of a book. I had noticed how rarely any of us talked about books or ideas or even good films these days. Almost as if we had packed all that stuff away with our degrees and now we just talked about rent and jobs and salaries.

'Norah is a musician too! She's a singer,' Kiran said.

'Classical?' Conor asked.

'Oh, no – nothing like you guys,' I said quickly. 'I do jazz covers in pubs. Cole Porter and stuff. It's mainly for fun really.' This wasn't false modesty; I wasn't prepared to embarrass myself in front of these guys, who were clearly all going to be career musicians. I didn't know what I was going to be, but I was pretty sure I wasn't going to be competing with the real Norah Jones.

'So what are you planning for this evening?' Andrew asked me later, while the others were wrapped in an animated discussion of the horrors of house and flat shares (Niall was winning: his flatmate boil-washed her underwear in the communal saucepans).

'Probably a shower and bed. It's been a long day,' I said, before kicking myself. Did I really need to sound quite so grandmotherly? 'What about you?'

'I want to go to the opera.'

'That opera?' I say blankly, pointing at the giant amphitheatre in front of us.

Andrew grins. 'The very one. The others aren't so keen, so I was going to go on my own.'

'But you're musicians! Don't you all love opera?' Caroline says.

Conor said, 'No, now here you're making a very common mistake – sorry, misconception. Chamber musicians generally have no time for opera. It's too big and brassy.'

'Noisy,' said Niall. 'So much yelling. So few good bits.'

Andrew said, 'Ignore them. It's *Carmen* – that's basically nothing but hits. Tickets go on sale from seven, so we'd have to queue. I'll be going anyway, so no pressure.'

'Sounds great,' I said, before I could chicken out. 'Anyone else?'

'Oh,' Caroline said. 'I'd love to, but I am knackered. Also broke. I could do with a shower and beer at the hostel . . . would you be up for that, Ki Ki?'

I knew that Caroline would have loved to go to the opera; she was a hopeless romantic and loved all things Italian and dramatic. She was opting out because she didn't want to cramp my style. That's how good a friend she was.

Kiran didn't seem to have picked up on all the subtleties; she just seemed exhausted. I had always known she loved her sleep, but she was famous for it on this holiday; she could go all day but then she needed nine hours minimum every night. We practically had to drag her out of bed in the mornings. 'I am *dying* for a shower,' she said.

So that was how I ended up going to the opera in Verona with Andrew, barely hours after meeting him. The sun was casting long shadows across the soft ochre stones of the amphitheatre as we queued for tickets, and then climbed inside to take our places, perched above dozens and dozens of gently curving rows. Below us was a sea

35

of humanity, chattering and occasionally flashing a camera light – there were no smartphones, so nobody was filming it. Above the amphitheatre we could see the hills of Verona darkening from mauve to indigo as the stars started to spring out from the sky, one by one. It was utterly magical.

'This is not where I expected to be this evening,' I said, fanning myself with my programme. It was still oppressively hot at eight o'clock, and I was bare-shouldered in my one black dress, my denim jacket folded on my lap. 'I still can't believe we woke up in Florence and tonight was supposed to be Rome – and here we are in Verona. Isn't that crazy?'

'Didn't the train stop in Bologna?'

'No, we were hoping it would, but the first stop wasn't until Verona.'

'Worked out well for me, then,' he said, grinning shyly. He was dressed in the same shirt and trousers from earlier, having offered to queue so that I could go back to the hostel and shower. I felt much better for having a set of fresh clothing and even some make-up and perfume, applied with a shaking hand.

This throwaway comment kept my heart hammering as the roar of conversation died down and the orchestra began to tune up. Did he mean it was nice to have company for the opera – or more?

'I love that sound,' I said to him. 'The orchestra tuning up. There's nothing like it, is there?'

'I know! I just hope it doesn't rain, is all.'

'Oh,' I said. Because now that he had said it, I could feel the humidity in the air – the gathering heat, almost audible like a low hum. Then the orchestra started up with the overture. I knew the opera, but I'd never heard a live performance. I got absorbed in the story too – soldiers and factory girls flirting on the street, and then Carmen, singing her famous 'Habanera'. But as act two began, I felt a drop and then another one. As Carmen read the cards foretelling her death, there was a crackle of lightning. And then a clap of thunder, and then real rain; light at first then heavier and heavier. People had started leaving at the first signs of rain, but the cast were still going. Andrew and I exchanged glances and hung on, vainly trying to shelter under our soggy programmes.

'Are you sure you don't want to leave?' he said, even as people were pushing past us. 'Let's not drown ourselves for culture.'

'I don't want to leave before the singers do,' I whispered back; the tenor was valiantly giving his all with 'Toreador'.

'Sure. They've suffered for their art and now it's our turn,' said Andrew. 'Well, we might not be able to see them, but we can still hear them, just about.'

By now it was coming down in sheets, and the cast and orchestra finally ran offstage, after a final bow.

'We heard the best bits anyway,' Andrew said, as we joined the solid queue of people fleeing downstairs. 'Oh, God, you're soaking. I wish I had an umbrella, but it's against the backpacker's code. You can carry several kilos' worth of waterproof gear, but never an umbrella, or they kick you out of the hostel.'

It was so unfortunate, but we were laughing so much that it didn't matter. And less opera meant more time talking to Andrew.

The rain did stop, as abruptly as it had started, but our conversation flowed. As we walked slowly back towards the hostel, I found myself telling Andrew all sorts of things – like the fact that I had hated my name for years and had begged my parents to let me change it. Dad had wanted to call me Ella or Nina, after two of the greatest female jazz singers, but my mum had wanted to name me after her mother, who had died a few years before I was born.

'I think it's a cool name, though, Norah. It's strong. And I don't think it's old-fashioned, it's a classic.'

'Thanks,' I said, smiling. 'I do like it now.'

'I'm maybe not the best judge of what's old-fashioned, though . . . the thing is, I basically grew up in the 1980s. My parents were quite a bit older when I was born – my mum was forty-five and my dad was fifty. And I have three older brothers – Patrick, Peter and Fergus. Gus is thirty-two now.'

'Wow.' I couldn't imagine being as old as thirty-two; or even having a sibling that old. We were back at the hostel now, which was as beautiful as the rest of the town; it was an actual villa, with ceilings sixteen feet high and frescoes on the interior walls. We had gone inside for long enough to change out of our damp clothes and now we were wrapped up in jeans and sweaters, sitting under a huge cypress tree in the garden, looking at the stars and the half-moon, as bright as a torch. The cicadas were loud all around us, a magical sound.

'Yeah, so I got all their hand-me-downs, which were mostly from the 1970s. You'd want to see photos of me – with my long pointy collars, I could have had someone's eye out.' He laughed, obviously not too traumatized by the memory.

'So are your parents musical?'

'My mum, no. My dad – was.'

'Oh, I'm sorry.'

'Thanks. Anyway, he was musical. He played the piano and he taught me some of the basics of improvising – when I was fifteen or so, I suppose.'

'Is that what you want to do? Composing?'

'Yeah. I mean, I am doing it – I write music all the time. But I have to earn some money with the fiddle too. Hence hawking ourselves around all these gigs in Italy. But I'm off to study composition in September – I'm doing a diploma.'

Next month. 'Oh, where?' I couldn't help but hold my breath; London had music schools. I even managed to fit in a fantasy of him playing the piano while I sang, in some cosy little bar, in the seconds before he said, 'New York. A place called Juilliard.'

'Oh.' I mustered a smile. 'I've heard of it. That will be exciting!'

He nodded.

'Anyway – what about you? How is the singing going?'

'It's going OK, in that I'm getting gigs and getting asked back – but long term I'm not sure how realistic it is to keep going. The thing is that I don't write my own music. I have tried but I can't. I just do covers, and there's not that much demand for that.'

'Join a band, then. Team up with someone who does write.'

'I've been trying, but it's hard . . . it seems like singers are ten a penny.' Lest I sound too downbeat, I added, 'I'm doing a recording, though, the week after next – a proper one, in a studio with a pianist. So I'll have a demo CD, which is what I need.'

'Nice! What's the set list?'

'Um, "A Foggy Day" . . . "Bewitched, Bothered" . . . more Gershwin and Porter, and some Doris Day numbers. "Secret Love" is one.'

'Oh, nice. She is a seriously underrated artist.'

'Yes. That's why I love doing covers. I just don't see the point in trying to write anything better than songs from that era . . . Oh, sorry. I don't mean your stuff.'

'I'll have to write you something,' he said. 'Something special.'

My heart was thudding so hard I was positive he could hear it. I summoned up all my nerve and reached for his hand. He touched the side of my head, gently, and drew my face to his. We kissed. And it was that very, very rare kiss where the reality was just as wonderful as the anticipation, if not better. I knew that nothing else I experienced, as long as I lived, would ever be quite like that particular kiss.

'I really am glad that train didn't stop in Bologna,' he said, at one point.

'Me too,' I smiled.

Then Andrew said something that I wrote down word for word in my notebook the next day, even though I probably would have remembered it anyway.

'It's funny isn't it, how we agonize over these supposedly big choices we have to make that actually make no difference in the end. But the little decisions – that seemingly mean nothing – they can change everything.'

'Like getting the wrong train in Italy,' I said.

'Or the train not stopping 'til Verona.'

He turned my hand over, running his fingertip over my wrist.

'Stay here with me,' he said. 'Just one more week. We're finished with the performances – I was planning on doing some travelling by myself. We can stay here, or maybe even travel, go to Venice or Lake Garda . . .' He looked at me tentatively. 'Would you? I know it's crazy.'

I opened my mouth to say no, because obviously it was. My flight was already booked; I had no idea how much it would be to change it, but I doubted Ryanair were flexible. The temp agency were expecting me to be available for work on Monday. If I stayed, I'd have to use

my credit card, which was strictly for emergencies ...
And what would the girls say?

But then I remembered something my dad, of all people, had said to me as he was driving me to the airport bus stop. 'I hope you enjoy every minute of it,' he had said, sounding a little wistful. 'This is such a special time in your life, love. You'll never be quite so carefree or independent again – so make the most of it.' He had followed this with some more dad-type advice about foreign ATMs and currency exchange rates that I didn't pay much attention to, but his other words had stuck with me. This probably wasn't quite the type of scenario he'd had in mind, but I decided to follow the spirit of his advice anyway.

'OK. I'll do it,' I said to Andrew.

'You will? Really?'

'Yes – really,' I laughed. New plan. I was staying in Italy.

Back at home, in Turnpike Lane, I let myself into my top-floor flat and start turning on lights. It's not the world's biggest home – 'deceptively spacious' was the estate agent's code for 570 square feet – and it's not the best area. My friend Paul refers to my street as Murder Mile. We get regular visits from the police and 'debt recovery agents', and the Wetherspoons at the end of my road is packed by 10 a.m. every day. But I've made it as nice as I can, with maidenhair ferns and Etsy posters disguising the beige bathroom tiles and boxy rooms, and with my dad's record collection taking pride of place all along one wall of my tiny living room. I was only able to buy this place because of my inheritance from him, and I'd give it away in a heartbeat if I could have him back, but here I am.

Joe and I have already booked our trip for next Saturday, so I'll have to pack now because I won't have time in the week with school. Also: I want to get on with it before I lose momentum and think about what I'm actually doing and how very mad it is. When I pull my suitcase down from the top shelf of my wardrobe, I realize how long it's been since I actually went anywhere, except to my mum's in Ealing, and on a yoga holiday in Turkey by myself last summer. I had vague thoughts that I might meet someone on that holiday, which was obviously very deluded of me: all the other yogis were women, and ten out of twelve had just recovered from a break-up.

With the suitcase, a soft bag falls down – one of those things I've obviously stuffed into a crevice years ago and forgotten about. I open it with no idea what's inside.

It's full of old clothes: things that I've put aside either to be repaired at some point or because they might come back into fashion, or because I'll magically lose weight and be able to get back into them. In the last category is a black summer dress, the cheap one that I wore that night at the opera in Verona. It's been washed since then (probably), but when I shake it out I

43

swear I can smell the sunscreen I used then, and the perfume I sprayed on so nervously in the hostel bathroom. *You can't go back*, says my pragmatic side. *Maybe, once in a while, you can*, replies my other half, the half that's packing for Dublin.

# 4. Have You Met Miss Jones?

## *Friday, 20 December 2019*

It was a good thing that I packed on Saturday night after getting back from Joe's, because for the rest of the week I barely have time to breathe between lesson prep, reports, carols in the old peoples' home and general end-of-term madness. Greencoats Academy is a girls' school perched in the foothills of Alexandra Palace in the outskirts of North London. It's not flashy or high-flying, but I love it. I love my commute, which is a fifteen-minute cycle through the park on my Miss Marple bike, I like my headteacher and my colleagues and, most of all, even though it's the world's biggest cliché, I love the kids. I love introducing them to obscure old bands they've never heard of – like U2 and the Beatles – and learning from them as well; I know all the new music and slang ahead of even Joe, with his Soho media job.

It's 8.15 a.m., and I'm in one of our practice rooms for a final run-through with Ashanti Evans, my soloist for the Christmas carol service this evening. This is a big deal: held in the local church on the last day of term, it's a hot ticket for the whole school community, including parents and staff. I've got my Good Black Dress hanging in the staffroom for the occasion and I've already wrestled my hair into submission in a low chignon. I wore it loose last year, and one of the parents complained they couldn't see their kid through my mass of curls. Which is a bit mad, but I don't want to cause any distractions; it's obviously all about the choir tonight, especially since this is the first time the junior chamber choir is taking part.

The only problem is that Ashanti doesn't seem like she's eager for her moment in the spotlight.

She's painfully shy, with such serious acne that it's been on my mind to speak to her pastoral tutor, to see if her parents might be open to a GP visit about it. But Ashanti has the voice of an angel – pure and clear like a choirboy's. The first time I heard her, when she auditioned for the JCC, I was blown away, and I knew I wanted her to do a solo. I even wrote this arrangement of 'O Holy Night' with her voice in mind, with the choir singing the chorus in two-part harmony so she's not overstretched.

'Let's take it from the top,' I tell her. 'Just don't forget to breathe after "brightly shining" so you don't run out of breath during the next line. Have you got all your breaths marked in your score?' There's a noise from outside. 'Hang on a second.' I hop up to investigate. It's a bunch of Year Tens who've decided to use the next-door practice room as an informal breakfast space, breaking multiple rules in the process.

'You know you can't be here right now – off you go,' I tell them, and they scoot. Aside from my first and scariest placement, when a student threatened me with some broken-off piano keys and I had to hide in a stationery cupboard, I've never had a problem with behaviour management, touch wood. 'Miss Jones is *bulletproof*,' I heard one Year Ten tell another once, and I honestly consider that to be the best compliment I've ever received on my teaching.

But there are different kinds of behaviour management, as Ashanti demonstrates when I get back.

'Right! From the top – ready?'

'I'm not sure about it actually,' she says quietly.

Uh-oh. This doesn't sound good. 'What do you mean?'

She doesn't say anything or look at me but closes her score and shakes her head. I notice her nails are completely bitten down. 'I don't think I want to do it any more.'

I'm about to launch into the 'Of course you do' pep talk, but something stops me. With any other student I'd put this down to nerves and wanting some last-minute reassurance, but Ashanti is different. I've had a brief worry myself that maybe tonight was too soon for her, but her tutor agreed with me that it would be a great confidence boost. If she pulls it off.

'How come?'

She shakes her head. 'Just don't.'

Helpful. I'm considering my options – call her bluff

47

and tell her I'll give it to someone else? Give her a pep talk? – but I force myself to stay quiet and see if anything else comes out, a trick that sometimes works. After a few seconds, she adds, 'I heard some girls talking, in the loos.'

'Saying what?'

'That it should be someone else – like Emmy.'

Aha. I wouldn't be surprised if this view was being put around by Emerald Pitt-Kay herself, but she's already captain of the under-sixteens hockey A-team *and* had the lead in the junior musical last year. More pertinently, despite her years of private voice lessons, she sings frequent flat notes, and I can't rely on her to actually look at me while I'm conducting, unlike Ashanti, who watches me like a hawk.

'They don't decide who sings the solo,' I tell her. 'I do. And I know that you are going to do a great job. I wouldn't have chosen you otherwise. It's normal to be nervous – even Beyoncé is nervous before a performance, that's why she invented Sasha Fierce.'

She doesn't show much reaction, but she's listening, so I press on.

'I'm going to tell you a trick my singing teacher told me, when I had my first solo in school.' Ashanti looks at me in surprise; it's obviously never occurred to her that I went to school too, once upon a time. 'What you do is focus on one person in the audience. Think of that person, and sing the song just for them. Can you think of someone?'

She nods slightly.

'Great. You think of them and sing – like you're telling them the story. Just think of the meaning of the song, and everything else will fall into place.'

She nods, and I feel a bit of a hypocrite for a moment. It's easy for me to tell Ashanti that performing is a breeze, but it's been exactly six years since I sang a note in public. That's different, though, of course. I made a conscious decision to step down. Sort of.

'Right – time for us to get going, somebody else needs the room. I'll see you this afternoon at the church for our dress rehearsal.'

Watching Ashanti set off for the library, I wonder if it was actually a good idea to put her forward for the solo or if I should have chosen something less pressured for her to start with. But it's too late now; we have to commit to it and style it out, whatever happens. I learned a long time ago to lock any sadness or insecurity away inside me, so it never shows in the classroom. I keep my private life hermetically sealed while I'm at school. I've only had one major slip-up, and that was on the way back from a school trip to Bath, just after I started four years ago. We were watching *Finding Nemo* on the bus and I started crying like a baby at the bit where Nemo tells Marlin, 'I love you, Daddy.' The students were nudging each other and looking genuinely worried; thankfully, that cohort have all left now, and I'm bulletproof Miss Jones again.

'That was sounding good,' says a voice. I turn and

see Chris Nagle, my colleague and fellow music teacher, in a Santa hat, as it's the last day of term. He gives me a double thumbs-up.

'Oh, thanks, Chris,' I say. 'I should have asked you to sit in and accompany her to give her some practice.' Chris will be playing the organ this evening while I'm conducting below.

'I was dealing with some creative differences back there.' He indicates the practice room behind us, where a three-piece band is doing interesting things with the Beatles' 'Yesterday'. 'It will be great, though. Honestly. And the arrangement's sounding – great.' He leans forward to pat me on both shoulders, which strikes me as a bit odd. Is this Christmas spirit, or flirting? 'I must dash – staff meeting! See you there?' he continues.

'Yes, I'm just coming.'

'Miss! Sorry, miss, but have you read my Mozart essay yet?' Help: now I'm being accosted by Samira Barker, whose essay I have *not* yet read. Also, I've still got thirty djembes to set out before my first lesson, African drumming with Year Seven. Sometimes, after a day of music lessons, music theory and band practice, my ears are actually ringing. I'm convinced that if I ever keel over on the job there will be a chorus of 'Miss! Miss!' and fists banging on the doors of the ambulance as it drives off. But there's no other job I would rather be doing.

The hours go by in the usual last-day blur, with the high point being the staffroom presentation to Gloria

Simmons, our colleague who is retiring after twenty-five years' service teaching English. Gloria is a bit of a legend in the school, having actually attended it herself back when it was a sleepy little place with just two hundred pupils. I can't imagine teaching at my old school, not until enough people have retired or maybe even died. She's really pleased with the gift I helped choose – a set of luggage for her new adventures – and comes over after her speech to say thank you.

'Oh, it's no trouble! It's a big occasion after all. We'll all miss you very much,' I say, sincerely. Gloria is a bit nuts – she believes that there are 'question marks' over the moon landings, for instance – but she keeps her more outlandish views to herself and she was very kind to me when I first started. 'And twenty-five years – that's something to celebrate! Any plans for retirement?'

'Oh, haven't you heard? I'm moving to Spain.'

'No, I had no idea! That's exciting.' How exactly is that going to work, post-Brexit, I wonder but don't say. 'I envy you, on a freezing-cold day like today,' I add, without really meaning it.

'Well, it will be you next, won't it?' she says, chuckling.

'Um, how so?' Does she think I'm near retirement age?

'Oh, you know how it is. When I started, I thought I'd only be here for a few years and then I would go off travelling or move out of London or something. I wanted to move to Spain when I was twenty-five. But that's not what happens, is it? A year goes by and then another . . . you blink and you're sixty. Oh well, better late than never. You're halfway there!' She chuckles and moves off to chat to someone else, obviously not noticing that I'm frozen on the spot with horror.

'What was Gloria telling you? It's obviously given you a few white hairs?'

Maria McCarthy is my favourite colleague: even taller and curlier-haired than me, at nearly six foot to my five foot eight, she's a forthright Liverpudlian who proves my theory that the best teachers were often the naughtiest students. Maria's school exploits go way beyond lighting up a cigarette in science class; she was, in her own words, a holy terror. Now she teaches history and geography, but she still causes a stir on Friday afternoons by roaring away on her boyfriend Dave's motorbike.

'Oh, just that I'm going to be following in her footsteps and staying here for ever, with nothing more to expect from life except retiring to Spain in thirty years.' I shrug, seeing the comic side now; I can already picture myself telling Caroline or Joe about it.

'Thirty years? Haha – Gloria really is on happy pills if she thinks we're retiring before we're seventy,' Maria says cheerfully. 'And I'm off to Spain tomorrow! Well, Tenerife.' Like me, Maria is going away first thing tomorrow, except she's going on an all-included beach break with Dave. 'When are you heading to your mum's?'

We've both been so busy, I haven't even had the chance to tell Maria about Dublin yet. 'Change of plan actually. I'll explain tonight – are you coming for a drink after the carol service?'

'Of course! End-of-term drinks at the Crown? I don't think I've missed one in the past ten years, not going to start now!'

I smile at her, thinking that perhaps Gloria might have had a point. *Are* we a bit stuck in our ways? Am I going to end up staying here, being Miss Jones, until I retire? *You blink and you're sixty.* I remember an expression my mum used recently: the days are long but the years are short. Well, this day isn't long enough to pack in everything I need to do, if I'm to have a hope of getting out in time, so I hoover down a slice of Gloria's retirement cake in lieu of lunch and rush off to my next lesson.

'Girls.' I clap my hands, and the shrieks and giggles stop immediately. 'Five minutes until we're on. So that's five minutes to check your folders and make sure you all have your music in the right order – *not* to check your hair and make-up.'

We're in the vestry, waiting to go on; there are so many performers that we're taking turns to use the backstage space. There are a few last surreptitious glances in the mirror and a few compacts flipped out of pockets, but I turn a blind eye; I've checked my own reflection more than once in the past ten minutes. I can hear Tony Shields, our headteacher, who sounds uncannily like Alan Rickman, winding down the end of his reading. 'Good luck, everyone,' I say. 'Just remember to watch me – and smile. Enjoy it.' I give an extra beam to Ashanti, quaking at the end of her row, but she doesn't smile back.

In our planned formation, we walk out into the silence of the packed church, its lofty ceilings lit by dim lamps and dozens of candles. The scent of incense mixes with the faint hint of a hundred perfumes from mums and colleagues; our footsteps are loud on the Victorian tiles. I feel that combination of nerves and calm that always descends on me before a performance; there's nothing like it.

The girls file into their places beneath the altar, and then Chris, up in the organ loft, starts playing the intro to 'O Holy Night'. I lock eyes with Ashanti, smiling encouragingly and counting her down: one two three, one two three, one two three *go*.

There's nothing. She opens her mouth a centimetre and closes it again, gazing at me in panic. *Shit*, I think but I don't show my fear; just keep conducting while Chris keeps playing the opening bars on a loop. I reckon we have about four more bars of this before it will start sounding very odd, and then I'll have to sing the opening line in hopes that Ashanti can pick it up. I notice Emmy Pitt-Kay pointing discreetly to herself – me, miss? – and I have to give her props for her presence of mind; she will go far in life. Two more bars and I'll probably have to let her have a go.

I focus my full attention on Ashanti, beaming her a

reassuring smile and telegraphing: no biggie, try again, one two three, one two three *now*. And she does it. The first phrase is hesitant but then she's flying; the notes are soaring into the darkened vault above: you can almost see them floating. Shivers are coursing down my spine at the sheer beauty of her voice. *A thrill of hope, the weary world rejoices.* Now the choir swells in behind her, making the biggest and best sound they have to date: *Fall on your knees, O hear the angel voices.* Ashanti catches her breath while they sing, and I'm relieved to see that she's not crushed by her blip; she looks radiant. It's a Christmas miracle.

Afterwards, there's the usual standing around and chatting to parents before my gang of pals breaks away for Christmas drinks. First, though, I have to find Ashanti – she's standing by her mum with her two little brothers bouncing off each arm.

'That was lit, Ashanti! Lit!' her littlest brother is saying, and I have to agree.

'Shush, Malachi! Oh, miss, I'm so sorry I was late coming in,' she says, obviously torn between guilt and joy, and looking to me to see how bad it was.

'That was nothing! You did brilliantly – nobody noticed.' I give her a big hug. 'Thank you. It was really gorgeous. Hello, Mrs Evans! I hope you're proud of Ashanti – she's worked so hard.' My throat is hoarse by the end of this sentence and I hope I haven't lost my voice completely, which sometimes happens at the end of term.

'Yes, very proud.' There's no hiding the beam on Mrs Evans's face.

'I used the trick you said – of singing it to one person in the audience,' Ashanti tells me, while her mum is distracted with her little brothers.

'Oh, great! Who did you sing it for?'

'You, miss.'

I'm pretty overcome by this and I'm not sure what to say – luckily Mrs Evans chooses this moment to scoop Ashanti off for a celebratory milkshake with her family. What with the emotion and exhaustion, I feel like having the same thing but with a generous shot of something inside.

# 5. But Not for Me

Half an hour later, I'm in the bar of the Crown Hotel with my cronies: Maria, Chris and a few others – mostly women, as tends to be the case with school staff. When I first started at Greencoats, the nights out were positively wild, and more than one staffroom romance got started over a pint or five of Fosters. But now we're all a bit more settled down; we've had four staff weddings in four years, and Chris and I are the only single ones. We've adopted the Crown because the other pubs are too close to the school; there's always the risk that parents, or even a stray sixth-former, might come in for a drink. Like police officers, we have to socialize off our beat. I even chose my flat because it was close enough to cycle to work, but too far to be in the school's usual catchment area.

Chris and I are queuing together for drinks at the bar. As a romantic prospect, Chris is less 'I would' and more 'I should' – in the sense that he's perfect on paper. He's nice, he plays the piano, he doesn't have any convictions or substance abuse problems . . . I'm not crazy about his long ponytail or the fact that he vapes (pineapple flavour – urgh), but those wouldn't be deal-breakers. There's just no spark. He's a good sport, known for doing zany things like dressing up as Mozart or David Bowie when teaching their music. I have to hand it to him: anyone who can carry off full Star Man make-up and jumpsuit in front of thirty-two fourteen-year-olds deserves respect. But he's not for me.

'That dress really suits you, Norah,' he says, blushing slightly. 'Is it new?'

'This old thing?' I laugh. 'Chris, I have literally now worn it for three years in a row. But thank you.'

The barmaid hands us our tray of drinks – beers for Maria and Chris, Brandy Alexander for me – and we bring them back to a squashy sofa that Maria has bagged for us in the corner. We all clink glasses, full of euphoria. Christmas has begun!

'Thanks for earlier, Chris – you really saved the day with your intro playing,' I say. 'How long were you going to go on for?'

'All evening, if necessary,' he says. 'Luckily Ashanti pulled it off. She's not very aptly named, though, is she?'

'In what way?' I ask, necking my creamy cocktail. I probably shouldn't be drinking these with my early train tomorrow, but I always have one on the last day of term; it's tradition.

He starts singing in a falsetto. ' "Always on Time"? Ja Rule featuring Ashanti? Norah! How can you teach the national curriculum if you don't know your noughties R'n'B?'

'Sorry, Chris. Before my time.' I laugh as he mimes being shot in the heart.

'What? Of course it's not before your time! When did it come out . . . can't be earlier than, let's see, 2004? I'll look it up.' He checks on his phone. 'Oh gosh, 2001. But that was five years ago, right?'

'I'm afraid not. It was nearly twenty years ago.'

'How did that happen? The noughties were just yesterday,' says Chris, shaking his head. 'How did I get so old?'

'Oh, you're not old,' I tell him.

'Do you mean that, Norah?' he asks, looking at me mournfully.

'Absolutely,' I say, stifling a yawn. Chris has just turned forty, but that's twenty-five in man years; in dating terms he's actually younger than me.

'Oh God, look at that – it's EPK,' Maria says. 'In the Crown, if you don't mind!'

Emerald Pitt-Kay has indeed put her blonde head around the door, flanked by two pals; when she sees us, her eyes widen, and she goes immediately into reverse, bashing the door open, and the other girls back out with her voluminous puffa coat.

'I'll let her think I'm coming after her. I'm going to the loo, though,' Maria says, getting to her feet.

'Oof,' I say, stretching out on the vacated space and half closing my eyes with fatigue. 'I wasn't expecting that – I'm glad we didn't have to deal with them.'

'You wouldn't have had to do a thing,' Chris says valiantly. 'I would have dealt with them. You've had enough to do today – you put this whole evening together!'

'Hardly. But thanks, Chris – you're a sweetheart,' I say, patting his hand.

'Do you mean that, Norah?' he says, again. I'm just getting worried that he's got the wrong idea, when I get a shock that's even worse than the surprise appearance of EPK. Chris leans across to try to kiss me. I recoil just in time to stop him, and we look at each other in horror.

'Oh God! I'm sorry, Norah!' Chris says. 'I shouldn't have done that!'

'It's OK, Chris,' I say, once I've recovered my ability to speak. 'These things happen. Christmas spirit and all that. I'm sorry. You're great, but . . . there's someone else,' I add, wishing this were true.

He shakes his head. 'I got carried away. You're so lovely, Norah. I hoped maybe there was a vibe. But there obviously wasn't, and I am really sorry I misread the situation!'

I'm glad he said that, because I was just thinking that my hand-patting must have been misconstrued. I am, obviously, fully against any kind of harassment in the workplace, but Chris looks so miserable and petrified; I don't want him worrying over Christmas break that I'm going to make an official complaint. And it is flattering – just not in a way that I want. It's typical. When it comes to dating, I'm like one of those bird feeder tables that only attracts squirrels.

'It's fine . . . I think you're lovely too, Chris. Just not for me. If you did internet dating, I bet you'd clean up.'

I'm half tempted to advise him to cut his hair, but I'm not his mum; hopefully he has some other female friend or other who can step in and make him over.

Thankfully, Maria reappears then, breaking up the awkward atmosphere.

'So what's all this about a trip to Dublin?' she asks, flopping down between me and Chris.

'A bit of an impulse. My mum changed her plans so we got a deal . . .' There's no way I can explain the whole Andrew thing to her. It's too complicated, and I don't want to go into details in front of Chris.

'Who's we?'

Damn, did I say we? Well, it's going to come out at some point. 'Me and my friend Joe? You remember, he came in to talk to the Year Twelves about animation.'

Her eyes light up. 'Dreamy Joe? Of course I remember. So is this a romantic trip? Is he still single?'

I'm quite surprised – I wouldn't have thought Joe was Maria's type, but of course he is dreamy enough in his own way. Gloria certainly thought so; she put out all the good biscuits when we entertained him in the staffroom – foil-wrapped Viscounts, no less. I can see Chris looking despondent, and I realize he must think that Joe is the 'someone else'. Maybe I should let him think that – it's easiest all round. 'Yes, he is. I mean he is for now.'

'You dark horse!' Maria looks thrilled. 'So romantic – a little away break to Ireland. My ancestral home, don't you know.'

61

'No, I didn't know that. Really?'

She points at herself. 'Maria McCarthy? From Liverpool? Of course it is. It's a pity my surname's not McCartney or I'd be Liverpool royalty. But yes, my grandad was from County Cork. I have loads of rellies still there, used to go for holidays in Allihies every summer. Great days. And Dublin's a fantastic city, you'll have a laugh. It's not cheap, mind, but great fun.'

'I hope so. What about you, Chris? Any plans?' I ask, to steer the attention away from me.

Chris describes his plans, which involve multiple choir and organ gigs in numerous venues all around London. I don't need to worry about him; choirs are absolute hotbeds of shagging and flirtation, for straight men at least, and he's bound to meet someone soon. He leaves soon after, which is a relief. I'm glad we have at least two weeks before we have to face each other again. It's going to be *so* awkward.

'What was up with him?' Maria asks as soon as he's left. 'It's not like him to bail out so early. Especially at Christmas.'

I shrug, trying to keep a poker face. I'm so tempted to tell her what just happened with Chris, purely to see her face, but I restrain myself. She wouldn't mean to spread it, but it's the kind of school gossip that would go round the building twice and enter student lore, simply by osmosis.

'Anyway,' Maria says. 'Speaking of performing. We're going to do another one of our tribute nights in

62

February, in the Greyhound. Can I put you down for an act?'

'Oh – maybe. I'll see . . .'

She shakes her head. 'I know that means no. Come on! I've done karaoke with you, I know you can sing. Why can't you just get over yourself and do one tune onstage? Dave's going to be there with Journeying On.' That's Dave's Journey tribute band. 'You could do a little jazz number. Wear that.' She nods at my dress. 'Chris is even going to do an Elvis. "Love Me Tender", bless him.'

'I don't know . . . I always feel like footage is going to end up online, and the kids will see us,' I complain, which is true enough.

'Footage!' Maria says. 'You're not Lady Gaga. Honestly, if little Ashanti can get up in front of the whole school and sing, what's stopping you?'

She's right. And I know that my refusal to sing in public is ridiculous; but when it comes down to it, I also know that I just wouldn't be able to do it. But I tell her I'll think about it, which buys me enough time to think of a proper excuse. At least the discussion steers her away from asking me any more questions about Chris, whose sudden departure is pretty out of character. What a mess; but this time tomorrow, I'll be in Dublin, leaving it all safely behind, for now at least.

# 6. All I Want for Christmas

Normally I cycle to and from school but I didn't cycle in today – not just because of the three cocktails I drank but because of my massive end-of-term bag crammed with my laptop, presents, cards and papers. So I get the 144 bus, thankful that it's travelling away from Muswell Hill towards the grittier environs of Turnpike Lane, so I'm unlikely to see Emerald Pitt-Kay or any of her other friends, wherever they ended up. I might have a quiet word with her in the New Year, but I don't have the heart to take any official notice of it. After all, I was underage when I tried to get into a very similar bar, also at Christmas, and got turned away. Which turned out to be lucky in the end, because that was how we first got to know Joe and his friends – and how I made my stage debut.

I rub the steamy bus window with my woollen glove, smiling at the memory. It was Christmas 2004, and Caroline, Kiran and I had decided that we *had* to spend the evening of the 24th at the pub. We had been talking about it for weeks, and it was the one bright spot of rebellion in our otherwise very tame A-level year. We had identified the bar of the Drayton Hotel on The Avenue as the ideal place, because we knew it was off the beaten track for people our age. We thought we'd have a better chance of getting served there than in any of the known teenage haunts, which were often raided by the police.

'The other tip is: know your drink,' Kiran had said on our last day of term, in the sixth-form common room.

'How do you mean?' Caroline asked, looking up from an interview with her crush Orlando Bloom in *Heat* magazine. Caroline and I were both fascinated by celebrities and discussed them endlessly as if they were people we knew. Was anyone looking after Britney Spears? Was Ben Affleck ever really in love with J-Lo, or had it all been a publicity stunt? And how on earth was Jennifer Aniston ever going to get over Brad? We could spend literally hours discussing these topics, making Kiran roll her eyes.

'You need to sound as if you're used to ordering drinks, so when they ask you what you want, you don't just say "Uh, um, an alcopop?" You say something very specific, like "I'd like a Bombay Sapphire and tonic, please, with lime *not* lemon." Then they see you're an experienced drinker so they don't question you.'

'What's a Bombay Sapphire?' I asked.

'It's a new kind of gin that's really trendy,' Kiran explained. 'Or you could ask for a very specific kind of wine. Like "I'd like a 2004 Chardonnay, please, but only if it's French. I don't drink Australian wines."'

'But I only really like Bacardi Breezers,' said Caroline. 'What about our fake IDs, won't they work?'

Kiran's older brother Azad, who was studying

economics at Kingston University, knew a guy who had made us very dodgy-looking fake IDs with new dates of birth, supposedly from various universities. Mine was from Leicester Regional Technical College, which wasn't even a thing. Not only did we have to remember our new ages and what we were studying, we had to memorize our birthdays *and* star signs; it was like method acting, or being a spy.

Nonetheless, Christmas Eve saw us dressed up to the nines and ready to hit our first ever pub together. Kiran had recommended that we dress 'professionally', so I was in my favourite red top, with a low-cut square neck, a black pencil skirt and knee-high boots, very much channelling my style icon, Monica from *Friends*. Not yet knowing about the rule of doing 'eyes or lips', I went heavy on both, and then ran down to tell Mum and Dad I was going out.

They were in the kitchen, which was in its usual pre-Christmas state of code amber alert. Every surface was full of potatoes and vegetables soaking in bowls of water – I had spent the afternoon peeling carrots – and Mum was bashing stale bread for her famous stuffing. Dad was polishing the silver, ready to lay it out for Christmas lunch the next day, and surreptitiously eating one of the home-made mince pies cooling on a wire rack. He was listening to jazz on his headphones, because Mum always wanted Radio 4 while she was cooking. I had heard her say on the phone to a friend the week before, regarding Christmas, 'It's just three days of housework, isn't it?' I didn't really know why there had to be such a fuss. Dad, Miles and I had repeatedly said to Mum that we didn't care if there weren't fifty different side dishes at lunch, to which she always replied, 'I care.' I had offered to do it all, but she had said no, so I hadn't pushed the point; I was bound to get it all wrong anyway.

'Mike, those mince pies are for tomorrow! Honestly, you're worse than the kids,' Mum said exasperatedly. 'You look very pretty, Norah. What are you all dressed up for?'

'Well – I'm going to meet Caroline, and Kiran,' I said. 'At the Drayton Hotel, for a drink.'

I hadn't really thought this through, vaguely assuming that Mum and Dad, who occasionally gave me a small glass of wine, would be fine with me going to a civilized hotel bar. I would be eighteen in January, after all. But Mum immediately put down her rolling pin and put her hands on her hips. 'Are you joking? Absolutely not. Mike, you agree with me, don't you?'

'Well – honestly, I don't see the harm,' he said, carefully adding a bit more polish to his cloth. 'A few drinks in a hotel bar? That's better than cider on the bench in Ealing Common.'

'But it's so unnecessary! She'll have plenty of years to go drinking with her friends.'

'Well, hang on,' said Dad. 'Didn't you used to go to pubs when you were seventeen?'

'It was different then! There's so much crime about

now . . . Anyway, I wanted us all to play Cluedo later – have a nice family evening. You agreed to that, Mike.' This was obviously turning into one of their rows, and I wasn't surprised when she said, 'Norah, go and watch TV with your brother.'

I sidled out of the room, berating myself: why had I been so stupid? I should have known it would cause ructions. I went into the living room, where Miles was sprawled on the sofa watching *Shrek*. Once, I would have circled it in the *Radio Times* with huge excitement and looked forward to watching it all day. A little part of me did still wish I was watching it with him in my pyjamas, eating Cadbury's Heroes in the multicoloured light of our artificial Christmas tree.

Miles didn't say anything when I came in, but he moved his leg on to the footstool so I could sit down. He had a finger injury from rugby practice earlier that week, so had been absolved of any Christmas chores today. Mum was really proud of his sporting prowess, a big rarity in our indoorsy family, and treated him like a kind of prize racehorse, buying entire loaves of Hovis and packets of Kellogg's Crunchy Nut that were just for him, while Dad and I made do with generic corn-flakes. But generally we got on fine, occupying parallel grooves and never really clashing, because we were so different. Despite being named after Miles Davis, he was completely uninterested in jazz or any kind of music at all, to Dad's despair.

'You're all fancy – what's happening, a party?' Miles

asked, idly. He liked knowing what the girls in my year were doing so that he could report back to his own pals and feel like a real fifteen-year-old man about town.

'No, I'm supposed to be going to the Drayton, for a drink . . . Mum freaked, and now they're fighting.' We could hear them, low but angry, what felt like a constant backdrop to Christmas and, actually, our lives together. I almost didn't notice the knot in my stomach any more.

'You are an idiot, Norah. Why can't you just lie, like a normal person?' Miles said. It was true; that was what he had always done. Whenever Mum and Dad told him to do something, he smiled and nodded and did exactly what he wanted to, making sure they never found out.

'Maybe I will,' I said.

I put down the tub of Heroes and went into the kitchen and stood there until they noticed me and fell quiet.

'I texted the girls. We're going to hang out at Kiran's instead.'

Both of them looked relieved, and I felt guilty but relieved too; it was so much easier to lie. I could see why everyone did it.

'I'll give you a lift, love,' Dad said, getting to his feet. 'It's very cold – you could be waiting ages for the bus.'

'Oh – that would be great, thanks Dad.' Kiran only lived around the corner from the Drayton, and I could always text her en route to ask her to wait for me. And something told me that Dad wouldn't press me too hard on the details anyway.

Twenty minutes later, we were clattering up to the front of the Drayton's bar with high heels and higher hopes. However, the barman, an older man with no nonsense about him, didn't even let us finish our orders. He asked to see our ID, and then shook his head with a brief smile.

'Sorry, girls,' he said. 'Come back in a few years. And Merry Christmas.'

'Well, at least he was nice about it,' Caroline said, as we trailed slowly back out. 'And he said we can come back.'

'Are you joking? I'm never giving this place my custom,' Kiran said crossly. 'Honestly. Twenty quid we paid for those IDs! Don't worry, though, I'll get our money back.'

'Where do we go now?' I said. 'I suppose we could go to McDonald's. Or Pizza on the Green.'

'No, we have to go *somewhere* for a drink like we said we would,' Kiran said. 'This can't be the night we get broken up with by a Post-It note! It has to be the night something else happens.'

Caroline and I understood the reference to *Sex and the City*, but we didn't really love it the way Kiran did; the women all had fabulous lives, so why were they always complaining? I was so busy trying to think of somewhere else to go, I didn't notice the boys walking past us, until one of them turned around.

'Norah?'

It took me a second to place him, but then I remembered; Joseph Lee, from West Ealing Junior Arts Academy – WEJAA. I was in a production of *Jesus Christ Superstar* with him last year, when I played Mary Magdalene. I remembered Dad giving him lifts home a few times, but I had lost touch with him after that. I was too busy nursing crushes on the main cast; Joe couldn't sing a note so he was in the chorus. I remembered, though, that he had drawn the poster for the production, and it was brilliant: trippy and seventies-looking, complete with rainbow psychedelic lettering. Joe was nice, but not really my type with his emo fringe and baggy jeans.

'Happy Christmas! What are you guys up to tonight?' Joe asked. I vaguely recognized a few of his friends, though of course they all went to a different school.

'Oh, we've just been kicked out of this place,' Kiran said. 'They wouldn't accept our IDs.'

Caroline and I winced; we would probably not have admitted that.

'Of course they didn't,' said one of Joe's friends. 'It's over twenty-ones.'

'We're going to Finnegan's – want to come?' Joe said.

We all looked at each other. 'Isn't that place massively dodgy?' Caroline said. I knew what she was thinking: it was well known you could get groped at Finnegan's, though I was ready with a karate chop for anyone who tried it.

'Exactly – that's why they'll let us in,' said Joe.

'All right, then,' said Kiran. 'Finnegan's it is.' It was a come-down from her *Sex and the City* hotel bar dreams, but we had to start somewhere. We set off, Joe introducing us to his friends Paul, Will Palmer and Simon Martin. I got a start when I realized Paul was *the* Paul Slovinski, who was famous in both our schools for being a junior tennis champion *and* writing poetry that had been published in their school annual, which Miles brought home. I had been quite taken with his sonnet 'Desolation' and had shared it with the girls, after looking up his picture and deciding that he was hot. He looked like a poet, tall with dreamy cheekbones, black hair and piercing blue eyes. He started chatting to Kiran, and I heard him tell her he was hoping to go to Edinburgh.

'Ostensibly to study English,' he said, while I blinked. I had never heard anyone use the word 'ostensibly' in conversation before and I wasn't entirely sure what it meant. 'But that's just my excuse for being there. I'm going to write plays and get them put on at the Edinburgh Fringe Festival.'

'Brilliant!' Kiran said, looking smitten: she loved a man with a plan. 'You'll have to send us tickets!'

'I will,' Paul promised. I was impressed by his

ambitions; Paul obviously had it all worked out and was thinking much bigger than anyone I knew, including me.

'What have you applied for next year, Norah?' Joe asked me. 'Going to study music?'

'Oh, no – history,' I said. 'I'm hoping to go to York. They have a great music department, so I'd love to join the choir – if I get in.'

'Of course you will! I thought you'd be training to be an opera singer or something.'

I laughed. 'No way. It's practically impossible to make a career as a professional singer, so I thought I'd do something useful instead.' I wasn't sure what I was going to do with my history degree; I vaguely thought something in the Civil Service – something steady and reliable, anyway.

'Like history?' Joe said, with a twinkle in his eye. 'Very useful.'

'Well, how about you – are you studying art?' I said tartly.

'Nope. I'm hoping to do engineering, at Imperial. I'll make my millions developing some kind of green aviation and then I'll retire and do art.'

Another big thinker. This must be the kind of confidence they taught them at their boys' school. 'You do that,' I said, burying my nose in my scarf. It was freezing; I hoped Finnegan's wasn't much further. 'Actually, if you want to make millions with your art you should start by making fake IDs. Ours were rubbish, and we paid twenty quid for them. Have you got one?'

'Not needed – I'm already eighteen,' Joe said, sounding cocky. 'October 15th, in case you want to send me a card next year.'

I tried to think of a smart reply to this, but none was needed, because we were already at Finnegan's, being whooshed inside without even the pretence of an ID check. Once we were in, we all rushed to the bar to arm ourselves with Bacardi Breezers. We had no problem obtaining them except that we had to yell to the barman to make ourselves heard over the music. There was a live band called the Nine Inch Nialls doing covers of U2, in keeping with the Irish theme – the walls were papered over with tourist posters of Ireland, vaguely discernible through the pub's red lights. It reeked of stale beer and cigarettes; the floor was sticky; everyone there looked about sixteen. But it was decked out with tinsel and fairy lights for Christmas, and we were all ecstatic to have finally made it to a real live pub.

It was too loud to talk, so we just danced and drank – although Joe did keep trying to chat, at one point asking me if he could have my email address to send me a petition to open a skate park in Ealing.

'Do you even skate, Joe?' I asked.

'No, but I would if there was a skate park.'

I laughed, and we started talking about other local haunts. We were deep in an argument about where had the best pizza in Ealing – Pizza on the Green or the Pizza Express – when I saw that it was already ten o'clock; time had flown by. Feeling a bit guilty again, I decided to send Dad a text.

'Dad, just so you know – we ended up in Finnegan's pub. I wanted you to know in case anything happened. I'll be home by midnight.'

Then Caroline ran over and nudged me.

'Norah, did you hear? The singer's just gone off stage to barf, and they're asking if anyone wants to do any covers.'

'What?' Kiran shushed Joe, and we heard the lead guitar player, tapping on the microphone. 'Hi there again, just to say ... our singer's had to, um, take a health-related break, so we have ten minutes left, if anyone wants to come up and give us a few tunes. That's a big opportunity, coming to you here from the Nine Inch Nialls. Thank you.'

'You should do it,' Joe said, giving me a gentle push.

'What? I haven't got anything ready – I don't know any U2,' I said. But Kiran and Caroline were already frog-marching me towards the 'stage', a small platform on the sticky floor in the corner of the room.

'OK, we have a volunteer,' the guitarist said. 'What's your name?'

I certainly wasn't telling him my real name; there were people here from school, and other schools, and this was the kind of thing that made you an urban legend and not in a good way. But at the same time, I was a few Breezers to the good, and I'd just remembered I did know a U2 song: 'I Still Haven't Found What I'm Looking For'.

'We already played that,' said the guitarist. 'Tell you what, how about some Christmas tunes?' And he played thirteen notes, up and down a scale.

'Oh, I do know that.' My doubts and hesitations all vanished, pretty much there and then. 'All I Want for Christmas'? To sing. The singing part of my brain had been switched on, and I was ready. I took the microphone and sang the first few bars, quietly at first but then more confidently as the room fell quiet.

If I was going to sing 'All I Want for Christmas Is You' I was going to do it properly. I did the full gospel-style intro complete with improvisation, and then we were away. It was such a fantastic song, all I had to do was remember the words and go along for the ride, while the keyboard and guitars did their thing. People were dancing; Kiran and Caroline were shrieking, and I could see Joe, drinking his beer and watching me with a huge beam on his face. I threw in a bit more improvisation at the end, and as I sang 'You, baby' I pointed into the crowd, who all went wild. But I didn't have anyone in particular in mind. Instead of *you*, all I wanted was *this*. Singing my heart out; watching everyone dance and sway and sing along – it was an absolute rush.

But then, just as I was singing the final 'You, baby', Kiran and Caroline ran up and signalled to me. 'Norah!' Kiran called over the music. In a stage whisper, she

77

mouthed, 'It's the police!' I didn't even think twice; I bolted from the stage, grabbing my coat and the girls' from the pile beside the front door, where we had left them, and we ran outside, breathless and giggling, not daring to look back until we were halfway down the street.

'Do you think it really was the police?' said Caroline. 'We should check if the boys are OK.'

'They should be – Paul's eighteen, so is Joe,' said Kiran. 'I don't know, maybe it was just a rumour. Some guys at the bar told me.' She looked unusually embarrassed. 'Maybe they were pulling my leg.'

'Don't worry,' I said. 'At least we left on a high. Oh my gosh – it's my dad!'

It was Dad. He was ten feet away, looking a bit stern at first. Then, as he came closer, his face broke into a huge beam. 'You sounded great, Norah,' he said. He bent down to give me a big hug. 'Really great.'

'Were you listening, Mr J?' Kiran asked, looking scared.

'I was outside, having a sneaky cigarette – don't tell your mum – and knew it was Norah. How did you end up onstage, love?'

'It just happened,' I said, at the same time as Kiran said, 'The singer of the main band had to go and puke.'

'A classy joint,' said Dad. 'Well, I'm glad you told me where you were. I wouldn't want to have missed that. Would your friends like a lift home?'

Joe and Paul appeared after that, having come to see

78

what had happened to us, and it was decided that Dad would drive Joe, me and Caroline home, while Paul walked home with Kiran. And that was the beginning of us all hanging out together: a few more times over the Christmas break and then all through the summer that followed our A-levels. We even spent results night together, ending up in a paddling pool in Will's parents' garden. Even after we all went off to uni, we still met every Christmas Eve in the pub; through different jobs, relationships, milestones, Christmas Eve drinks remained a constant. So of course I can't be too hard on Emmy Pitt-Kay – she's only doing what I once did myself. As I see my bus stop approach and ring the bell, I decide I must ask Joe, tomorrow morning, if he remembers that night.

# 7. Sentimental Journey

## *Saturday, 21 December 2019*

It's 8.35, and I'm pacing up and down on the concourse at Euston station, near the Paperchase concession, watching the destinations flash orange and waiting for the 9.00 train to Holyhead to appear. It turns out that flying to Dublin for Christmas at the last minute is quite expensive, so we're getting the train and ferry. Joe and I couldn't believe it when we started looking at flights.

'This is outrageous,' he said. 'I mean – I know it's last-minute, but we could literally fly to New York for these prices. Low season, but still.'

'I suppose lots of people want to go home at Christmas. Look, it's really cheap the opposite way,' I said, showing him. 'Even with Mum's air miles the flights are too outrageous.'

'What about the train?' Joe asked.

'The train? I know geography's not your strong point, but . . .'

'Train and ferry. Look!' Joe held out the results of his search. 'It's *much* cheaper. Leave Euston station at nine, and you can be in Dublin by five. Plus, more eco-friendly. Win-win.'

I knew Joe adored train trips; when the girls and I were backpacking around Italy, he got the Trans-Siberian railway from Moscow to Beijing. This sounded like it would take almost as long.

'Won't it be really grim – being squashed on the train for that long, and then a boat?'

'Grim? Are you crazy? Train journeys are magical. For these prices, we can upgrade to first class on the train if you really want to treat yourself. And look, there's even a cinema on the boat!' He said this in the tone of someone describing first class on a luxury Caribbean cruise.

'OK,' I said. I was happy enough to go along with his suggestions; the more ownership he took, the more I could pretend this was a joint idea, rather than my own crazy plan.

The concourse is mobbed with frazzled and festive crowds wheeling suitcases and carrying totes stuffed with presents; everyone in London appears to be going home for Christmas via Euston station. Unsurprisingly Joe is late. There won't be any reason for it; he's just a late person. I had originally suggested meeting at eight and he wanted to meet at 8.45, so we compromised on 8.30. So I'm relieved to see him appear while it's not quite 8.40, two coffees in hand.

'I don't know what you're so worried about. We have our seats pre-booked, and there's loads of time,' he says, handing me mine.

'We have to watch for the platform and as soon as

the train is listed, we have to run for it or someone might steal our seats.'

Joe obviously doesn't share my travel philosophy.

'I might go and buy the paper,' he says.

'No! We don't have time!'

'I didn't know train travel was so triggering for you,' he says. 'Look, it's just been announced. Platform ten – this way.'

'I just don't want to get on the wrong train, that's all,' I say, as we join the crowd rushing for seats. It's obviously going to be packed, and I'm glad that I insisted on pre-booking first class. I don't know why I'm in such a flap – I'm not usually a nervous traveller. I just know I'm going to feel a little tense until we're safely installed in seats 46 A and B, with our bags in plain sight.

'Hey, how did the concert go?' Joe asks.

I shiver at the thought of Chris as our embarrassing encounter comes back to me. 'I'll tell you when we're on the train,' I say briefly.

It's a bit of a zoo on board – every carriage is packed, and there are even people sitting on suitcases in the aisles. But there's a real festive spirit – quite literally in the case of some tables, which are already having a livener even though it's 9 a.m. – lots of Santa hats too, and people writing out last-minute cards. Everyone is going home. This mass migration, every Christmas, always makes me feel emotional. It's true that everyone is headed for their individual little pods, but the travel part is a communal effort; we're all homeward bound – except me and Joe. I don't know where exactly I'm going, but at least I have Joe with me.

Soon we're in our first-class carriage, which is comparatively empty, and we find our seats without drama – we have a four-top table and we're able to sit opposite each other diagonally.

'Dream formation,' says Joe. 'Here.' He produces a chocolate croissant from a paper bag – my snack of choice whenever I'm hungover. 'I thought you might need this. So how bad was it?'

'Thank you! It was a bit hairy, but we pulled it off.' I explain about the last-minute drama with Ashanti.

'I thought you were going to say that Emerald stepped in and started singing the solo,' Joe says. 'That's how I would storyboard it.'

'No! But then there was more drama afterwards . . .' It is a relief to be able to tell someone about the encounter with Chris.

'I think you missed a trick there,' Joe says, when I explain what happened. 'Imagine all the fun you could have had with sexy cos-play. Don't tell me you don't dream of a man in a David Bowie jumpsuit.'

'Thank you for that visual,' I say, shuddering. 'Anyway, it's going to be hideously awkward, but never mind, we've got two weeks to forget about it.'

Now the train is chugging past the familiar landscapes of North London, looking strange and distant from this angle. I can see the bridge at Chalk Farm where I used to meet my old boyfriend Matt, a glimpse of Primrose

Hill, where the girls and I spent what feels like endless summer days after browsing Camden Market. Then we're going past Ealing, the site of our childhoods, and then northwest, out of London towards Chester, not a million miles from where my dad grew up. Joe was right; there is something magical about a train journey. It unrolls more slowly; it gives you time to think. And to have conversations that you might not have otherwise.

'Joe, this is very cheesy, I know, but do you believe at all in the concept of fate?' I ask him. This has been on my mind lately, for obvious reasons.

'No,' he says. 'I think life is random, and we've dreamed up the idea of fate or destiny to make ourselves feel better about it.'

'Right. Thanks for that.' I don't know why I bothered asking; I should have turned to Caroline or Kiran for a discussion about fate.

'It's funny you should ask me that, though, because we just covered it in my Cantonese class.'

'Really? That's interesting.' Joe started these a few years ago, as part of a general mission to learn more about his Chinese heritage. His dad's Cantonese is quite rusty at this point, and they never spoke it at home, so Joe decided to take matters into his own hands. 'What did you learn?'

'So the expression we learned is *yuan fen* . . . it's mostly used in the sense of a connection or an affinity, I think, between people but also between people and places. So my dad would say he had *yuan fen* for the UK. But you could also say that it was *yuan fen* that you met someone, or worked with someone.'

'So, it's like saying something was meant to be?'

'Yes. There is a catch with it, though. Just because you have this connection and you're fated to meet, it doesn't mean you are fated to stay together. Some couples have fate without destiny – that's an expression people use.'

'Oh, right.' Now I wish I hadn't asked.

'It derives from Buddhism – the idea being that you met in a past life. Or I think it does, anyway.'

'I see,' I say, thinking that Italy in 2009 might qualify as a past life. It certainly feels like it.

I haven't had time to give the girls much information on my trip. When we were younger, I wouldn't have imagined taking such a step without endless phone calls and ideally discussions over drinks. But we're older and busier now, so I just explained briefly on our WhatsApp group, embarrassingly entitled Yass Queens.

*Is it ten years already? I can't believe it!* 😲, Caroline wrote. *Norah this is so exciting. I am sure he'll be there. I'm so glad you're doing this* ❤️❤️.

Kiran's reply took a bit longer to come through. *Wow. Big news!! Lots of luck and hope it goes well* ✌️. *I'd love to chat this eve but I've been awake since 4 am, going to try and go to bed when the twins do.*

*Poor you. What time are they waking up for the day now?* Caroline wrote.

*Atticus wakes between four and five, and then he wakes up Roxy. It was 4.35 today*, Kiran replied. *Basically I live in a*

*different time zone now. Please enjoy the holiday for me, Norah.*
*I can't imagine the freedom* 😃. *Keep us posted?!!!*

Poor Kiran. She needs her sleep more than almost anyone else I know. I hadn't actually told them yet that Joe was coming with me, but it doesn't matter; I can fill them in properly, later.

I know I wasn't awake at four like Kiran, but I am exhausted after my late night. I can feel my eyes closing as I drift into a bizarre and stressful dream in which Chris and I are taking the girls on a school trip to Lake Garda. Emerald Pitt-Kay is performing some kind of sold-out concert in an amphitheatre, with Andrew accompanying her on the organ.

When I wake up, I can tell that we've come a long way. The towns and buildings have given way to proper countryside; low stone walls, green fields and sheep. The coastline is unfolding beside us as well, rising up to a castle here and down to a beach there, and then past a vast caravan site. The clouds that were squatting over the West Midlands have parted, and biblical rays of light are touching the grey sea and the white waves. It's beautiful, and infinitely nicer than sitting on a plane – I'm so glad we came this way.

'Welcome to Wales,' says Joe.

'Already?' I shake my head, sit up and yawn. I hope I haven't been drooling or anything, but Joe looks like he's been immersed in his book: something depressing and arty-looking in the Don DeLillo vein. 'I can't believe we're going to Ireland.'

'I can't believe you've never been,' Joe says.

'Have you?'

'Sure. Dublin for a wedding, Kilkenny for work – and once just to explore – why wouldn't you?'

'I suppose . . . I've never got round to it.' And also, if I'm being honest, I'm not sure what there is exactly to draw me there. Even in Dublin, I'm not totally sure what there is to see. Paris has the Eiffel tower, Edinburgh has the castle, but what does Dublin have? A Guinness factory, which isn't very appealing, since I don't like beer, and the Book of Kells – which I'm sure is great, but isn't it a long way to go just to see a book? And of course there's Andrew, but the idea of going there and not seeing him is somehow worse than playing it safe and never going at all.

That's the simple answer. The less simple answer relates to my dad.

'Didn't you tell me once your dad was Irish?' Joe asks, as if reading my mind.

This is one of the things I really appreciate about Joe. Most of my friends never mention my dad at all, ever. If the subject of fathers comes up, they change it as soon as they remember about mine. I know that it's kindly meant, and that they want to spare me the sadness of thinking about him. But what they don't understand is that I like talking about him. It gives me the chance to remember the good things again; it makes me feel as though he's not forgotten.

'Well, his mother was Irish, from Dublin. She came

over in the 1950s I think, to Manchester, and she got work in a factory . . . but he had a kind of rocky relationship with her. I think she was quite harsh. And my guess is that he actually didn't want to visit much for that reason. I don't know if he even went himself.'

'Oh.' Joe digests this. 'What about the rest of his family? Your grandfather, for instance?'

'Well, that's the thing. I . . . don't exactly know about them.'

'You mean they died?'

'It's complicated . . . They were somewhat estranged, I think. Dad got a scholarship to Manchester Grammar School, and then he went to uni in Manchester, and after that he got work as a trainee quantity surveyor in London. Which is where he met my mum, sharing a flat in Earls Court, or a squat really. They had an argument over nuclear power by the Teasmaid, or something very eighties like that. And I think he just left that whole life behind after he and mum got married and his parents died. I mean, I think they died.'

'So you don't know if your grandparents are alive or dead,' Joe says slowly.

I nod, feeling an odd sense of shame. 'You must think we sound like such a mess.'

'Not really, actually,' he says. 'I was thinking it's not that different from my dad. You know he came over here for boarding school when he was nine – he was sent here, and my uncle went to relatives in Canada, and they basically never came back. And since my grandparents died I am honestly pretty hazy about who's left in Hong Kong – some aunties, I think, but my dad's not big on detail.'

I nod, feeling a bit better that it's not just my family that's like this. Though it is sad to think that I have the same amount of connection to Ireland as my colleague Maria does – but no 'rellies' like she has to spend the summer with.

'Anyway. He was really nice, your dad,' says Joe. 'I remember he used to give me lifts home from drama because I was always forgetting my travel pass. He always had jazz playing in the car.'

'I remember.' Dad was horrified at Joe's lack of musical knowledge and considered the noughties a cultural wasteland, so he took the opportunity to catch Joe up whenever he drove us back from drama group.

'He was also the first person to play "Bohemian Rhapsody" for me,' Joe says. 'He kept me in the car to listen to the whole ten minutes of it, or however long it is. Do you remember that?'

'No! When was that?'

'It must have been when he was dropping me home one time. Remember he'd sometimes drop you off first and then me? We had some good chats,' Joe continues. 'He actually encouraged me to apply to art college – did you know that?'

'No! Joe, did he really?'

'Yes. He said that I'd never regret taking a risk to do something I loved . . . though I'm glad I studied engineering. It's pretty useful with character modelling.'

I'm beaming; I love hearing anything new about my dad. On the rare occasions when it happens, it's as if he's been brought back to life – just for a second, just for a flicker. I wonder what he would say if he knew I was going on this crazy adventure. I think he would tell me to go for it. I think he would tell me, like he told Joe, that I'd never regret taking a risk for something – or someone.

'I think the person who taught me the most about jazz was you, though.' Joe adopts a high-pitched, know-it-all voice. 'Now, Chet Baker . . . most people think of him primarily as a trumpeter, but I think you'll find his best work was actually as a *vocal* artist . . .'

'Very funny.' I aim a kick at him under the table, but I'm laughing. 'Oh, that reminds me . . .' I tell him about Emerald trying to get into the pub and backing straight out when she saw us. 'Do you remember that first night we went to Finnegan's? And we thought the place was being raided?'

'You were such drama queens,' says Joe. 'You obviously thought a raid would be like prohibition with flappers screaming and everyone hiding in their double bass cases. What would really happen was that a plain-clothes officer or two would arrive, cough gently, and say, "Ladies and gentlemen, we will shortly be conducting some ID checks, so please do have your identification ready," and then people would start to sneak out. And there would always be one very smug eighteen-year-old left sitting alone proudly with their pint.'

'Generally you,' I say.

'Always me,' says Joe.

I laugh again. I haven't thought of this in years, before last night, or discussed it with Joe. I remember reading somewhere that the sign of a friendship that's past its sell-by date is when you only ever talk about the olden days. So that's a good sign for our friendship, I suppose. But people don't always remember the past the same way. What if Andrew has a completely different recollection of what happened between us? Or worse, no memory at all? I'm prepared for this to happen, but it's still going to hurt if I've come all this way for nothing.

The bilingual train announcement starts up again. 'In a short time we will be arriving at Holyhead – Holyhead our next and final destination. We'd like to wish all our passengers a good stay in the Holyhead area, or a safe onward journey, and a very Happy Christmas.'

Again, the panic rises up inside me. I'm normally not a terribly anxious traveller, especially if it's just me and not a bunch of fifteen-year-olds. But by the time we get out of the train, I'm in a lather of anxiety, imagining that the boat will never materialize, or that we'll get on the wrong boat to Scotland, or that all transport will close down and we'll have to spend Christmas in the ferry terminal in Holyhead, surviving on mini catering packs of shortbread.

'I'm sure that would be fine, if it did happen,' Joe says, when I disclose some of these ideas. 'We'd get a B&B or something.'

'B&Bs aren't open over Christmas,' I remind him. 'And what about our reservation in Dublin?'

'Norah.' Joe puts down his bag, oblivious of the crowds around us, and grabs me by the shoulders. 'It's going to be OK. We're going to get on the boat successfully – that's something we can do. And have a drink, and look out of the window and read our books. Maybe do the crossword. And then we'll have a good time in Dublin.' He gives me a look. 'Are you freaking out about Andrew?'

'I suppose I must be,' I admit, realizing that of course he's right.

'Don't worry about that. Whether you believe in fate, or *yuan fen* or whatever – it's beyond your control. So whatever you do or don't do, it doesn't make much difference to whatever is going to happen. It's out of your hands.'

I'm not sure if this reassures me completely. But as we queue for the ferry, the anxiety starts to dissipate a little. I'm just going to take the next step, and the step after that, and try not to freak out and over-think every little thing. After all, I took a risk in the first place when I stayed in Italy with Andrew, and that turned out well. More than well: it turned out to be one of the best things I've ever done. So maybe, just maybe, lightning will strike twice.

# 8. How High the Moon

Andrew and I stayed up almost the whole night, after going to the opera, only heading to bed just as the sun was rising. I woke up to find Caroline shaking my shoulder and knew it must be late by the heat of the day.

'Norah!' she said. 'Wake up, Sleeping Beauty. We have to check out. It's noon. And the train for Rome leaves at two!'

'Oh gosh, is it?' I sat up and rubbed my eyes. 'I got to bed quite late . . .'

'Yes you did,' said Kiran, who was perched on the other bed. 'Spill! What happened?'

'Oh, it was – it was wonderful.' I filled them in briefly on our evening together. 'And . . . I know this is going to sound a bit mad, but . . .'

'What?' they said, in unison.

'Well, I'm not going to fly home today. I'm going to stay on with him here, for another week.'

In reply, Kiran fell backwards on to her bed and waved her legs, still in their smart fabric shorts, in the air. She covered her mouth with a pillow and shrieked into it.

Caroline said, '*What?* You're joking, right?'

'She's not joking,' Kiran said, coming upright again.

'I bloody love it. This is so cool. This is what should have happened in that film, where they meet on the train – what's it called again?'

'*Before Sunrise*,' Caroline said automatically; she and I had watched it and the sequel back to back at the Prince Charles cinema, in the summer after A-levels. 'Yes, but Norah, are you sure about him? I mean, you don't know him – are you sure he's not dodgy? What about your flight and what about work next week? And what will your dad say? Isn't he collecting you tomorrow?'

'Yes, he is – I'll have to phone him. I'll just tell him I'm staying on. He won't mind. I won't tell him about Andrew, though,' I said. I had learned my lesson on Christmas Eve 2004; sometimes it was better to ask for forgiveness than permission. 'And work is just me phoning up the temp agency on Monday morning. I'll pass.'

'And he's so clearly not dodgy,' said Kiran. 'Do keep in touch, though, Norah. I want all the details.'

'Oh, so do I,' said Caroline wistfully. 'It's so romantic. But be safe, Norah. Don't let him take you to a second location.'

'I won't,' I said. 'Honestly, don't worry, Caroline. I think he's a good one.'

Once they had left for the train station, I went to meet Andrew, as planned, at the hostel reception. I had just finished booking myself into the women's dorm room for another night, when I heard him behind me.

'Hi,' he said, with that crooked half-smile I already loved.

'Hi,' I replied, beaming all over my face like an idiot.

'I was worried you'd change your mind and hop on that train back to Rome after all.'

'Nope, I'm here,' I said. 'The girls thought you might be kidnapping me, but I said I already ran a background check with Interpol – and you passed.' I added shyly, 'Were your friends surprised? What did they say?'

He grinned. 'Conor's exact words were: "That must have been some opera."'

We walked out of the hotel and down the narrow lane that led to the river. I noticed the huge medieval doors, set within the ancient high walls, all coloured rose, lemon and that orangey-ochre shade that seemed quintessentially Italian. It was a quiet summer Sunday lunchtime; a few young men flew by on mopeds, but the street was otherwise as still as a forest. I glanced up at the perfect blue sky, and my heart soared at the thought that we had a whole week together. Then we reached the river, and Verona opened itself up to our gaze, with its tiled roofs, towers and belltowers, its shuttered buildings and ivied brick walls, all ours for the taking.

'Imagine – you could be heading back to Rome for your Ryanair flight right now,' said Andrew.

'Don't.' I shuddered. 'I don't think I'll ever want to go back.'

I was worried for a moment that he'd think I was proposing something – that we run away and live in Italy together? – but he just grinned back. 'I know exactly what you mean.'

A stone-tiled bridge, the Ponte Pietra, led us over the wide brown river, and we wandered under an arch into the old town, talking and drifting until we found ourselves outside a place where a little crowd was gathered, obviously waiting for some attraction to reopen after the lunchtime rush. I looked up to read the much-graffitied sign.

'Casa di Giulietta. Oh, of course. Juliet's House.'

'Juliet who?' Andrew asked. I turned to look at him in surprise, to find him grinning again. 'I'm only codding you . . . I did *Romeo and Juliet* for my Junior Cert. *Two households, both alike in dignity, In fair Verona, where we lay our scene.*'

'*From ancient grudge break to new mutiny, Where civil blood* something something. Sorry, I need a translation. Codding me? Junior Cert?'

'Ah. I think it's the GCSE equivalent? And codding – gosh, that must be a Dublin word. I never knew that. Do you want to go in?'

We passed through another cobbled alcove, where bricked walls were crammed with tiny pieces of paper, pasted thickly on the walls and stuffed into every available crevice.

'Those are the letters to Juliet,' said Andrew. 'People come from all over the world with their love messages and leave them here so Juliet can – well, I'm not sure what they're expecting her to do, but they leave them here anyway. A triumph of hope over experience.'

The alcove opened into an ancient, brick-walled

courtyard, where a slim bronze statue of Juliet, rubbed smooth by the hands of generations, stood before a wall that was thickly covered with tumbling, glossy vines. Fifteen feet above our heads, a little stone balcony budded from the wall, and further up were arched windows where you could almost expect Juliet, or her nurse, to emerge to look for Romeo.

'Is it real?' I asked.

'Well – it depends what you mean by real. The house is from the 1300s, but the balcony is from the 1900s . . . Juliet didn't exist, but there was a family here with a name that sounded like Capulet. So I suppose . . . it's real if you think it is?'

I looked around, imagining it for a minute as it would have been in the fourteenth century. Maybe Juliet wasn't a historical figure, but who was to say there wasn't a grain of truth in the story? In any case there was something special about this place. And whether it was just the beauty of the old house or something everyone was bringing to it, it didn't seem to matter.

'Do you want to go in?' he asked.

I looked at the window, saw the admission price and let out a gasp of horror. I hadn't budgeted for an extra week's holiday on top of a week of no wages. I certainly couldn't afford things like this if I was going to be able to eat or sleep anywhere that wasn't a park bench for the rest of the week.

'What is it?'

I hesitated. Andrew probably knew that I was on a

budget, but I didn't want him to think that I was being miserly, or worse, hinting for a loan. Luckily, he guessed what the problem was.

'Not to worry. It's nice inside, but nothing unmissable. The courtyard is the best part, I think.'

'So you've been inside already? Andrew, you should have said.'

'I just wanted to show it to you,' he said.

I swooned inside and wrote this down in my mental notebook, which was already filling up with innumerable things I knew I would never forget. 'I think I can imagine it,' I said.

'You're right,' he said. 'Here – I want to show you something else.'

Andrew led me towards another square nearby, the Piazza dei Signori, where I let out another involuntary gasp, this time of sheer delight. The jumble of styles, the medieval turrets and Renaissance arches, the brown-and-cream striped palazzo; the statues in the middle, all under a bright blue sky – it was simply all too beautiful to be true. And yet here were people walking home from lunch, boys on mopeds, people having coffee, children chasing pigeons; just living their everyday life, here in paradise.

'See?' said Andrew. 'All we need is the city, each other – and maybe a cup of coffee.'

We sat and drank espressos at a zinc table outside a café under an umbrella, and once again I had to remind myself that I wasn't dreaming; this was happening, now, on 14 August 2009.

I had phoned my dad earlier, using the hostel pay-phone, to explain that I wouldn't be flying back the next day from Rome, as previously planned. I hadn't intended to tell him about Andrew, but it all came out within minutes; it was hard to keep a secret from Dad. Even though I was twenty-two and all grown up, in theory, Dad was fairly dubious about the sound of Andrew – until I mentioned that he was a musician. On hearing that Andrew played the violin and was going to Juilliard, Dad revised his opinion and just told me to be careful.

Andrew smiled when I told him that last part. 'It's funny that you live in London and your dad tells you to be careful in Verona . . . I mean it's not exactly a crime hot spot, is it?'

I didn't think it was worth mentioning that, in Dad's view, the danger was sitting opposite me shaking sugar into his second espresso. We chatted some more about home and discovered that we both came from large suburbs of capital cities – Andrew was from a town called Bray, south of Dublin.

'It's a great place,' Andrew told me. 'I mean Bray itself is a bit of a faded beauty. It was a big seaside resort, back in the day – not so much now. But the setting is lovely, with Bray Head sweeping down to the sea. Dublin's answer to the Bay of Naples, apparently.' He laughed, and a second later he added, 'That's not true, by the way. I've been to the Bay of Naples, and it's very different. But Killiney Bay is a beautiful spot.'

'I've never been to Dublin,' I admitted. 'Never been to Ireland in fact.'

'Really? We'll have to set that right.'

I thrilled at the hint that we might stay in touch, but I didn't want to pin him down to anything so early on. 'When's the best time to visit?'

'Well, the summer is nice – that's generally a few days in July. But personally, I like Christmas. That's a great time to be in Dublin. So many people come home, you see.' His face grew thoughtful. 'I remember as a kid, how every year all these aunts and uncles and cousins would reappear as if by magic. I thought they were part of Christmas, like the Three Wise Men. Walk down Grafton Street on Christmas Eve and it feels like you could see anyone: whether they belonged in the past, or far away or both – you'd almost expect to see a ghost. Until the decorations came down and they'd all vanish again to wherever they came from. I'm not explaining it very well.'

I shook my head. 'I think I know what you mean.'

'Even if I end up living abroad, I think I'll always want to spend Christmas in Dublin,' Andrew said. 'In fact, Norah, I'll make you a promise. If you come to Dublin, in ten years' time, I'll be there to meet you.'

'Oh yes?' I was laughing.

'Absolutely! I'll see you at six o'clock outside Bewley's Café on Grafton Street, on Christmas Eve 2019. Anyone will tell you where it is. I'll meet you under the clock.'

I was still laughing and shaking my head, because it

sounded so nuts. But Andrew was taking out his note-book. 'Look, I'm writing it down. And your email address. And your number, just in case. But here's the date: 24 December 2019, 6 p.m. Andrew. Write that down! I'll write it too.'

'Why in ten years?' I asked.

'Well, let's hope it won't take that long. But in case life gets in the way . . .'

I watched him write it down and I remembered what his friends had said; once it was in the notebook, it was a done deal. I got out my notebook and wrote it too, along with his email address: andrew_power21@hotmail.com. I knew Power was his surname, or I might have been confused.

'OK, then,' I said. 'You're on. I'll be there.'

He held out his hand, and we shook on it solemnly. I was grinning, because it was all so silly. I hoped it wouldn't be ten more years before I did see him again, but at least this seemed like a start.

'Meanwhile . . . I have something else I'd like to propose,' said Andrew.

I looked at him in alarm. Obviously it wasn't going to be that kind of proposal, but . . .

'Nothing too crazy,' he said, a faint flush growing along his cheekbones. 'But there's a Swedish guy in the hostel who wants to sell his guitar. So I thought: how would you like to do some busking? We could have some fun, and it's not bad money, or so I'm told. I've never done it before.'

'You mean with me singing?'

He laughed. 'Well, unless you have a triangle. Sure, with you singing. I can't sing a note.'

I knew by now that Andrew's musical tastes were eclectic, but I was still taken aback by this suggestion. In my experience, most classically trained musicians wouldn't be keen on busking with a guitar. But obviously, I was thrilled.

'Well, OK – I mean I'd love to. But, Andrew! What about your violin?'

'Conor took it home for me,' Andrew said, smiling. 'I love that you ask that – you're such a musician. Now, what should we play? Do you know any Mamas and Papas? "California Dreamin'"?'

'Of course! Oh, wait, I just thought of something.'

'Permits,' we said in unison.

'Not a problem – it's twenty-five euros from the police station. You just go there with your passport. There was even a guy with a piano on one of the bridges the other day, by all accounts.'

'This is so exciting! OK, let's write down a few songs so we don't waste rehearsal time,' I said.

We both got out our notebooks simultaneously, then looked at each other when we realized what we'd done. And then we laughed and laughed until we had to stop, because we were attracting such odd stares, though even after that, it only took a glance at each other to start us laughing again.

\*

Andrew said we should check out the situation with permits before doing anything else, but I suggested we try practising together first.

'They might ask us to perform, like an audition,' I said. 'We'll have to have something ready.'

'Ah – good thinking,' he said. 'This is not your first rodeo, is it?'

'It is, actually. I've never busked before! But we won't tell them that.'

I waited in the garden of the hostel while Andrew went to get the guitar. I sat on the bench where we had sat the night before – was it really less than twenty-four hours ago? – under the shade of the cypress tree and looked down at the red roofs of the town, sleeping in the afternoon sun. I could hear the cicadas, fainter than they had been last night but still there. I kicked off my sandals so I could feel the dry grass under my toes. Sitting there, knowing that Andrew was minutes away and that we had a whole week to spend together, I knew I was the happiest I'd been in a long time, maybe ever.

Soon, I heard his footsteps scrunch on the gravel, and he sat down again.

'God, it's out of tune – good thing he left town or we could arrest him for crimes against music. OK. What should we start with?' He started strumming the first chords of 'Bridge Over Troubled Water' and I joined in, making up the words I didn't know; I could look them up later on the hostel's computer. He smiled, when he heard me. 'Wow! Nice sound.' When we finished he said, 'Beautiful. You have a really gorgeous voice. What's next? Slow songs are good, I believe, because they make people stop and throw the coins. And I think the older the better.'

'Let's see ... "Both Sides Now" by Joni Mitchell? Do you know that?'

'Joni who?'

'Andrew! Really? You'll definitely know it.' I started singing, and he picked up the chords, singing along. He hadn't been quite lying when he said he couldn't sing a note; each individual note he sang was in tune, but together it sounded – wrong.

'I can sing the notes, but not the music,' he said mournfully.

'Well, I can barely play the guitar, so we're a good team,' I said, smiling. 'I only play the piano really now. I haven't picked up my trumpet in years.'

'I didn't know you played the trumpet!'

'Yes, in the school orchestra – it wasn't a very happy experience, though.'

'How so?'

'Oh, just I was the only girl, and the rest of the section liked playing practical jokes on me – telling me we were all going to stand up during a particular section, then I'd be the only one. That kind of thing.'

'Bullying, in short,' said Andrew. 'It's true you don't see many girls in a brass section, and I suppose that must be why. I'm sorry to hear it.'

'Thanks. But I prefer singing now anyway.'

'I'm not surprised. The brass section's loss is my gain. You know who you sound like? You sound like Dusty Springfield,' he said. 'Do you know many of her songs? There's a gorgeous old song of hers – hang on, actually. I have it on my MP3 player.' He took it out of his bag and put the earphones straight into my ears; the light touch and the intimate gesture made my heart skip a beat.

I listened and I felt the thrill you get when hearing a great pop song for the first time. A piano playing chords that sounded like a sweet old memory, and Dusty's voice – singing about going back to a time when she was young enough to know the truth, which I didn't fully understand. Then the sound built, in that very 1960s way, with the flutes and strings getting louder and more elaborate, and Dusty's voice more and more triumphant; it started like a ballad, but it ended like an anthem.

'That's beautiful,' I said, handing him back the earphones. 'What's it called?'

'It's called "Going Back". I think it was the Byrds originally, but loads of people have covered it.'

'Oh! The Byrds – we must do "Turn Turn Turn". I don't know about this song, though, Andrew. It's gorgeous, but won't it sound a bit odd without all the orchestration? I think it really needs that or it might sound a little flat, to be honest.' I thought for a minute. 'And it's the same with "Turn, Turn, Turn" actually. It needs a bigger sound than we can make.'

'You're absolutely right. To everything there is a season.' He nodded, a slow grin spreading over his face. 'We make a good team, don't we?'

I smiled back, thinking: you're telling me.

After we got our permits – which involved both an audition and lots of form filling – we set up camp on the Castelvecchio bridge, on the way out of the old town centre. We started with 'I Still Haven't Found What I'm Looking For' and finished with 'California Dreamin', after a haphazard journey from the nineties to the sixties and back. On the first evening we made nearly forty-five euros; on the next one, nearly sixty – more than enough for a celebratory dinner at one of the trattorias beside the river, with cheap red wine and the biggest, most delicious pizza I'd ever tasted, with blackened edges that overspilled the plate. We sat outside and ate under the stars, marvelling at our good fortune.

'It feels like a dream, doesn't it?' I said shyly.

'I know. Making music, and getting paid for it – it seems too good to be true.'

That wasn't *all* I meant, but I knew what he was talking about too, of course.

'So . . . you're not tempted to throw in Juilliard for a life of busking?' I said, teasing but also wondering if, by some mad chance, he might be reconsidering his trip across the Atlantic.

'No,' he said. 'I didn't come from money, you know,

Norah. The next ten years of my life will be about chasing work, doing anything that will pay me and getting contacts more than anything. So this scholarship to Juilliard – I can't tell what doors it might open or what it might do for me. I can't turn it down.'

I nodded. I had already sensed this in Andrew. He was laid-back and utterly without pretensions, as happy strumming U2 as he was playing Vivaldi in a fifteenth-century chapel. But underneath the jokes and the banter was a completely steely dedication to his music. I didn't have a single doubt in my mind that he would do whatever it took to be a success.

'Of course you can't turn it down,' I said, sitting up a little straighter. I didn't want him to think that I'd been hinting at anything. I had ambitions too.

'I know the timing sucks,' he said.

He reached out a hand and put his on mine, sending shivers coursing up and down my spine again. I had spent two full days with him now but I couldn't imagine ever getting tired of it, or of him. We were getting on so well, without even having any artistic differences. The only time we had actually argued – if you could call it that – was when Andrew had referred, in passing, to Ella Fitzgerald as 'just a vocalist'.

'What do you mean, just a vocalist?' I protested.

'I only mean it literally in that she didn't play an instrument . . .'

'Yes she did! Her voice was her instrument. She used it exactly the way Charlie Parker or Benny Goodman used theirs. In fact, she did more than them, because she didn't just scat – she made up lyrics, she invented poems – she even did comedy! Have you heard her recording of "How High the Moon", live in Berlin? It's eight minutes long, and that's mostly her swinging it, doing variations exactly like a trumpeter or saxophonist would . . . nobody could do what she did. I've tried, and I can't even come close.'

To his eternal credit, Andrew didn't laugh indulgently at my passionate defence of Ella. He did smile, but he held up his hands and said, 'Consider me schooled. Respect is due. I'll get a recording of it.'

Now part of me was suddenly desperate for plans, for assurance that we could find a way to be together after this week. But at the same time, I didn't want to put pressure on him – or spoil the time we did have. I wanted to enjoy every moment of it, while it lasted.

'But, regarding Juilliard,' said Andrew. 'It's only for a year. So after that . . .'

'That's a long way away,' I said. 'Let's just enjoy this week, for now.'

'Good plan.' He smiled at me. 'What about your music, though? Your voice is really gorgeous – you've got something special there, for sure. I hope you'll send me your CD, when you have it done.'

'Of course.'

'In fact,' Andrew said. 'Do you want to practise the set list with me, for the recording? You know what you're doing, of course – but I'm happy to have a listen and see if I can make any suggestions. I'd like to hear it anyway.'

'I'd love that,' I said, touched.

We wandered back up to the hostel and spent a while in the garden, on our usual secluded bench under the cypress tree. The moon, which had been a crescent on the first night, was now swelling towards being full. It was getting increasingly hard to tear ourselves away to our beds in separate dorms.

'I have an idea,' Andrew said after a while, his forehead resting on mine.

'Another idea?' I said, teasing him. 'What now – we put on an opera?'

'Tempting! No, I was going to say: with all the money we're making . . . tomorrow, or the day after, we could get the train somewhere. Maybe Lake Garda? It's meant to be beautiful. We could stay in a hotel . . .'

'I don't know about a hotel,' I said, jokingly. 'What are we, millionaires?'

He put his arm around me. 'Right now, I wouldn't trade places with all the millionaires in the world.'

I took his hand and tilted my face up towards his kiss. Oh, that kiss. I would never get enough of it, of him. It was already Wednesday; my new flight back was booked for Saturday night. What would I do at the end of the week? How could I bear to say goodbye to him? But I pushed the thought away; we had the moment now. We had to stay in the present, and soak every bit of it up, while we still could.

Two days later, after an extra morning performing, we got the train from Verona to Descenzano del Garda, where we waited for an hour at a little bar beside the ferry station, drinking lemonade with our feet propped on our backpacks and watching two young tabby cats dozing in the sun. I was wearing my black dress again, the one I'd worn to the opera, since everything else I had brought badly needed washing.

'Smile,' Andrew said suddenly. I turned to look at him and smiled when I saw he was taking a picture of me. I hadn't even known he had a camera with him.

'Let me take one of you?' I asked, and he smiled for the camera while I snapped. I was so glad I would have one of him – I hadn't even thought about it. 'Don't forget to email it to me,' I said. I knew that he didn't use Facebook, and I used it only minimally, with no profile picture. And nothing else – not Instagram, not Snapchat or Twitter – yet existed, so our contact after today would be by email, phone or nothing.

A ferry took us around the headland, to Sirmione, which we had picked for no real reason except that it was where the next boat was going. We had been talking all day, when we weren't busking, but on the ferry we stayed quiet and looked. The lake was perfection: a pale azure sheet, whose edges dissolved into the foothills of impossibly high blue mountains. After the bustle of Verona, it seemed so quiet; the only sounds were the ferry's engine, the cry of a few gulls passing overhead and the other passengers talking, their Italian still sounding like music to me.

Sirmione was a peaceful little town right on the lake shore, dominated by an impossible-looking medieval fortress with square towers, rising straight up out of the water – three sides of it were only accessible by boat. We found a small hotel near the ferry landing and took the room without even asking to see it, which Andrew joked was also against the backpackers' code. After putting our bathing costumes on under our clothes, we made our way to a brief sandy beach beside the castle and swam out into the lake, heavenly and cool after our hot wait at the shore. We floated on our backs, looking up at the blue sky and the fortress walls, and at any moment I half expected the castle's walls to open and for us to be swept in with the current, into some medieval pageant or fairytale. But that didn't happen; instead I felt Andrew's hand reach for mine in the water.

'When we're back in rainy London and New York – when the wind is cutting through us and the rain's soaking our boots – let's remember this,' he said, and I nodded, thinking: as if I could forget.

We stayed on the beach until we were dry, when we wandered up into the town and saw the shuttered yellow villa, guarded by ancient cypresses, where Andrew told me the opera singer Maria Callas had lived with her Italian husband before leaving him for Aristotle Onassis.

'How do you know all this?' I asked, wondering if he was some kind of opera superfan. I hadn't had that impression; he seemed eclectic in his tastes more than anything.

'I read it in the guidebook, while you were changing earlier,' he admitted, making me laugh.

Leaving the villa, we walked a little way down the hill, where we came to a fork in the road. One way led back down into the town; another led along a path up into the hills, probably some kind of scenic trail. I glanced back at Andrew to see which way he wanted to go, but he had an abstracted look on his face, which I knew by now was a sign that he was hearing music in his head. He hadn't offered to play me any of his compositions, and I hadn't asked, but I had seen him early in the morning, or late in the evening in the hostel garden, jotting in a composition notebook.

'Which way?' I asked him. 'Into the hills, or back into town?'

'Um.' He looked around vaguely – obviously, he hadn't even noticed the junction.

'You choose,' he said, so we turned back down, into the town; it was getting late, and the air was cool.

Back in the harbour, we stopped in one of the trattorias for a dinner of grilled fish and a glass of wine – a white wine called Lugano, which the waiter told us was local, not just to this part of Italy, but this part of Lake

Garda. It tasted crisp and almondy, and was a gorgeous greeny-gold colour, like the stones at the bottom of the lake which we'd seen earlier through the transparent water.

'This is delicious,' I said. 'I would buy a bottle and take it back for my dad, if it wasn't for the stupid liquids rule.'

'Would it travel, though?' said Andrew. 'You know I had that summer job in Alsace, playing the piano in a hotel. They had this dessert wine we used to have every night after we cleared up and I thought it was the best stuff ever . . . I brought a bottle home, but it just wasn't the same. That's because wine is about the moment, apparently. Or so one of my Trinity classmates told me.' He grinned. 'That's the kind of thing I learned there.'

'What does that mean exactly – wine is about the moment?' I asked, not because I didn't understand but because I wanted to hear his explanation.

'Well, partly it's about where and when it was made, the earth the grapes grew in, the sun and the weather. But it's also about where and when you taste it. It's one thing on a terrace in Italy, with your feet in the water and the stars so close overhead that it feels you could touch them . . . it's going to taste different back in your kitchen in Ealing.'

I nodded. 'Jazz is like that too, I suppose. It's all about the performance and the improvisation, and who's playing: the chemistry in the room. Even if you get a live recording, it's never going to be the same as being there.'

'But that's what makes it special,' said Andrew.

We finished dinner not long after that and went back to the hotel. Our room was small and simple, with heavy dark furniture and a double bed with starched white sheets. But it had a lake view and even a balcony which we could sit on and look out over the lake, now almost dark except for the full moon rising across the water. We didn't even turn on the lights in the room; just stood there looking down at the unearthly beauty of the moon, the sky and the lake.

'Well,' said Andrew. He sat down on the bed. 'Here we are.'

'Yes,' I said. 'Here we are.'

This was our last night together. Tomorrow morning we would pack our backpacks for the last time and get the bus to the airport at Brescia. My flight for Stansted was leaving at noon; his was leaving an hour later, for Dublin. We hadn't discussed the future at all, except in the most general terms – 'When I'm next in London' or 'If you come to New York'. I did wonder if we should talk about it more explicitly, but at the same time I didn't want to press too hard or look too far ahead.

'Come over here,' said Andrew.

I went to sit beside him, and he leaned down to kiss me. We kissed for a while, and then he slipped down the strap of my dress, and kissed my skin where the strap had been. I unbuttoned his shirt. It was the same one he'd worn to the opera, and I thought how funny, and also sad, it was that we were wearing our 'good' outfits again, for the occasion: our last night together.

'What are you smiling at?' he asked.

'Nothing, just – look at us, all dressed up with nowhere to go.'

'I don't want to go anywhere. Do you?'

I shook my head and he pulled me towards him.

Much later, I got out of bed, leaving Andrew asleep behind me. I gazed out of the window at the lake and the moon, higher now and completely full. It had lost its golden haze and was shining as bright as an electric light. Looking back at him, I felt the first hairline crack inside my heart. What had I done? I had laid myself open to be completely devastated, falling for someone who was about to move to the other side of the world for at least a year. I turned back to the window, wishing that somehow we could stay here for ever, just the two of us, busking or maybe working in a bar . . . I remembered my question to him in Juliet's house. *Is it real?* Was it genuine or just a romantic illusion?

Or maybe that was the wrong question. Maybe it was just too unrealistic to think that we could continue any kind of relationship, or even that we should after just a week together. We were a student and a temp; we couldn't afford transatlantic visits. Not to mention that he was starting the most thrilling chapter in his life, and I was returning to a temp job and my music career, which was effectively busking indoors. We were heading in different directions, and it would probably be less painful, in the long run, to acknowledge that now.

'Norah?'

'Sorry. Did I wake you?'

'Of course not. Come here.'

I went to the bed and knelt beside him; he held out a hand.

'It sucks to say goodbye, I know. But we'll figure something out.'

Looking down at my hand in his, I realized that I couldn't bear to prolong the agony – emails and silences and waiting, and wondering if he still felt the same. 'I don't know, Andrew. I think realistically – this is probably it, isn't it?'

He opened his mouth to protest but then a minute later he said, 'Well, I suppose for now it is. Yes.'

I nodded, feeling something close to relief. It was easier to say goodbye now than it would be in six months' time. Weirdly, I was reminded of the long drive up to York with my mum, after my Christmas break in my second year, when I asked her several times if something was happening with her and Dad. When she finally told me that, yes, they were splitting up, I was devastated but also, in a strange way, almost glad. At least now, I didn't have to wonder.

'But can we keep the door open?' Andrew said. 'I mean, I should be back in Dublin at Christmas – I can arrange a stopover via London. If you would like that?'

'Of course I would! And I'll write to you.'

'Do that,' he said. 'Look, we don't have to hold each other to anything. But we could just see what happens. I'll be finished the course in June, and I'll most likely head back to Europe then. I could even end up in London. And if I do . . .'

'OK,' I said, and added, 'And if all else fails, there's Christmas 2019.'

I knew that all we could do for now was hope for the best. Of course it couldn't be like this for ever; this was a temporary, stolen time, as fragile as a soap bubble. But he would only be in America for a year, and who knew what would happen after that? It was just like Juliet's house: it was real if we thought it was.

# 9. Has Anyone Seen My Man?

*Saturday, 21 December 2019*

The ferry terminal isn't huge, but there's a long wait between the boat actually arriving and us being able to disembark. I can't see much through the window beyond a few amber lights strung here and there, reflected on the dark water. But I'm conscious of an ever-growing buzz that's gathering among the passengers, every single one of whom is obviously going home for Christmas. As we get closer to Dublin, everyone starts chatting to each other, swapping acquaintances and general Christmas cheer. Then the exit is announced, and we filter through passport checks into the arrivals hall, where the solid ground feels like a shock, after nearly three hours of constant gentle rocking.

And then, unbelievably, I can feel my eyes start to prick up again. What is wrong with me? I haven't needed to cry in years, and now it seems to be turning into a near-daily danger.

Maybe it's the long hours of travelling. Or maybe it's seeing all the families gathered to welcome each other – people clutching home-made signs and banners, kids bouncing up and down for a sight of uncles and aunts, elderly parents preparing to welcome their adult kids home. I see a dark-haired girl, who I noticed on the ferry because she was so gorgeous, run into the arms of a tall young man. Couples are in the minority, though; it's mostly family reunions. This place obviously takes Christmas seriously.

I am *horrified* at the thought that I almost came here alone.

'Do you feel a bit friendless?' I say to Joe. 'Where's our banner?'

'We don't need a banner – I've got our bags.' He pats me reassuringly on the arm. 'Come on, let's grab a taxi.' And he strides on ahead, before I remind him that we need to find a cash machine first to take out euros. I suppose we are a good travelling team. He focuses on the big picture, and I remember the details. And by 6 p.m. we're in a taxi, heading along the quays towards the Shelbourne Hotel.

The question of where to stay was the subject of long discussion. I wanted to do Airbnb, but all the ones in the centre were booked up.

'It seems wrong to stay in a hotel,' I said to Joe. 'It's not Christmassy.'

'What if it was a really nice hotel?' he suggested.

'We can't afford a nice hotel,' I said. But then I remembered Mum's air miles and how they counted towards some hotels. An hour later, we were booking two balcony rooms at the Shelbourne Hotel. Mum was thrilled at the idea that she could help me book it, as it made her feel much better about dumping me.

'It's the best place to stay in Dublin,' she told me. 'You'll have a fantastic time.'

She was pleased that I would have company on the trip but a bit doubtful when I told her I was going there with Joe.

'He's a nice boy but . . . I just worry about "friendships" like that,' she said, the quote marks hanging heavy in the air. 'If he's not boyfriend material . . . he could stop you meeting someone special.'

'He's not stopping me, Mum! He's going to . . .' I stopped abruptly. There was no way I was going to tell her about my reunion with Andrew. She would say I was out of my mind. 'He's going to introduce me to some of his friends,' I said lamely, to get her off my back.

'Well, just as long as you're getting something out of it,' she said, slightly mollified. 'Otherwise . . . well, you don't want him to be getting all the benefits of a girlfriend without you getting anything out of it.'

'He's not getting any *benefits*, Mum,' I told her. But the conversation lingered uneasily in my mind. I realized it was probably more likely that *I* was preventing *Joe* from meeting someone. What if our conversations and texts were fulfilling his emotional needs and preventing him from committing to Julie or FiFi or Jess or all the other figures who've come and gone? But I can't worry about his life for him.

By now we're in our taxi, whisking along redeveloped quays with glossy high-rise office buildings, and a beautiful modern suspension bridge with curving girders, shaped almost like a guitar or a harp.

'That's the Calatrava Bridge,' says our taxi driver, an older man with grey hair.

'Oh. It says here it's the Samuel Beckett Bridge?' I say, consulting my map on my phone.

He laughs. 'Yes, that's the real name, I suppose, I just call it the Calatrava because that's who designed it. Everything has two names here. Like the Aviva stadium, you still hear that called Lansdowne Road . . .'

He reels off more examples, and I try to listen, but I don't take it all in: I'm too busy looking out of the window. All the buildings are lit up with Christmas projections, and I just catch a glimpse of a huge Georgian building with a copper dome before we cross the river – the Liffey – and stream up a side street. The streets seem somehow darker in Dublin, as if there's been a power cut, but the windows of each building shine all the brighter. I see cafés with fairy lights, and lively pubs with people spilling out on to the street – there really does seem to be one on every corner. And I can't help but scan all their faces, wondering if one of them will be his. I remember Andrew's words: *Even if I end up living abroad, I think I'll always want to spend Christmas in Dublin.* So he must be here, right now, somewhere in this city.

'The Shelbourne Hotel,' announces our driver.

It's another grand red-brick Georgian building,

covered in green creepers. I peek out the window and get a quick impression of red carpets outside, and black cast-iron statues of women with Ancient Egyptian-style headdresses, carrying lamps. It looks extremely swanky, and I hope we're not going to lower the tone.

I let Joe pay the driver, since I got lunch on the ferry, thankfully dodging the awkwardness of a tip, and we go inside to check in. Inside is just as beautiful as the exterior, from the marble floor to the gold and plaster ceiling: there's also a chandelier the size of a baby heli-copter, plus a twenty-foot Christmas tree. Quiet piano music is twinkling from a bar next door. Joe and I are practically nudging each other, barely hiding our glee that we actually get to stay here.

As we wait at the reception desk to check in, I notice a woman nearby sitting on a couch reading the news-paper. There is something striking about her, and I gaze at her trying to decipher what it is. It's hard to tell her age – she's one of those people could be anything from forty-five to sixty-five. Her face has plenty of lines, but they suggest sunshine and smiles rather than worries or smoking. There are white streaks in her chestnut hair, but her posture is very upright and youthful. But what draws the eye isn't her clothes, or her make-up or hair, though all are very elegant. It's her general air of being content with herself and with the world, of enjoying the moment without worrying about how she's coming across or what's going to happen next.

Obviously noticing me staring at her, she looks up

and smiles. I smile back, awkwardly, hoping she doesn't guess that I'm wondering what her secret is and how I might be able to copy it.

'Now! Ms Jones?' says the receptionist, interrupting me from my reverie. 'Was it a double or two singles?'

Thankfully she has two rooms for us rather than a bridal suite. Both are gorgeous, all done up with silk striped wallpaper and thick red carpets. They're not adjoining, but they're next door to each other; not huge, but with a bathroom each, and every conceivable little luxury from a box of chocolates to headed notepaper. The ubiquity of Airbnb is such that I can't think how long it's been since I stayed in a hotel – months? Years?

'What do you want to do?' Joe says. 'Room service or go out to eat?'

'Oh, let's go out,' I say, suddenly excited. 'I mean it's not every night we're in Dublin, is it?'

'Do you want to try and book somewhere?'

'Let's just wander. I'm sure there are lots of places nearby . . .'

'Now hang on.' Joe holds up a warning finger. 'I'm not going to be caught out by that. Remember Snowdon?'

'Oh yeah.' We had all decided to climb Mount Snowdon for Paul's thirtieth and came down after six hours starving and freezing, to find that nowhere in the town had a table for food. We ended up scavenging some chips from a van at 9 p.m., by which time everyone was completely broken and snarling at each other – even Joe was as close to grumpy as I've ever seen him.

'But we haven't just got back from a six-hour hike,' I point out.

'No – it was an eight-hour train and ferry journey,' Joe says. 'Let's get a reservation. I'm not having our holiday end in homicide before it even begins.'

Fifteen minutes later, we're setting off, on the recommendation of the hotel concierge, to an Italian place called The Steps of Rome. It's right off the top of Grafton Street, which is lit up with garlands of Christmas lights, still thronged with shoppers at nearly seven o'clock. I gaze down it, remembering Andrew's words: 'Walk down Grafton Street on Christmas Eve and it feels like you could see anyone: whether they belonged in the past, or far away or both.' We turn on to Chatham Row, and as we make our way to The Steps of Rome, I notice a small red-brick building with a sign: the DU Conservatory of Music and Drama.

'Look, Joe,' I say, remembering something Andrew told me in Italy. 'Andrew told me he had lessons here, as a kid. And he taught here as well. Except he called it the College of Music.' Again with the two names. 'He said it was really magical how you could walk by it and hear a flute or a saxophone, just a stone's throw from the busiest shopping street.'

Joe makes a polite noise, and we head on towards the restaurant. It's a cosy hole-in-the-wall place with square slabs of pizza displayed behind a glass counter and minuscule tile-topped tables. It's crammed with Christmas shoppers, but our reserved table is ready for us at the back.

'So . . . what do you want to do tomorrow?' Joe asks. 'Where do you want to go first?'

'I'm not sure – I haven't really had a chance to do any research,' I say, feeling slightly guilty: normally I plan my trips in a bit more detail. 'Maybe we could go and look around Trinity College? That's where Andrew studied,' I add, before realizing how I must sound.

'Mm,' says Joe. 'Just to check, though, Norah. Is this trip going to be some sort of pilgrimage to take in everywhere that Andrew might have had a pint or bought cornflakes? Because if so, it's going to be a long few days.'

'Ha, ha,' I say, opening my menu.

With my exhaustion and hangover from last night, pasta *and* pizza seem the logical choice, so I have a slice of margherita pizza to start, and then pasta with melting slivers of mushroom, blue cheese and thyme, actual heaven on a plate.

'Fun water?' Joe asks, pouring me another glass of sparkling water; he's referring back to a time when I referred to sparkling water as a 'fun' drink, which he still finds funny. He's having red wine, but I can't touch it: I still feel poisoned from last night.

'Thank you . . . Can I just say one thing?' I say. 'About Andrew? Since that's why we're here?'

'Sure,' says Joe.

'What really puzzles me is *why* I can't find him on the internet. I mean, I thought maybe he stopped doing music, but actually that doesn't seem possible. He was so dedicated – I mean music was his life. Is his life.' I pause uneasily, the past tense suddenly seeming ominous in this context.

'I'm sure there's some explanation. Maybe he's just teaching, or doing something else that doesn't put you online.'

'Even teaching, he would be online,' I say. 'It just seems so strange. And he was obviously really talented – I mean he went to Juilliard, he worked in Hollywood. But there's no mention of him, after about 2013.' I hesitate, not wanting to sound alarmist. 'Sometimes I wonder . . .'

'What – whether something happened to him?' Joe shakes his head. 'I'm sure it didn't. Or if it did you'd find some mention on the internet – even if it's just a local website or something.'

'I suppose,' I say. It's not the first time I've thought of this but I imagine that if a tragedy did occur there probably would have been a mention online, given Andrew's youth and talent. I give myself a shake. 'Yes, I'm sure you're right. But then why can't I find him?'

'I don't know, Norah. Maybe he joined a cult. Or he got mixed up in something dubious and went into witness protection? I'm just blue-sky thinking here,' Joe says. 'But . . . I do think you should prepare yourself for the idea that he won't show up.'

'I know,' I say, feeling unreasonably irritated at Joe's scepticism. 'But he might, you know.'

'OK, let's say he does. And let's say that you get on like a house on fire. What would you do then? Would you move to Dublin? Go long-distance?'

I sigh. 'I don't know! Anything could happen. He might be engaged . . . or be married with three kids.'

'He might have a mullet,' Joe offers. 'Or be really, really into making his own craft beer.' I laugh at this because I know he's referring to a date I went on where the guy could literally talk of nothing except his adventures in home brewing.

'Yes. Or he might have a tattoo on his face.'

'Or even just a beard,' says Joe. 'Everybody has a beard now, so you should genuinely be prepared for that.'

I shiver. I hate beards, which has been a real problem on the dating scene in recent years.

'Let's worry about that later,' I say, borrowing Joe's favourite phrase. 'For now . . . I'd like to make a toast.'

'A toast?' He looks around theatrically. 'When have you ever made a toast before? Aside from at Kiran's wedding.'

'Shut up, would you? I want to toast to you, Joe. Thank you for coming with me. Because I don't think I would have had the nerve to come by myself. And even if I had, it would have been a slightly sad trip. But with you here . . . I think it might almost be fun. So cheers to you.'

'Any time. I mean, not any time. I won't spend every Christmas haring off with you in pursuit of an old boyfriend. This is a one-time offer. So make the most of it.'

'I will,' I promise, solemnly.

# 10. Don't Stop Believin'

From: Andrew Power
To: Norah Jones
8 December 2009

Dear Norah,

Thanks for sending me your demo CD – I thought it was great, especially 'A Foggy Day' and 'Every Time We Say Goodbye'; that's such an old standard, but you managed to bring something new to it. I'm actually playing it as I write to you, so if any impresarios come down my corridor they'll be sure to hear it.

I don't know if I ever described my accommodation to you. I'm on the thirtieth floor of the Meredith Wilson Hall, which has everything you could want, including a hot chocolate bar and a 'rec room' where they play Twister on Friday nights. I haven't got involved in the Twister yet – I'm older than most students here and I think it would be creepy. But there's a gym on the top floor with a treadmill where I can jog while looking down over the Lincoln Centre and the Upper West Side, and feel like a right old Master of the Universe. The only odd thing is that some of the undergraduates share a room – I can't get my head around that. Even in Trinity, where we were fairly barbaric in other ways, we always had our own little cell. Graduate students are seen as the ancient mariners on campus, and the undergrads generally steer very clear of us, and who can blame them.

New York is still wonderful, and all the clichés are still true: it is very hard to use the subway, though I'm getting a bit better at it, and it is also very, very cold in winter. I nearly froze to death the other evening coming home from the Met, which is literally next door to us. So I went downtown to Macy's the next day and bought myself a proper padded puffa coat, like a rapper. I look an awful fool but it has possibly saved my life – we could have had a real-life *La Bohème* situation on our hands.

Speaking of operatic singing, the other night we went out and did karaoke in Hell's Kitchen with a bunch of the performing arts crowd. Norah, if you've ever seen anything worse than a load of performing arts students doing karaoke, please tell me. It saps all the fun out of it when they're all doing it so perfectly, belting out songs in five-part harmony. One of the waiters there thought we were from some kind of cult. They weren't wrong.

Now, I come to the bad news. You know I had hoped to come home for Christmas, but, sadly, it looks like it won't be possible this year. The airfare is astronomical – I was being over-optimistic thinking that my scholarship would cover it. One of our professors has invited us waifs and strays to his house in Brooklyn – he owns a brownstone, which is apparently a big deal. He is very well-connected and he has also invited a Very Well Known Composer in Hollywood who sometimes hires assistants from my course. It would have been hard to turn that down, even if I could afford the air-fare to Dublin. I am sorry that I won't be able to fit in a stopover in London – but hopefully next time. I'll be coming back to Ireland next June anyway – unless I get a job here, which between you and me is fairly unlikely.

I hope you're keeping the faith and still singing. I'm sure you'll make it if you don't give up. That's what I'm trying to do, anyway. I hope you have a good Christmas, when it comes – I'll be thinking of you.

Ever yours,

A x

*I hope you have a good Christmas, when it comes – I'll be thinking of you.* I had exchanged several emails with Andrew since we'd parted in Italy, but this one was the one that I reread most often. I had been so disappointed when he had said he couldn't be here or in Dublin for Christmas, but I could see that he couldn't help it. I had already replied, but now I took a minute to write him a quick email to wish him a Merry Christmas, and best of luck if he did get to meet the famous composer tonight. Then I stood up to look through my wardrobe for my favourite Christmas jumper. It was Christmas Eve, and I was off to meet my Ealing friends for our now-traditional drinks.

Kiran had been very reluctant to give the Drayton her

custom after being turned away from there five years earlier, but it was the place to go these days – plus, she had an added incentive. Handsome, high-cheekboned Paul Slovinski had been a crush of hers ever since our night out at Finnegan's. We hadn't seen much of him in his last two years of university at Edinburgh, but Kiran had bumped into him at Ealing Broadway shopping centre a few days earlier, and he had seemed keen to catch up. He was going to the Drayton with Joe and some others tonight, as were we, and now Kiran was in a state of high excitement, planning and re-planning her outfit in anticipation of seeing Paul under the mistletoe.

'Don't worry,' Caroline had said. 'There will be plenty of us there, so it won't be too obvious either way.'

'Oh, I don't mind being a bit obvious,' said Kiran. She was planning to wear her cropped pink mohair jumper, which left her bare brown midriff on display, plus her favourite skinny jeans. Caroline and I still had mixed feelings about the skinny-jean trend, but Kiran had embraced it from the get-go, pouring herself into pairs so tight they made her seem five inches taller as well as half her usual size.

Getting ready in my bedroom, it felt like being seventeen again, except that I was in my dad's bachelor pad instead of my old house; my parents were now occupying their own three-bedroom flats at opposite ends of Ealing. I was still living with my dad to save money, and

Miles and I were also at his place for Christmas – our first time doing Christmas alone with him, since we had been at Mum's last time. There had been talk of me doing all Christmases with my mum while I was living at Dad's, but I had been adamant: alternating meant alternating, regardless of who lived where.

It was all a bit of a mess. But there was no point in worrying about my life choices, or theirs. And at least I was saving money by living at home.

'Dad!' I called, running down the corridor. 'Could you give me a lift to the pub?' God, it really was just like being seventeen again.

I wasn't prepared for the sight of the kitchen. I had thought that we were doing a low-key dinner with only the good bits – just turkey, roast potatoes and stuffing. But Dad had obviously had a last-minute panic and had gone out and bought tons more vegetables, cranberry sauce and special Christmas napkins, so that the place looked exactly the way our old kitchen used to. Sleeves rolled up, he was busy making Mum's special mince pies, painting them with a glaze of beaten egg just the way she did – except he was using a fork, not very effectively, and he had Billie Holliday playing in the background. His flat was open-plan, with his record player and vinyl collection taking pride of place in the living area: seven hundred in total, including lots of rare pressings and signed albums. He once told me that if he sold them they would be worth thousands, but

Dad would never have sold them; he loved and played them all.

'Hello, love!' Dad said. 'Let me just get these in the oven and then I can think straight and talk to you. No, don't do that – you'll get your nice clothes all mucky.'

'It's fine, Dad.' I had found a pastry brush, by some miracle, and started painting as well. 'You didn't need to do all this! It would have been fine with just the turkey.'

Dad sighed. 'I just wanted it to be nice for you both.' He picked up the finished tray and put them in the oven, before wiping his forehead and crossing them off a list on the table. I had a pang as I saw how much grey there now was in his curly hair, which used to be the same chestnut colour as mine, and how much older he suddenly looked. Why was he killing himself doing the same stressful Christmas dinner Mum always had? I wanted to say, 'It's just food. It isn't love,' but I stopped myself in time. 'I'm sure it will be lovely,' I said instead.

I still didn't completely understand the reasons why Mum had left Dad, but I was inclined to blame my mum for most of it, since she was the one who had an affair – with the father of Maisie Salter, who was in my year in school. I had been horribly afraid that she would end up marrying Mr Salter, who was a widower, and that I'd have to be stepsisters with Maisie, whom I barely knew and didn't much like. But I had been even more confused when the relationship seemed to peter out. Dad had seemed open to a reconciliation, yet Mum still wanted to be on her own. What was the point of them splitting up if she wasn't even going to stay with the guy? It would be a long time before I understood that it wasn't that simple.

'Let's hope so. Did you say you wanted a lift? I didn't know you were off out.'

'Oh. Well –' I thought he knew that I always went to the pub on Christmas Eve. 'Not if you need help. Would you like me to peel some of these? Where's Miles?'

'He's gone to Finnegan's,' Dad said with a smile. 'I'm sure you remember those days.'

I did and I cursed Miles inwardly for not telling me. I wanted to go out, but I didn't want to leave Dad alone on Christmas Eve. While Mum's life had picked up since they split up, with book club, choir, pilates, trips and new friends, Dad's circle seemed to have shrunk. He had his three golf friends – 'the girls' as Mum called them – but he didn't seem to go many places, except, of course, jazz gigs.

'Ah – listen to this,' Dad said, turning up the sound. 'Have you heard her recording of this?'

I nodded; it was Billie Holliday singing 'I Get Along Without You Very Well'. Such a sad song: it made me think of Andrew. But at least we were in touch, I reminded myself.

'I was just listening to Rosemary Clooney's version – do you know that one?'

'I do,' I said, smiling; this was a game we could play for hours. 'Too up-tempo.'

'Yes. The definitive version, of course . . .'

'Chet Baker,' we said in unison. Dad beamed. 'Shall I put it on for you?'

'Oh –' I felt bad, but I was conscious that Kiran might be waiting for me in the pub; Caroline had warned us that she might be late, as her mum wanted her to go to a neighbour's drinks with her.

Dad smiled. 'Don't worry, love. It's your night out with your friends – we'll have plenty of time together after this. Where are you going, the Drayton? That's fine – these can bake while I drop you. Anyone to pick up?'

'No – I'm meeting Kiran and Caroline there.'

'Just you girls; good. I'm glad we sent you to a girls' school.'

I laughed. 'No, I'm afraid there will be boys there. Men, actually. Joe Lee – remember him?'

'Ah, yes, the little fella with the fringe. Did he ever go to art school?'

'No, he studied engineering. And he's six foot now, Dad, not so little.'

Dad shook his head. 'Never. I hope you have your fake IDs?'

'Very funny,' I said, remembering the furore when Mum discovered mine. She had never found out about the night in Finnegan's, though: Dad had kept that secret, just telling me not to pull any similar tricks again, and a month later I was eighteen anyway.

Dad smiled. 'I remember those days of trying to look older than you are . . . it lasts about three years, then you spend the next fifty trying to look younger.'

'You'll always look thirty-five, Dad.' I felt bad that I was leaving him alone on Christmas Eve. 'Are you sure you don't want help with all this? I could stay home, you know. If you wanted to do something together.'

I did mean it, but at the same time I really wanted to get out and see my friends. So I was relieved when he said, 'Not at all . . . Now come on, hop to the car.'

The Drayton was just the same at it had been five years earlier, when we'd first tried to enter it: same brass lamps, same wood panelling and tasteful tinsel; even, we thought, the same barman who had turned us away before. Joe and Caroline were already there when I arrived. His ridiculous fringe had gone, to be replaced by quite a cool hairstyle, and he was wearing a smart navy-blue jacket that was a step up from his previous eternal denim and slogan T-shirts. When he got up to give me a hug, I noticed he seemed broader somehow, as if he'd been working out.

'Hi Joe!' I said. 'How's life in Marylebone?'

'In Marylebone? Is that where you live? Wow. I wish I was an engineer,' said Caroline.

'How's the new job?'

'It's really, really boring. I knew it would be boring, but still. You know there's a joke about engineering jobs – it's like in *Lord of the Rings* where Gandalf does endless meetings, spreadsheets, reports and then magic for about two minutes. Except I haven't got to the magic part yet. It does leave me time for my hobby, though.'

'What hobby?' I asked.

'My cartoons. I haven't spammed you with my You-Tube link yet? Consider it done.' He whipped out a smartphone – one of the first I'd seen – and showed us the link. 'I'm also doing a part-time diploma in animation – this is my homework.'

'Joe, these are really great,' said Caroline, taking the phone from him – which struck me as an oddly intimate gesture. I took a quick look. It was a short clip of a boy wandering in a forest, which turned into a railway track that then turned into a wave. I was still watching with interest when Joe took the phone back.

'It's a bit long,' he said. 'I'll send you the link. Do you want a drink, Norah?'

'Oh, look, it's Kiran!' said Caroline.

Kiran, still with her coat on, had gone straight to the bar when she arrived to take advantage of what she said was a bit of a lull. She was fighting her way back from the bar with two gin and tonics for me and Caroline, and a Bacardi Breezer for herself. We were old enough now to genuinely enjoy those drinks we'd previously ordered to look sophisticated, but Kiran remained loyal to her Breezers. 'I'm sorry, Joe, I didn't see you,' she said, giving him a hug.

'No worries ... I'm heading to the bar anyway. I won't be long. Or rather, given the queues here, see you next Christmas.'

'I'll keep you company,' said Caroline, to my surprise.

There was a huge queue as ever, but Joe and Caroline

seemed happy enough chatting away, not trying that hard to get the barman's attention.

'Is there something going on there?' I asked idly. 'Does he look different to you?'

'No . . . I think he's just been hitting the gym. And, no. He is not her type . . . Where is Paul?' Kiran looked distractedly around the pub, pulling at the hem of her fuzzy cropped jumper.

I decided she was probably right. Caroline was a hopeless romantic and had been ever since I'd known her. We had met in Year Nine, when we were in cross-country club together. It was at the end of the day, and we had discovered that you could run, or rather walk, straight home and nobody would be any the wiser, so we had just run towards her house where we ate biscuits and discussed Jilly Cooper novels, both of which we devoured by the dozen. Caroline was looking for a grand romance, but there was something vulnerable about her; she attracted men easily, but too often things seemed to end in tears. She had said, herself, that she wasn't interested in British men because they were unromantic and drank too much – which I had to admit was fair enough. Joe was as British and unromantic as they came. He didn't drink too much – but he certainly drank more than the one-beer limit most European men seemed to observe. He was an engineer, too, which wouldn't interest Caroline; her ideal man was a writer, artist or musician.

'There he is!' Paul had just arrived, looking as

handsome and high-cheekboned as ever, wearing a green-, black- and white-striped scarf and carrying a pint. Kiran was eager to talk to him, but she soon got roped into a discussion with Will Palmer and some other girls from our year – the place really was like our sixth-form common room. Paul and I caught up instead, and he asked me all about my singing.

'Did you write your play in the end?' I asked him. 'You were going to get it put on at the Fringe . . .'

I hadn't been taking the piss, but Paul flushed anyway. 'Oh, God. Did I say that? What a pretentious little git I was. No, I did have one put on by Bedlam – that's the university theatre company. But I didn't make it to the Fringe, shockingly. I'm still writing in the evenings, though. And temping in the day.'

'Cool! I'm temping too,' I said, clinking my drink against his. 'Isn't it the best?'

'So fun,' Paul grinned. 'It's fine, really, isn't it? And it's flexible, so I can visit someone in Edinburgh . . .'

'Oh – really!' I glanced instinctively at the back of Kiran's head, but she was deep in conversation with the others. 'You're seeing someone?'

'Yes, Sandy – Alexander,' he added. 'He was on my course. Now he's doing a master's degree, so . . .' He started explaining about Sandy's dissertation on Robert Louis Stevenson.

'That's cool. I mean, long-distance is hard, but he sounds great.' I was surprised to hear that Paul was with a guy, but I was mainly worried that Kiran didn't know yet that he was in a relationship at all and would feel quite foolish when she did find out. Just then she turned around, having finally got rid of Will and the girls. 'So, what are you up to, Paul? Temping! That's so cool. Tell me more about your writing.'

They continued chatting, while I wondered whether Paul was going to mention his long-distance boyfriend. But instead, he went to the bar, and Kiran turned to me with a glowy look on her face.

'I think it's going really well!' she said. 'What do you think?'

'Kiran, I'm really sorry, but Paul just told me he's seeing someone in Edinburgh,' I said quietly, before anyone else could interrupt us. 'Long-distance. His name's Sandy.'

'What? You must have got that wrong,' Kiran said. 'There's no way. He would have said, surely?'

'Well, I don't know if it's common knowledge, but that's what he just said. Someone from his course.'

Kiran looked completely baffled, and I couldn't blame her. It was a surprise. 'You must have got that wrong,' she said again. 'I'm sure he's not gay.'

It was frustrating that she wouldn't believe me, but I had done my duty as a friend so I dropped it. We started talking instead about Kiran's work, which was as demanding as ever, and my career, or lack thereof.

'It's going OK, thanks,' I said, in reply to her question about my music. 'I got my CD demos made, and I've dropped them into all the live venues in London. And I mean all. And I've had a few calls back . . .'

'Yeah? How many?' Kiran was looking slightly distracted, watching Paul talk to Joe and Caroline.

'Three . . . well, four. One wanted me to do a wedding, but then he changed his mind when he found out I didn't have a website, or a backing band.'

'Hm,' Kiran frowned. 'Well, that's not bad – three out of – how many CDs did you make?'

'Um, a hundred.'

Her eyes widened; she obviously thought that three to a hundred wasn't a great return on my investment. 'That's – that's a lot! How about a video?'

'A video? Like a music video?'

'Yeah! Like, wear something sexy . . . make sure they can see you as well as hear you.'

I made a face. 'I don't want to wear something sexy . . . and I don't have the money to produce a video, not a proper one. Also, I hate the whole video thing, to be honest. It's just another way to judge female singers on how hot they are . . . Think of all the great jazz singers. Most of them would never have made it based on looks alone.'

'Fair point,' said Kiran. 'I'm guessing men don't have to make a video where they writhe around on the hood of a car.'

'No, they don't. Well, Andrew might do some kind of video at some point – I'm not sure.'

She nodded, as though she had finally decided something she'd been in two minds about before. 'Norah, don't take this the wrong way,' she said.

'Whenever someone says that there's so obviously no other way to take it.'

'No, listen! I think if you want to do music, you need to put everything you've got into it. Like, it's great that you have a CD, but now you need a website. And don't waste time posting your CDs, for God's sake – you might as well send them a gramophone. Just email them an MP3 file. You need professional headshots. And you do need a video. Even if it's just to show your performance style . . .'

'OK.' She was being a little overbearing, but it was good advice. 'I'll try.'

'Well, no. Do or do not. There is no try.'

'I am doing!'

'Are you really, though?' said Kiran. 'I mean, it doesn't look like it. And Andrew: it's great that you're still in touch, but don't you need to think about meeting someone who actually lives in the same country?' She paused for breath. 'I just . . . I totally get the whole post-uni, where-am-I-going sort of haze . . . but I hate to see you noodling around like this.'

'*Noodling around?*' I said, suddenly furious. She knew nothing about me and Andrew, and she also didn't know anything about music or how hard it was. And I was doubly annoyed that she saw fit to criticize me while also completely dismissing what I had just told her about Paul. Kiran always saw things the way she wanted them to be, which was fine for her, but I didn't need her telling me what to do. 'You know what, it's getting late. I'm going home.'

'Norah! I didn't mean it like that –'

I wasn't listening; I was already halfway out of the pub. I was sick of them all anyway; it wasn't my night. I walked right by Joe and Paul – Caroline had presumably gone to the loo or something – and I noticed them clocking me, but I was too distracted to do more than give them a quick wave.

'Hey! Norah!'

I looked around, as I opened the door. It was Joe, looking concerned.

'What's wrong? Why are you leaving?'

'Nothing! I'm fine. Just tired.'

I walked outside, realizing I might be overreacting, but not caring. I wished I hadn't come out. I wanted to go home and spend the evening with my dad, which was what I should have done in the first place. I would text Caroline later. I wouldn't call Dad, because he would probably have had a drink by now, and I didn't want to make him think he'd have to come and get me. I would just get the bus home and have a good old pity-party while I stared out of the window at these suburban streets, just like when I was seventeen.

The worst part was that I knew Kiran was right. Of course I should be doing a video; of course I should have a website. But I didn't want to do those things. I'd rather eat bees than do self-promotion and I was already doing as much as I could face. I just wanted to sing. Was that so bad? And was it so bad that I was in touch with Andrew, and that my heart skipped a beat when I saw his name appear in my inbox? I was also stupidly down-cast by the fact that Paul was successfully managing a long-distance relationship. But obviously, Edinburgh was a lot closer than New York.

'Wait! Norah, wait!'

I heard gasping behind me, and turned to see Kiran, who had run, or tottered, the entire length of the street in her four-inch heels.

'I am sorry,' she said. 'I'm really, really sorry, babe . . . that was so shitty of me. I didn't mean it. Or I did mean it, but I shouldn't have said it.'

'It was pretty shitty,' I agreed. But I let her grab me for a hug, feeling how cold she was in her thin coat, with her crop top.

'I am sorry, honest,' she said. 'I just really want you to make it. Because, Norah . . . I'm going to be working my arse off, in a pretty boring job, for the next forty years. And most of the time it's fine. I'm good at it, and I like being able to go shopping for clothes without worrying that I won't be able to eat. And I want to buy a house, and go on holiday and all that stuff. But you have the chance to do something different. And I really want you to make it.'

That felt like a lot of pressure to put on a friend, but I was touched at the same time. I knew that Kiran believed in my ability, more than I did myself a lot of the time. Then I smiled, as an idea began to take shape. 'I know. If you're that keen – why don't you help me?'

'Help you? How?'

'Well, with a website, and getting me bookings and finding a photographer. If you want.' I hesitated. 'Unless you're too busy?'

'Well, I am too busy but I also really want to do it,' she said. 'That's a brilliant idea, Norah! Yes. I'm in. I can be your manager!'

'Manager?' I echoed. I had just been imagining help with a website, but Kiran was already, though the word wasn't yet used in that sense, extra.

She slung her arm around me, and we started walking back towards the bar.

'And about Paul,' she said. 'I'm sorry. You were right! I've just heard all about Sandy. He's coming down for New Year's, apparently.'

'I'm sorry, Kiran. I know you liked him.'

'Oh, it's all right,' she said, as we went inside. 'It obviously wasn't meant to be. At least someone's found love tonight, though.'

'What? Who do you mean?'

'Look over there.' Across from Paul, at our table, were Joe and Caroline – nose to nose, his hand on her knee; next thing, he leaned in and kissed her.

The whole thing was so ridiculous, we looked at each other and burst out laughing. The next moment, 'Bad Romance' came on, and Kiran grabbed my arm again. 'This is the new Lady Gaga song!'

'I know!' I yelled back. 'It sounds just like the old one!' Before too long, Caroline joined us, and we shrieked at her, this being too good an opportunity for taking the piss out of her.

'Look at you, snogging an engineer!' said Kiran.

Caroline laughed but she didn't reply; we were all too busy dancing. Joe had been joined at this point by more boys from his school, and even more of our old school friends had arrived. The end of the night was a big sweaty sing-along to 'Don't Stop Believin''. I had never heard of it before this month, but now everyone was going nuts as if it was their favourite song from child-hood. Kiran was belting along and pointing at me while she sang the chorus. I knew what she meant, and I was going to take the advice, regarding music *and* Andrew. I would not stop believing. I would hold on to the feeling.

# 11. A Face in the Crowd

*Sunday, 22 December 2019*

Waking up, the first thing I have to do is unplug myself; pull my earplugs out, take my eye mask off and remove my mouthguard. I sleep with practically every orifice plugged up. It started when I was being driven mad by the traffic outside my flat, and the streetlamp right by my window. And the mouthguard is because apparently I grind my teeth at night. But now, instead of my narrow grubby window overlooking an Edwardian terrace in Turnpike Lane, I see the sun shining over St Stephen's Green. And instead of my threadbare old duvet I have those magic hotel sheets, soft and silky in the way that only hotels can make them. I snuggle down and sigh luxuriously. There's nothing at all like a hotel for making you feel free and decadent.

Even better is the knowledge that I have nothing at all to do today. I often wake up in the middle of the night in a flap about something or other to do with work, whether it's Samira's essay or Ashanti's solo or a friendship meltdown between two Year Sevens. But all of that seems very far away right now.

There's a knock at the door. 'Norah? Are you ready?'

Grumbling, I go to open it, still in my pyjamas.

'Don't you have your phone? It's a bit early to go banging on people's doors,' I complain, rubbing my eyes.

'I don't want to miss breakfast.' Joe takes a step back to look at my pyjamas, which are my favourites: brushed cotton with pizza slices on them. 'I didn't know they made pyjamas like that in adult sizes.'

I close the door on him, leaving him protesting outside, and tell him I'll meet him downstairs in twenty minutes. I don't want to miss breakfast either: obviously it's the best thing about staying in a hotel. He's lucky I can get dressed so quickly, too. A holiday with Kiran and Caroline always means at least twenty minutes' extra down time for me every evening while they put the finishing touches to their hair and make-up; I probably should make more of an effort but I can't be bothered. I'll save all my pampering energy for Christmas Eve. Even though it's likely Andrew won't show up, I'd still like to look my best when I'm waiting around outside Bewley's.

The Shelbourne's breakfast doesn't disappoint, and I'm soon sighing and exclaiming over all the starched white linens, sparkling silver and buffet, plus the menu with everything from waffles to egg Benedicts. We order a full Irish breakfast for Joe, and French toast for me, which is what I always order when I'm out for breakfast. I know it's dull but I love having the same thing every time. Life is confusing enough as it is.

'What do you want to do today?' he asks.

'Well . . .' I feel dismayed as I remember I have no idea what we should be seeing. Normally I like to have a full itinerary for sightseeing, with an A-list and B-list of things to see. 'I don't know! Oh God. I haven't prepared anything.'

'Relax,' Joe says, sipping his coffee. 'It's a holiday, not an exam. I have some suggestions.'

'Oh good,' I say, relieved. I remember this from other trips: Joe is a good travelling companion. He always has ideas but he's not wedded to them.

'I'd like to see the Book of Kells . . . but if there's too big a queue then someone at work recommended the Chester Beatty Library, which has even older manuscripts, but it's not as crowded. And the National Museum of Archaeology, lots of Celtic artefacts there.'

'Sounds good. Let's see, what time do they open?'

I'm horrified to find, when we look up opening times, that most of the things we want to see are closed this Sunday until 1 p.m. I know we could do other things, but I can't understand why museums would be closed on a Sunday morning.

'Monsters,' Joe says, when I complain. 'Imagine wanting to give their employees the Sunday before Christmas off with their families.'

'But I wanted to do some sightseeing,' I sigh. 'And if we don't have the morning I don't know how we'll fit it all in.'

'I know, but if you think about it,' Joe says, 'everything we see will be a sight. So it will all be sightseeing.'

The older woman I noticed yesterday when we were checking in walks past me, on her way back from the buffet, to join another woman at their table. I'm not at all surprised to see her breakfast consists of plain yoghurt, fruit and muesli. I bet she's a yoga teacher or something similar and rises at 5 a.m. every day to do asanas before having some hot water and lemon. She gives me a friendly smile as she walks past, and I smile back, thinking again how cool she is and how much I wish I could be like her, or befriend her. I can probably start by being a bit more Zen about sightseeing. It doesn't matter about sightseeing anyway, I remind myself – we're here to find Andrew, not look at museums.

'Well, I'm sure we can find something to do,' I say to Joe. 'Let's ask at reception.'

The receptionist suggests a walk in Stephen's Green, or around the 'Purple Flag District', which is a little network of streets between Grafton Street and Dame Street.

'What do you think a Purple Flag District is?' I ask Joe, as we stroll out of the hotel. It's cold but unexpectedly sunny, so I'm glad I've got my sunglasses as well as my big blue mohair coat.

'Who knows. Something to do with Prince?'

It's such a crisp, blue day that we decide on a walk in Stephen's Green – I've discovered everybody drops the 'Saint' – where we stroll around the central lake towards a summerhouse where Joe takes multiple photos. The water is so still and blue that it makes a perfect mirror image of the blue sky, down to the clouds and bare branches reflected in minute detail on the surface: looking at the pictures, they're perfectly symmetrical so that it's hard to know which end is up or down. Then Joe takes out his notebook and does a few sketches of me, with the summerhouse in the background, until I complain about the cold, and we move on.

'Have you ever thought about doing street portraits, Joe?' I ask, only half joking. His sketches are always so good – at least as good as any portraits I've ever seen.

'I would, if I had time. It would be a nice way to add to the character bank. Did I tell you I'm doing a main character, in the next film?'

'No, you didn't! That's amazing. Congratulations.' I know that Joe mainly works on secondary characters, so this is a big deal. 'Who is he?'

'She. A princess. Very brave and beautiful. It sounds easy, but it's hard to create something like that without making it generic. I'm doing some digital sculpts now, anyway, for early visual development.'

We talk about Joe's work a bit more, and I'm struck again by how challenging it is; both technically and technologically, and artistically. I honestly don't understand what he's talking about most of the time when he tells me about his work, but I admire the finished product – which is how he feels about music, I know. Soon our wanderings take us past a lawn with an abandoned football on it.

'Wilson!' Joe says, referencing the film *Castaway*.

'Wilson,' I agree. I start to laugh. 'You know who that always reminds me of . . . Remember Julia Stiles?'

'You mean Julie Fuglsang? Yes, of course I do.' This was Joe's ex from way back, who Caroline and I thought looked just like the actress Julia Stiles. She had trained as a dancer, like the real Julia, but then gave it up following an injury and got some high-powered job in finance. We were secretly obsessed with her and couldn't understand why Joe broke up with her, as she was so impossibly glamorous.

'How do you still remember her?' Joe asks. 'That was, like, ten years ago.'

'Oh, Caroline and I follow her on Instagram. Did you know that she's given up banking and started teaching dance again? And she's got a baby. Her husband's from Cameroon, I think.'

'No, I did not know any of that. That's – scary,' Joe says. I laugh again, while considering how odd it is that I can effortlessly track the activities of Julie Fuglsang, who I barely knew, but Andrew is lost to me completely.

When Joe's taken enough pictures, we walk out of the park and down Kildare Street into the campus of Trinity College. The noise of the city fades away, and we're again in a peaceful oasis, with grand buildings surrounding a network of green squares. The queue for the Book of Kells is insane, so instead we take a short stroll around the campus until we find ourselves in Front Square, a vast cobbled space with pillared granite buildings, green lawns and a campanile at one end. I stand there, remembering Andrew's tales of this place.

'The music faculty is based in House Five, overlooking Front Square,' he had told me. 'I remember walking along one Thursday night in winter, and hearing the sound of the chamber choir, rehearsing a piece I wrote for them . . . I knew there and then that there was nothing else I wanted to do but write music for people to perform.'

I decide not to share the memory with Joe, and instead we start strolling towards the arch at the other end of the square that marks the exit. I'm just wondering where we should head next, when I notice a figure coming towards us out of the darkness of the arch. I stop in my tracks. As he moves closer, my mouth goes dry. My heart hammers as I take in every detail, wondering if I'm seeing things. The dark head, held at the same angle, the height – the long dark overcoat which is exactly something he'd wear – even the loping, easy stride, just as I remember him walking in Italy. It's Andrew. I'm sure of it.

'Joe,' I hiss, grabbing his arm. 'It's him!'

'Who?' Joe asks, very unnecessarily in my view. But as he comes closer I exhale, feeling equal parts of relief and disappointment. It's not him after all – there's a certain resemblance, but this guy is younger, and his face is completely different. It must have been the hair, or the height. I feel so ridiculous, but I genuinely have to take a few deep breaths before I can straighten up and speak again.

'So I take it that wasn't Andrew,' Joe says.

'No – thank God.'

'But why thank God? Isn't the whole point of coming here to find him?'

I can't explain it to Joe, but I'm not ready to see Andrew yet – I need to be prepared.

'Well, that's going to pose a problem if you keep on freaking out at the sight of random strangers,' Joe says. 'So was that guy really his double?'

'Yes. He's dark-haired, tall, maybe just a little shorter than you – and he has pale skin and bluey-grey eyes . . .'

'Hmm,' Joe says. 'He'll stand out a mile here, then.'

'Haha,' I say, feeling somewhat recovered as we walk outside the campus and rejoin the normality of the crowds and Christmas bustle.

'Have you ever played Where's Wally?' Joe continues, and I give him a nudge to shut him up.

We've reached Grafton Street now; the shops are still closed, but some flower sellers are setting up, and a children's choir is singing 'God Rest Ye Merry Gentlemen'. I don't have any euro change yet so I go mad and give them a tenner. It's for charity, after all, and I'm also doubly grateful that I don't have to conduct them or organize them getting to or from their gig.

'Let's get you a coffee after your shock,' says Joe. 'Actually, why don't we go to the famous Bewley's? It's supposed to be very nice.'

'Oh.' I don't want to admit it, especially after what just happened, but the suggestion makes me nervous because this, of course, is where I'm headed on Christmas Eve, for my supposed meeting with Andrew. But I don't want to go there yet. Surely it would be a mistake – what if I jinx the possibility of Andrew's arrival by going there too soon?

Joe seems to sense my unease. In a more patient tone, he says, 'We can go somewhere else if you want.'

Looking up at him, I realize I need to get a grip, for his sake if not for my own. He has come for some kind of holiday, and I want to make sure he has some kind of a nice time. And anyway, we're not going to bump into Andrew; it's a city of over a million people, not a village.

'No, it's fine. Let's do it.'

It's not a mystic portal, I remind myself as we walk inside: it's just a café, albeit a very nice one. We walk through the opening lobby, which sells packaged teas and coffees behind glass counters, into a wide, high-ceilinged room with stairs and galleries rising above a twelve-foot Christmas tree. I notice high-backed red velvet booths, dark-green Chinoiserie wallpaper and beautiful stained-glass windows at the far end of the room. There's a bustling atmosphere and waitresses with white starched aprons that match the tablecloths. It's somehow dramatic and cosy at the same time. I can imagine Andrew in his student days, holing up here with a composition notebook and some earphones.

And I can imagine staying here all day, doing the cross-word over a pot of tea.

'Look at those windows – they're incredible,' says Joe. 'I'm going to take a closer look . . . But first, coffee.'

We order coffee for two, and some sticky buns, which are a house speciality apparently, and I return to a topic that interested me earlier.

'So . . . Julia,' I say, sipping my latte.

'Julie,' he corrects me patiently.

'Julie . . . I know it was a long time ago, but what happened there? Why did you guys break up?'

'Why? I don't know.' He looks vague. 'She was a bit serious, I suppose? For example . . . on this holiday, we would have been up since seven and we would have seen at least three sights by now. And no stopping for coffee either.'

'Hm,' is all I can find to say. I was hoping for a lamer reason, but that does sound rather exhausting.

'So what was the attraction? If she was so intense . . .'

'There's nothing wrong with a bit of intensity,' he says. I assume he's making some kind of sexual reference, so I decide to ignore this remark.

'What about FiFi, then? Why didn't that work out?'

FiFi, or Felicia, Lim was a Singaporean architect who Joe met through his old engineering friends, not long after he broke up with Julie. We all liked her; she was zany but fun and could always be relied on to turn up half an hour late with a crazy yet entertaining excuse.

'She was a bit *too* fun,' Joe says. 'Did I tell you about

the time I visited her in Paris, and she turned out to be homeless?'

'No!'

'It was after we broke up . . . I was there for a conference, so I emailed her in advance saying I'd be in town. And she said, that's great, you can see my new apartment. When I met her in the Tuileries Gardens, I noticed she had all these bags with her . . .'

'No.'

'Yes. She was "between places", she said. AKA, sleeping on a park bench.'

I refuse to believe Joe at first, but he maintains it and supplies so many details I have to accept it eventually. 'So where did she sleep that night?' I ask.

'Well . . .' He looks embarrassed.

'Say no more,' I say, rolling my eyes. 'I can see how that might take spontaneity a bit too far.'

I feel like I've heard enough about his love life now and I'm about to change the subject when he says, 'And Caroline . . .'

We're possibly crossing a line here, but I am intrigued nonetheless. I've heard Caroline's side of it – that he just wasn't serious enough, both about their relationship and in general – but I've never asked him about it. 'What about her?'

'She needed someone who adored her, and I didn't. I probably wasn't ready to adore anyone.'

I take a minute to digest this, before asking, 'So are you ready now?'

He shrugs. 'I don't know. Maybe if someone incredible comes along? But I'm not in a rush.'

This makes me lose all sympathy I might have had for him over his dating dilemmas. Call it biology or whatever you want, but that's the difference between us right there. We're both in the singles market, but he's window shopping and I'm panic buying.

'What?' Joe obviously sees my scepticism.

'That's the difference between straight men and women. You haven't settled down because you're choosy and you're not in a hurry. I haven't settled down because I can't find anyone – anyone functional – who I like and who likes me back. Plus I'm not going to meet someone at work, since I mainly work with teenage girls.'

'Have you tried online dating?' Joe asks.

I look at him blankly. 'Have I tried online dating?' I repeat. 'That's like asking if I've tried supermarkets, or air travel. Of course I have.'

'And?'

I just shake my head. Internet dating is a chasm into which I've peered, a few times, and then drawn back in terror. Too many deal-breakers – and I'm not talking about a ponytail or vaping or an inability to pronounce 'chorizo'. I know people do meet online – Caroline and Stefan, for one – but it's just a shop of horrors, as far as I'm concerned.

'I suppose some people just never meet anyone, and maybe that's what's going to happen to me,' I say, glumly.

'Well – that's why we came here, right?' Joe says encouragingly. 'To help you find the love of your life.'

Now I feel bad. I've been moaning about something that's not Joe's fault, *and* that he's trying to help me with. If I'm not careful, I'm going to dampen the holiday mood completely.

'I'm sorry, Joe. I don't mean to be such a misery.'

'No, I get it. My sister felt the same way for a long time.'

'Oh.' Joe's younger sister Amy is beautiful, and even more upbeat than Joe. 'Really? Didn't she have her big white wedding last year?'

'Yeah, she did, but you never know what leads up to these big white weddings, Norah. Or what follows them. Nobody has a perfect life.' He stands up. 'Come on. These sights aren't going to see themselves.'

'I'll pay the bill,' I offer, and Joe says, 'You do that,' with a grin.

I finish paying, feeling deeply embarrassed that I've just had such a meltdown, and it's not even lunchtime yet. If I'm not careful, this is going to be like that episode of *Friends* where Phoebe lends Joey a dog to cheer him up, and the dog ends up as gloomy as Joey. Not that Joe is a dog, obviously. I look for Joe and realize that he's wandered off; I can't find him anywhere. Eventually I track him down, examining the stained-glass windows at the far end of the room. He doesn't even notice me come up behind him, he's so absorbed. They are a marvel, backlit against the darkness of the room.

They look very old, maybe nineteenth-century, and they show different architectural columns, with all manner of wildlife twining and fluttering around them; not just butterflies, birds, flowers, but dragonflies, seashells and ammonites, all so intricately done I'm not surprised he's so lost in the detail. The colours are rich and mellow, glowing against the glass, which is the colour of faded parchment.

'I've never seen anything like this in a café before,' I remark.

'They're by an Irish artist called Harry Clarke,' Joe says, reading from a sign. 'I've never heard of him. Looks like Aubrey Beardsley, doesn't it? Look at the colours . . .' I watch him take a few photos. 'There you go,' he says when he finishes. 'That's what I meant about everything being sightseeing. You never know when you're going to find hidden treasure.'

I smile at him as we walk outside, hoping that this is a good omen for our trip – and my love life.

## 12. Girl in the Red Dress

With no particular plan we start exploring the side streets between Grafton Street and Dame Street, which are crammed with little boutiques, restaurants and cafés all decked out with fairy lights and red ribbon bows. We wander into the Powerscourt Centre, which is a bustling place converted from the courtyard of three Georgian buildings. A pianist is playing carols on the ground floor, and on the third floor we find a French café, where we sit with coffees overlooking the action – neither of us can face lunch after our breakfast and buns, or more coffee really, but, as Joe says, it's the price of renting the seat.

Joe sees an alert on his phone and shows me: it's a picture of his parents, on the slopes.

'Aw,' I say, smiling at the two of them. 'I love that they've embraced WhatsApp, but your dad still signs his messages "love Mum and Dad".'

I like Joe's parents a lot. His dad – also coincidentally called Michael, like my dad – used to play golf with mine, and his mum, Genevieve, is from Ealing and taught science at my school. My favourite anecdote about them is to do with Joe's birth. His mum went into labour on 15 October, which was the night of the Great

Storm of 1987, and his father was trying to keep the severity of the storm from his mum because he didn't want her to be frightened. Mr Lee was a structural engineer and he was picturing all the direst scenarios like Queen Charlotte's Hospital losing power – which could well have happened, by all accounts – and kept turning off the radio and shushing the medical staff whenever they mentioned anything.

'Oh yeah,' Joe says, when I remind him. 'That was classic Dad. Pretend a bad thing's not happening. Obviously Mum knew about the storm, but she says she didn't have the mental energy to worry about it, and it gave him something to do.'

I smile, thinking it's a shame my parents couldn't manage their disagreements that way. I don't think it was even the constant disagreements that broke my parents up, though that obviously didn't help. They just wanted different things: my mum wanted to go out and socialize, my dad wanted to stay home and listen to jazz. My mum wanted to go to a different place every year on holiday; my dad didn't really care for travelling at all. As my mum put it, they were just happier apart than they were together. For years I blamed her, thinking that wasn't a reason to break up – but eventually I had to accept that it wasn't my decision and that after all, maybe she was right.

I check my own phone and see that there are alerts from everyone on our wider friends WhatsApp, which is unimaginatively called Ealing. Kiran has said: *So is anyone going to the Drayton on Christmas Eve?* and it seems the answer is no. Kiran is too tired to go out past eight o'clock. Paul and Javier have a lot of prep to do as they're hosting Paul's parents for Christmas, plus a Friendmas celebration on Boxing Day. Caroline says if nobody else is free, she and Stefan are going to have a quiet night in. I'm expecting Paul or Javier to comment on the fact that Joe and I are both AWOL, but nobody seems to have noticed.

'What's wrong with everyone this year?' I say to Joe.

'What do you mean?'

'Well, why is nobody going to the Drayton? What about tradition?'

'We're all getting old, I suppose,' he says. 'We've got other commitments. I've been kidnapped by this woman who's taken me on a crazy trip to Dublin, for instance.'

'Ha, ha,' I say. 'Don't you think it's sad, though?'

'We'll do it next year,' Joe says. 'And at least I'll be with you. That's a tradition, right? We'll make a little Drayton tribute corner right here in Dublin.'

'Mm,' I say, feeling torn; that does sound nice, but I can't let go of the hope that I might end up having a very different Christmas Eve this year. To change the subject, I say, 'Do you think Stefan is going to propose this Christmas?'

'How would I know?' Joe says, which reminds me of his limitations; much as I love talking to him, it's not like talking to my female friends. 'Is he meant to be?' he asks a minute later.

'Well, that's the thing. Caroline is really hoping he

167

will, but she won't bring up the topic or discuss it with him at all. Do you think that's strange?'

'Not really. It's traditional, isn't it?'

'Yes, but I don't think it's a great tradition . . . I think it's weird that you wouldn't discuss it together and that he's the one who gets to decide when it happens. They share bills, they decide where to go on holiday together – why can't they discuss something as big as getting married?' I feel disloyal saying all this, not least because I do like Stefan a lot. He's an artist – or rather a painter, as he corrected me once when I said that – but dresses and acts like an accountant; he leads a very orderly life and is up at six every day to go to his studio before his day job teaching art. I think he'll come good.

'So I take it you wouldn't want a flashmob proposal or to be asked on, what's it called, a jumbotron?' Joe says.

I shudder. 'Nope. I think it's a big decision, and you should have a conversation about it first, like two adults.'

'Got it,' says Joe. 'I'll be sure to tell your intended that's what you'd prefer. Also maybe a list of pros and cons. A spreadsheet?'

'Very funny.' I look at my watch. 'Oh, God, Joe – it's already two thirty! How did that happen?'

This keeps on happening; we sit down for a cup of coffee, and I blink, and two hours have gone by. We're not really in a museum mood by now, so instead we wander along a cobbled lane towards a market called the George's Street Arcade, a treasure trove full of second-hand bookstalls and poster shops. I notice a vintage clothes shop and ask Joe if he'd mind us dropping in.

'Knock yourself out. I'll meet you in **Grogan's**.'

'What's that?'

'The pub on the corner, just behind us there. I had it as a backup plan, in case we had to invoke the Rule of Joe.'

I nod. I'm familiar with the Rule of Joe, which says that people on holiday together should spend at least half an hour on their own every day.

Entering this shop really is like stepping back in time – in the sense that suddenly it could be any year between now and 1970. Actually, it feels quite 1990s. There's a scented candle with a light woodsy smell, masking any mothball aroma. A girl with goth make-up is sitting behind the counter reading *The Mists of Avalon*, and they're playing 'Blue' by Joni Mitchell, which I introduced to Andrew. I swear I went months without thinking of him before this week, but lately everything is conspiring to remind me of him. I distract myself by flicking through the rails, running my hand absently over the brocade, silk and velvet, until my fingertips encounter something luxuriously silky and soft. It's a long red silk evening dress that looks like it's from the 1940s. My favourite decade.

'Will I hang that up for you in the fitting room?' says the girl, and I smile as I remember how puzzled I was when Andrew used to say 'will' instead of 'shall'. 'I don't have a crystal ball – I don't know if you will or not,' I used to tell him.

I duck into the changing room. I'm really not sure if the dress is going to fit, especially after that lunch, but to my amazement it zips up as if it's been made for me. The bias cut is so flattering, and the low-cut neck makes my skin look as creamy and lush as the head on a pint of Guinness. But then I glance at the price tag and gasp out loud; there's no way I can justify this.

'Oh, that's only gorgeous on you,' the girl says. 'That's the real bombshell look.'

'Thanks – I just wish I had somewhere to wear it.'

'It could be nice for a wedding? If you've any weddings coming up.'

'Only about a hundred.' I went to four weddings last year, and next year, 2020, is even busier: I have five between May and August. I don't think this would be appropriate for a wedding, though, really; it's way too attention-seeking, albeit in a good way.

'Let's have some fun with it, and you can take a picture anyway,' she suggests.

That's nice of her. I let her kit me out with a beautiful emerald necklace, some block-heeled shoes with a diamante clasp and a brown fur jacket – she checks first if I have any objection to fur, and I tell her not if it's vintage.

'Same here. I'm vegan myself, but I always say the animal's already been murdered anyway, so why let all their pain and suffering go to waste?'

I put the fur back on a hanger, but even without it the dress is gorgeous; a vision of pin-up glamour. And it would be a really great dress to perform in. I was never one for draping myself over the piano while singing 'Makin' Whoopee' through false eyelashes. But it was nice to have a reason to get dressed up every week. That part of my life is over now, though. I don't need it, so I put it straight back on the hanger, after thanking the sales assistant.

I'm getting ready to leave when I notice a pile of fliers advertising a 'Private Dinner at a Georgian Residence' – obviously some kind of supper club. It's tonight.

'Oh, take one,' the shop assistant urges. 'My friend runs it. It will be deadly. It's always a great crowd. It's probably booked up, but you could sign up to the list and get on to the next one. It's a bit like Henrietta Street – you know, the tenement museum.'

This leaves me none the wiser, but I take the flier, not bothering to explain that by the time the next one rolls around I'll be back in London, and go to join Joe in the pub. Standing outside, I have to double-check that I have the right place: one sign outside describes it as Castle Lounge while the other wall says Grogan's. Inside, it's a buzzy little place, with crazy-carpeted floors and wood-panelled walls displaying an eclectic collection of paintings and photographs. Little fringed lamps are suspended from the ceilings, casting a mellow light, and it's already full of people gathered around small tables on low blue velvet stools. I notice Joe at the back, sitting in front of a pint of Guinness with the comic book he bought earlier.

'See anything nice?' he asks as I sit down.

'No, there was a lovely dress – I was tempted. But I'm already on a lovely holiday, so I had to say no to it. Otherwise, I won't even be able to afford avocado toast, let alone my mortgage.'

'And the flat whites. Don't forget the flat whites.'

'I know. We are the generation that lives in a flat white. I didn't know you drank Guinness.'

'I don't. I said "a pint" and before I could say of what, he poured me a Guinness. So I guess a pint means a Guinness. What do you want to drink?'

'I suppose I'll have a Guinness as well. Do you want a top-up?'

'Watch this – they come to you.' He holds up a hand, and a girl comes over, carrying a tray, and takes my order.

'Very civilized, isn't it?' Joe notices the flier poking out of my pocket. 'What's that?' As soon as I explain what it is, he says, 'Why don't we go?'

'It's expensive . . . And it's probably booked out,' I say. 'Although I do like the idea of it.' I've been to two of these before, and it was fun meeting new people – and it would be nice to do it in Dublin and meet some locals.

'Ah,' Joe says. 'I forgot. You're a guesser, not an asker.'

'What do you mean?'

'A guesser just makes up their own mind that something will be booked out, or that they won't be allowed to sit there, or that someone wouldn't be willing to do them a favour … whereas an asker will ask the question.'

'Hm.' This makes sense. 'I see what you mean. I suppose I'm a guesser. I guess so, anyway. Are you an asker?'

'I'm an asker when it comes to stuff like this. I mean, it's a two-minute phone call. Do you want me to phone? I'm easy. If you think it's too expensive we can just go to McDonald's.'

It is expensive, but I'm pondering something else.

'How many weddings are you going to next year?'

'Me? I have no idea. A couple? I'd have to check my diary.'

'Well, I'm going to six. I mean I'm invited to six. And I only genuinely want to go to one of them. The other five all involve travel. Even if they're not abroad it means a hotel or B&B. And what with flights, tights and taxis, they each cost me between three and five hundred pounds, or even more for the ones abroad. What's funny?'

'*Flights, Tights and Taxis.* That could be the title of your autobiography. No, I hear you – weddings are expensive.'

'Yes! And I've just been guessing – or assuming – that each couple would be devastated if I didn't go. But what if they weren't? What if they were just inviting me to be polite, or they had someone else they really wanted to invite instead of me, or they just didn't mind either way?'

'All plausible options.'

'So I might just not go. And that will save me . . .' I have to get out my phone calculator, as maths isn't my strong point. 'Up to two thousand five hundred pounds. Or maybe more.'

'Nice to have – you'll have paid off that mortgage in no time.'

'I don't know about that.' My inheritance obviously gave me a good deposit. But I've still got many zeroes to go before I own the flat rather than the bank.

'What about you?' I ask curiously. 'Have you ever thought about trying to buy your flat?' Joe's flat is so much a part of him, I sometimes forget that he is still renting.

'Ah. Well, actually, I hadn't told you yet.' He wipes some froth off his mouth. 'I've put in an offer on a flat – a place in Acton.'

'In Acton?' I repeat, as if he's told me Mars. 'But –' Nothing wrong with Acton, but it's really far out west – next door to Ealing in fact. 'Where in Acton?'

'East Acton,' Joe says, which makes sense: it's the cheapest part. Joe is well paid, but this is still London – just about.

'Yes, the offer's been accepted – so now it's all in the hands of the lawyers.'

'So you'll be moving to Acton,' I repeat. I am surprised at how unsettled this makes me feel – much worse, in fact, than the idea of the friends all abandoning our Christmas drinks tradition. For as long as I can remember, Joe's place has been our haunt in central London, where we all gather after nights out or just on weekend afternoons. I can't imagine knocking on that door and not having him answer. Not to mention that, if he lives in Acton, we'll be at opposite ends of London, which often sounds the death knell for friendships. 'I'll never see you again,' I say, joking. 'Don't you need to be near Soho, where all the action is?'

'Not if we're moving the offices out to Brentford,' Joe says. 'And there are lots of other film and TV studios out west – Pinewood, the BBC – so it's a good location for me.'

'Of course. Well – congratulations. Have you got a picture?' He shows me the listing, and I try to act supportive and enthusiastic. I am happy for Joe, obviously. I suppose this had to happen – he couldn't live in central London for ever. But it seems like the end of an era.

Grogan's is filling up now, and people are standing at the bar as well as thronging the tables. We're crammed into a little alcove table, thigh to thigh, and it's getting dark outside, the roar of conversation building like a storm.

'Hey, look at that,' says Joe. I follow his gaze and see a blur on the wall, deep blues and purples and reds; I'm momentarily confused until I realize it's a stained-glass window.

'What are the odds? First a café, then we find one in a pub. Like I said – hidden treasures.'

But then, suddenly, I spot something else behind

him. Or rather, someone else. And this time, I know it's not a mirage – it's an actual sighting. Not of Andrew himself, but of Conor, one of his fellow musicians, who was in the sextet with him back in Verona. He looks a bit older now, of course, but it's definitely him, standing in a corner, pint in hand, laughing with two other guys. Thankfully neither of them is Andrew, but who knows when he might pop in? This is exactly the kind of place where I can see him whiling away a chilly evening at Christmas time. He could walk in at any minute.

'Joe,' I hiss. 'We have to go. Now!' And I zip out of the side door, grabbing my coat on the way, without even checking to see if Joe's following me.

'I hadn't even finished my pint,' he complains. 'What was it this time?'

'It was his friend. Conor. One of the guys in Italy! It was definitely, definitely him.'

'And you ran away from him like a fugitive because . . .'

I don't want to admit it but I can't really hide things from Joe that easily. 'Because if I see Andrew ahead of Christmas Eve, I won't know if he would have turned up of his own accord. I'll never know that unless I can avoid him – until it's time.'

I can see Joe is biting his lip in the effort to suppress all the remarks I know he wants to make.

'I know,' I admit. 'It's ridiculous. And superstitious and all the rest of it.'

'I didn't say anything,' says Joe.

176

'You didn't need to. I can see it all over your face.'

'I tell you what,' says Joe. 'If you want to lie low, let's do that tonight. We don't have to go out for dinner. What do you say we order room service and watch an old film, or something?'

I have to admit, that sounds very appealing. But I don't want to spend my whole time in Dublin in hiding. I decide I need to do something to reclaim my destiny – to make this trip less about finding Andrew and more about having an adventure; until the 24th, at least.

'No. Let's do the supper club,' I tell him. 'If they have space. And do you know what? I think I am going to get that dress.'

# 13. A Foggy Day

From: Andrew Power
To: Norah Jones
15 November 2010

Dear Norah,

Greetings from Los Angeles! I am sorry that it's taken me so long to reply to your email. My big news is that I got the job working for the Very Well Known Composer (VWKC), and I've been here since September. With all the Wikileaks stuff in the news, I am paranoid about my email being hacked so I won't use his name: I'll just say: think Boy Wizard or Vampire Teen film: not those but similar level. And now I'm his assistant, or rather his second assistant (there are also two interns, a PA and a sound engineer). And yes, if you're thinking *Devil Wears Prada*, you're not wrong, especially as regards his critiques of our work. 'Strings for a sad scene – ground-breaking'. I say this in jest, though. I am learning an unbelievable amount and he is very generous with his time. I am mainly doing orchestral mock-ups for him, plus taking notes, setting up equipment, booking session musicians and, obviously, getting coffee. But he has also asked me, and the two interns, to write some cues for him – the other day he had me play one of mine and he broke it down for me, telling everyone exactly what was wrong with it. You might think this sounds bad, but actually the others were jealous that I got feedback: I was suitably and genuinely grateful.

He works from his home studio, which is up near Laurel Canyon – that's the road up in the Hollywood Hills where all the great singer-songwriters hung out in the 1960s. So many of the songs we played together were written there. I can't even describe the place to you, Norah. You would love it. It's twenty minutes' drive from Sunset Strip, but it's like being in the Rocky Mountains: all cliffside gardens and wooden chalets, and pools and trees everywhere, and views you wouldn't believe. At night you hear coyotes and owls, and the sunsets are a sight like no other, because of all the smog. I really have to tear myself away at the end of the day. I'm living in a horrible apartment with three other guys in West Hollywood, all aspiring actors working as wait staff. We keep very different hours, so I'm generally setting out for work when they're coming home. One of them suggested we could actually sleep in shifts and get an extra roommate to save money – I'm seriously going to consider it. What with my airfare and buying a car, I'm practically paying money to be here; but it's all worth it, I hope.

I was thinking of you the other day because I was listening to 'Blue', by Joni Mitchell, on my way home in the car. We live about ten minutes from where her house was, on Lookout Mountain – it's like a little log cabin in the woods. I think *Blue* is one of my favourite albums now, and I can't believe I'd never listened to it before you recommended it.

That song 'River' made me think of you, too. I'm afraid I'm not going to be home for Christmas again this year. The fare is simply unaffordable, and we'll be working through the 'holidays' as they call them here – my mum and my brother Gus are going to visit me in the spring instead. So it looks as though I've missed my chance to see you again this Christmas. But who knows what will happen when this job ends – I'm here for another year at the most and I hope I'll be back in Europe after that. I find myself missing the small things: like a proper pint or a cup of tea. That's not the only thing I miss, of course.

How are you doing? I'm glad to hear the gigs have picked up, and it sounds as though your friend/manager is doing a good job. Your website looks great, and I especially like the photo on the landing page. I need to create my own website at some point, but I've been putting it off; I'm too busy and tired at the moment, plus I'm not as beautiful as you.

I'll finish now – I'm going to get some sleep because we have an early start in the morning, as ever. I hope you have a good Christmas, Norah. I am sorry that yet again we won't meet this year. I can only pin my hopes on a reunion someday – maybe at Bewley's, on Christmas Eve 2019, if not before?

Ever yours
A x

Hearing someone pass behind me, I minimized my screen quickly, hoping the telltale blue Hotmail interface hadn't been visible. While reading Andrew's email I had been transported to California, seeing him backlit against the blue sky, his grey eyes squinting against the Los Angeles sun. Now I was back in the solicitor's firm in Holborn where I had been temping for the past three weeks, on a foggy, chilly autumn day. It couldn't have been more different to Andrew's workplace, with its stained grey carpet tiles and dusty venetian blinds, and with the lunchtime microwave smells and constant wars over whether to open or close the windows. But all offices were like that, in my experience, and by now I hardly noticed it; my mind was always on something else, generally either music or Andrew's emails. I was disappointed that once again we wouldn't be meeting up at Christmas. Nor had he made it to London last June; his time in Dublin was too busy with family and work commitments. I knew it wasn't his fault – the opportunity he had now was clearly too good to give up – but I was beginning to wonder if we would ever meet in real life again.

It was nearly a year since my showdown with Kiran at the Drayton, and even though I wasn't a superstar yet, my singing career had come on considerably. Kiran had been as good as her word, and within about six weeks after our conversation I had a basic website, with audio clips and some black-and-white photos, taken by Joe on his Nikon camera. Caroline wrote the copy and bigged up my experience to date, not quite lying but definitely making the truth sound more impressive than it was. And I went back to the pianist who had played with me on the demo, a diminutive fifty-something called Ernie Everett, and asked him if he'd like to team up to do any gigs.

'I suppose we could,' he said. 'I do a few gigs in Soho – there's a member's club that might like a vocalist. And I play in an Italian restaurant called Ciao Bella's in Holborn. They did ask me if I knew anyone, too. Do you know any Italian songs?'

'No, but I can learn,' I promised. I was thrilled, thinking that maybe Ernie could be the Chick Webb to my Ella Fitzgerald. It wasn't quite like that, but within a few months we had regular gigs, in the Artists' Club in Soho, and at Pizza Express in Ealing on Monday nights as well as Ciao Bella's. Dad used to bring his golf friends to see me on Mondays, and even Mum would sometimes come by with her friends. My perennial memory is of them both clapping and waving at me from different tables – our version of a happy family. Andrew might be making waves in Hollywood, but I was getting big in Brentford, as the fabulous Norah Baker: Mum's maiden name.

Looking at the clock for the millionth time that morning, I saw that it was nearly 12.30. One compensation for being slightly underworked here was that I could take a full hour for my lunch break. Our friend Paul Slovinski, Kiran's former crush, was studying nearby, and we sometimes met for lunch on a park bench in Lincoln's Inn Fields. He had shelved his playwriting ambitions for now and was doing a law conversion course. His former boyfriend, Sandy in Edinburgh, had met someone else, and we spent a lot of time commiserating with each other about our love lives. I also loved exploring the Inns of Court, with their medieval walkways, hidden fountains and quaint arches, even more beautiful today with the clinging autumn mist. Walking briskly, I could feel as if I was going places, even if in reality I was increasingly aware that I didn't want to temp for ever.

I had just arrived back at my desk when I realized that I'd forgotten to copy fliers for my gig at Ciao Bella's that evening. I always brought along a pile to every gig; it was a good way to pick up extra work such as singing at private functions. I had learned that my clientele was older and liked to have a piece of paper to take away rather than just googling my name or my pianist colleague Ernie's. I hesitated, wondering whether to leave it or try and nip to a printers' before my gig. I would be cutting it fine, because I finished here at 5.30 p.m. and the closest printers, which were all the way down in the Strand, closed at six.

I was just wondering if I could ask my dad to print some, as he was coming that evening, when one of the paralegals dumped a pile of contracts on my desk.

'Can you make three copies of all these and bike them around to the address on top? Ta,' she said before rushing off. I watched her head off into a meeting room with Matt, one of the trainee solicitors who had caught my eye, being a tad friendlier than the others, and quite handsome in a clean-cut way, like a 1950s film star. He always arrived in all his cycling gear and walked to his desk at the back of the floor before putting his bag there and going downstairs for his shower. I could never get my head around this – why exactly didn't he go straight to the shower? – but I had to admit that I didn't hate the sight of him striding by in all his Lycra.

The meeting door closed behind them, and I came to a decision: I would print the damn fliers here. I justified it to myself by reminding myself that I never drank the office coffee, which was pure poison, and therefore never used any of the milk. The supply of milk was an extremely sore point in the office, and I had already been asked to draw up a sign forbidding anyone from using it in their cereal. As a result the fridge was now full of labelled pint cartons in various stages of grim decay.

I opened up my email and found the PDF of the flier, which Kiran had created for me, apologizing that she couldn't make any more after this as she was just too busy. I had reassured her that she had done more than enough. I knew I should have been trying to cash in on the success of Duffy or Adele with a copycat act, but I also knew that I wasn't as talented as them. The ongoing troubles of Amy Winehouse were heartbreaking to read about – I had snuck in to see her in the Camden Jazz Café when I was seventeen and had been in awe of her ever since. It also, somehow, scared me off even further.

If that was what fame and success was doing to someone like her, with her talent like a gift from the gods, what would it do to a minnow like me? My shameful secret was that I was perfectly happy with my current level of 'success', such as it was. I did sometimes worry about the future but I dealt with those worries in the same way I dealt with my alarm in the morning: by pressing the snooze button and hoping for the best.

I sent the document to the downstairs printer and then ran down to do my photocopying. I found the machine jammed but cleared it with a bit of coaxing – I had twigged long ago that this was by far the most important skill to have in an office setting. I made my copies and then waited expectantly for the flier to come out, feeling a twinge of guilt at the cost of the thirty colour copies – at about 4p per copy, I was costing the company at least £1.20 in printing costs, not to mention my wage of £8.50 an hour.

After a few minutes, though, my fliers still hadn't appeared. I despatched my copied contracts, after the usual banter with the man at the courier company, and ran up to check the hold-up on my computer. But when I opened up my recent print jobs, my blood ran cold. The printer downstairs, the one I normally used, was HP OFFICE3547. But I had somehow sent my flier to HPSOLO221, wherever that was. Which meant that my thirty fliers, with me in plunging black, advertising the Fabulous Norah Baker (with pianist Ernie Everett) could be anywhere at all in the building.

I immediately did a sweep of all the machines on the whole ground floor, then the floor above, busting as much of a move as I could in my pencil skirt and heels, but I couldn't find them. I was running late with my next job, transcribing a long interview with a client. But my trusty typing speed of 75 wpm was hovering more at 40, as I kept having to stop and wipe my sweaty palms. It was possible that HPSOLO 221 was a defunct printer that had been shoved in a cupboard somewhere; it was also possible that it belonged to the senior partner, or worse, to some trainee solicitor who was scribbling lewd messages on it and passing it all around the office. Why had I ever thought it was a good idea to use the work printer?

Just as my anxiety was becoming unbearable, the people in the meeting room opposite me all came out, and to my surprise, Matt, the handsome trainee, came walking over towards me. After looking left and right to check we weren't being watched he said, 'These yours?' and showed me a brown folder. I looked inside and saw my fliers. The relief was indescribable. Especially as the printer must have been inside the meeting room and my stuff could easily have been shared around the roomful of people if he hadn't picked it up.

'I am really sorry – thank you so much. I wouldn't normally use the work printer, but –'

'Not a problem,' he said. He was still holding the folder. 'Though it's probably best not to make a habit of it – you're lucky it was me that picked it up and not one of the partners! I just happened to be sitting nearby and I thought, hello.'

I nodded. 'Thank you so much.' I held out my hand for the folder, but he was still looking at it. 'So – this is you?' he said, looking from the fliers to me and back again. 'The Fabulous Norah Baker?'

'Well, you don't have to call me that but – yes. It's just a stage name,' I muttered. 'May I have them back, please?'

For a minute, he looked as if he was going to do some kind of playful withholding of them – dangling them out of my reach and saying, 'Not so fast!' If he had, things might have gone a completely different way. But he handed them back. 'Good picture,' he said, glancing from the photo to me and back again. 'What kind of music is it?'

'Jazz, really – jazz standards,' I said. There was a much nerdier technical description, depending on who you spoke to – the American Songbook, swing or just twentieth-century popular song – but there was no point in getting into that.

Matt almost sat down at the edge of my desk, before thinking better of it and standing back up. Thank God; already the entire office had clocked the fact that we were having a conversation, although nobody was sitting close enough to hear me; I was off in a little lonely corner by myself, away from the inner circle occupied by the paralegals.

He said, 'I live near the Jazz Café, in Camden. Have you ever been there?'

'Oh – yes, I have.' This surprised me for some reason. I don't know why, but I had assumed he lived in Balham or Clapham, where most of the trainees seemed to live. I never would have guessed Camden, and for some reason this, and the fact that he had heard of the Jazz Café, made me reassess him.

'Have you been?' I asked.

'No . . . not really my thing,' he said.

I nodded, unsurprised; jazz wasn't really anybody's thing, or nobody that I knew anyway – except me and my dad.

'Well, good luck with the singing.' He shuffled his papers and started moving off before pivoting back. 'Forgot to ask. Are you coming to the office Christmas party?'

'The Christmas party? No, I don't think so.' The party was on Thursday 1 December, at a nearby hotel. I wasn't invited, but I felt as if I'd already attended it, having heard so much about the planning of it: it was a buffet with a disco to follow, a disappointing step down from the three-course meal with live band that had been the standard before the crash. 'I think it's just for, um, permanent staff.'

'No, really? That's rubbish.' He shook his head, looking genuinely surprised, which struck me as a little bit naive. Had he really not noticed how incredibly petty and hierarchical his firm was, about everything from holiday allowance to milk usage? But Matt seemed nice, and genuine, and I felt slightly regretful when our conversation ended and he went back to his desk. So when he asked me out, the following week, I said yes. It was time to accept that I wasn't going to look up from my desk some day and see Andrew, fresh off a plane; I probably wasn't going to see him in London, or even in Dublin. I needed to face the fact that we were on different continents and would probably remain so. And meanwhile, after years of being single, I had to admit: it was nice to go on a date.

# 14. Family Reunion

Back at the hotel, I hang up the dress and wonder what to do next. Joe has managed to book two tickets for the supper club and is now taking a bath, but I feel restless. I decide to go down to the hotel bar with my book and just revel in the freedom of being on holiday with nothing to do. I've never actually been on city break alone, and I decide to add it to my list of things I'd like to do some day.

The Shelbourne has multiple bars, but soon I find my way to Number 27 Bar, with tall windows overlooking Stephen's Green. A fatherly barman called Gerry, who reminds me of the barman at the Drayton, makes me an Irish coffee, and I slip into one of the prize armchairs beside the fire, roaring in its marble fireplace. I have brought my book to read, but I find my eyes keep straying from the page as I consider everything that's happened since we arrived – my near miss with Conor, my phantom sighting of Andrew. And then I just let my eyes rest on the hypnotic flames and enjoy my Irish coffee, which is so delicious that I don't understand why I don't order them all the time back home, or make them myself: it's just coffee, sugar, cream – and, crucially, whiskey.

I almost don't hear the voice beside me saying, 'Excuse me – is this seat taken?' so that she has to repeat it a few times. Looking up, I'm thrilled to see that it's my friend – as I already think of her – from the breakfast bar and the buffet. She's gesturing to the arm-chair opposite me.

'Not at all, please sit down.'

'I won't disturb you,' she says, with an irresistibly friendly smile. 'I'm waiting for my partner – we're heading out for dinner but I thought I'd just have a little drink by myself first.'

'Oh, lovely!' I say, trying not to sound too effusive and probably failing. 'That looks like an interesting drink, what is it?'

'A hot port,' she says. 'Port, sugar and a slice of lemon with cloves. Great for the winter weather. Do they not have those in London?'

'How did you know I was from London?' I ask, smiling.

'Just a guess. Anyway, *sláinte*. Cheers and Happy Christmas.' She lifts her glass in a toast. We both open our books, but I still can't concentrate and find myself staring out of the window. After about ten minutes, my neighbour puts down her book and addresses me, smil-ing. 'So what brings you to Dublin for Christmas? Are you visiting family?'

'No . . . I'm meeting, um, an old friend. It's a sort of reunion.' This seems the easiest explanation, even if it doesn't quite cover everything.

She doesn't say 'What?' exactly, but her eyebrow arches in a way that indicates polite surprise.

'I see! Well, I hope it's a good trip anyway,' she says, and I decide she must be a diplomat or politician, or would make a great one if she isn't. 'We're here visiting from the west of Ireland – though we're both Dubs. We're spending Christmas with my partner's family, but we decided to stay in a hotel so as to have our own space.'

'That sounds like a *great* idea,' I say sincerely. 'I'm Norah, by the way.'

'Patricia – Pat.' She smiles and we shake hands. 'Norah. That's a lovely Irish name. But you've no family connections here at all?'

I put down my book, suddenly feeling like I would love to tell her more. 'Do you want the short answer, or the long answer?'

'Well, the wind is howling outside, and it's nearly Christmas. And we both have a toasty hot drink by the fire. So I'd say the long answer fits the bill.' She checks her little gold watch. 'Yes, we've loads of time.'

'Well – my dad's mother was from Dublin. She emigrated from here in the 1950s and she came over to Manchester. But she didn't really keep in touch with her family here, I don't think. At least, I'm not sure, because my dad moved to London when he was in his twenties, and he sort of repeated the process – he didn't keep in touch with his parents either. I know it must all sound unbelievably weird.'

I've known people to be shocked at all this – Kiran,

for example, couldn't believe it when I told her long ago. But Pat takes it all quite calmly.

'It's not that uncommon a story. Emigration is a painful thing, and families are messy. What does your father say now about it all?'

'I never asked him. And he died six years ago, sadly.'

'Ah, I'm sorry to hear it,' says Pat, sounding genuinely sorry.

'That's OK – it was a long time ago,' I say, my standard reply when anyone says this.

'You must wish that you could ask him now.'

'Yes. I don't know why I didn't really. I suppose I felt like, if he didn't want to be in touch with them then neither did I. And also, I wasn't that interested, I suppose,' I admit.

'But you feel differently now?'

I nod, realizing for the first time that this is true. It's not that I'm desperate to track down my grandparents. But I would like to feel as though I had some connection to Dad still, or maybe know a little more about what his family was like and why they all drifted apart.

'Well, there is so much help online for researching your family, as I'm sure you know,' Pat says. 'What was your grandmother's name? Her maiden name, I mean, assuming she married an Englishman? Do you know?'

'Oh, it was Byrne. Quite common, I know.'

'It is – a very common name,' Pat agrees sympathetically.

Remembering something, I add, 'And she grew up

somewhere called Liberty Street, or Liberties Row, or something like that.'

'Ah, you mean the Liberties,' Pat said. 'That's a very old inner-city area, right by the cathedral – St Pat's cathedral. I grew up in a place called Drimnagh myself, but a lot of families had come from the Liberties. In fact, I knew some Byrnes, who had moved to our road from the Liberties, around 1965 or thereabouts. What was your grandmother's first name?'

'Cora.'

'Cora. Well, I don't know the name myself but I could certainly see if I could get in touch with my old neighbours. And see was there a sister who moved to England.'

'Really? That's very kind. I wouldn't want to be a nuisance.'

'No nuisance, just a phone call. They were always a very nice family. I'm sure they're in the book. What's your surname now, just so I can tell them?'

'Are you sure? That's very good of you.' I tell Pat my surname, but I obviously don't expect anything to come from this; I can't possibly expect any genuine relatives to come out of a random encounter with someone in a hotel bar. But it's very kind of Pat to offer to do that on my behalf, and it's made me decide that I will research properly online myself.

'Ah, here is herself. Norah, this is my partner, Helena,' says Pat, a beam breaking out on her lovely face. 'Lena, this is Norah.'

Helena is tiny, dainty and dark, and is just as smartly dressed as Pat; they're obviously out somewhere fancy, unless they dress like that every evening – I wouldn't be surprised.

'Where are you headed to?' I ask them, thinking they probably have good recommendations.

'We're going to a supper club,' Helena tells me. 'It's run by my niece. She's an actress, not a chef, so I don't have the highest hopes of the food, to be perfectly honest. We're just going there to support her, hence we're setting off a bit early.'

'Oh! We are too! Is it the one in the Georgian house?'

'That doesn't really narrow it down around here,' says Pat, with a smile. 'It's in Mountjoy Square.'

'Joe and I are going to that too! That's such an incredible coincidence.'

I'm completely stunned, but the others don't seem at all surprised.

'There are no coincidences in Dublin,' says Pat, getting to her feet and shrugging on her beautiful silk-lined wool coat. 'The place is too small for that, there's no room for them. What's that line from the song? A quiet street, where old ghosts meet. That's Dublin: the world's biggest village. Well, that's great that you're coming, Laoise will be delighted, she might even sell out.'

The room is very warm now, filling up with festive crowds, and my cheeks are burning from the fire and the whiskey. But I feel a shiver at the mention of ghosts, since it reminds me so exactly of Andrew's words, about Christmas in Dublin.

'Before you go,' I say awkwardly. 'I just wondered, have either of you heard of an Irish composer called Andrew Power? Or a musician, even?'

They both shake their heads, and we say our good-byes as they head off, leaving me to my thoughts again, now even more crowded following our conversation and its series of coincidences. I notice Helena discreetly tucking her arm into Pat's as they move off. Maybe that's the secret to Pat's radiant appearance: she's one of those lucky people who found the love of her life years ago, leaving her free to focus on other little things like hair, make-up and inner peace. I wonder, if I had managed to be with Andrew somehow, would I be equally Zen and radiant by now? What would have happened if I'd actually managed to meet him – that time in London, when he asked me to?

# 15. Some Enchanted Evening

To: Norah
From: Andrew
2 April 2012

Dear Norah,

How are you? Berlin is good – as crazy and fun as ever. It's finally getting warm enough for me to think about dipping my toe into some of the open-air swimming pools they have here – they're mad for the outdoor swimming. I have an update for you . . . I will be in London for one night at the end of next week: Thursday 12 April. I entered a composition competition and I've come second. The finalists' music will be performed, at a venue in the South Bank – I don't know if you've heard of it, it looks to be somewhere central? (I am joking. I am sure you've heard of the South Bank.) The timing works out well because I will be in Dublin for Easter and I'll take in London on the way back. I very much hope you'll be able to make it? I can leave a ticket for you on the desk. Or maybe we could have a drink before – or after? I really hope that, after all this time, I will have the chance to see you again.

Ever yours,
A x

I closed my Hotmail with an inward groan. It was absolutely and completely typical. No sooner did I give up hope of ever seeing Andrew again *and* get a serious boyfriend than the universe taunted me with this email from him. I hadn't heard much from him since he had moved from LA to Berlin, eight months earlier, to take up a job managing a string quartet. Christmas had come and gone without any mention of us meeting up, though I had told him that I was seeing Matt, so that might explain his reticence. Now he was coming to London – he would be in the same city as me, for the first time in two and a half years. In fact, he would be less than two miles from where I was sitting right now, temping in yet another office, this time a big fashion magazine, in Soho.

I picked up another piece of sushi with my chopsticks – the whole office subsisted on sushi, and I had picked up the craze, along with wearing J-crew style combats. I had never thought of myself as a suggestible person, but after two weeks here I was addicted to Yoga Bunny Detox drinks *and* was also hankering after a large rose-gold watch like everyone had here. I opened up my gmail – another new acquisition – and wrote a g chat to Caroline.

*Guess what. Andrew is coming to town. He is doing a concert on 12 April and wants to meet. What do I do?*

I sent the message and hoped it would catch Caroline, over in her magazine office, also having sushi at her desk. Caroline had been doing brilliantly at work. She had started a blog and had joined Twitter – I still wasn't sure exactly what that was, but I knew that Caroline had been headhunted to join the staff of the glossy magazine of a weekend newspaper. And Kiran was the youngest director of her company in years – there were dozens of directors, she told us, but it was still impressive. As for me, I was still temping and still singing but I had moved out of Dad's house and into a flat share in Harlesden. I knew it was time for a change and I had set myself a deadline: either I would make it in some unspecified way that year or I would find a permanent job.

There was no reply from Caroline, and I was almost regretting asking her what to do. I normally preferred to make my own decisions. Plus, I was feeling more and more inclined to just go. True, I was with Matt, and had been for almost a year and a half. But I wouldn't be cheating on him with Andrew – I was just going to meet up with an old friend. What harm could that possibly be?

Just then, a message came pinging back from Caroline: *12 April? Isn't that Kiran's birthday dinner?*

I groaned again, out loud this time, attracting a puzzled look from the girl next to me, who worked in the advertising team but looked like a resting model, like all the staff here.

'I'm fine – sorry!' I told her, putting my sushi packet in the bin. Damn. It was Kiran's birthday dinner, and I was meant to be bringing Matt. I would have felt bad enough pulling out of Kiran's birthday – but I would feel embarrassed telling Matt the real reason I had.

*OK*, I wrote back to Caroline. *Maybe that is a sign. I can't cancel Kiran. And I can't do that to Matt – or could I?*

I half expected Caroline to tell me to follow my heart and meet Andrew, but her answer, a few seconds later, was kind but pragmatic.

*I think you're right*, she wrote. *You probably wouldn't be thrilled if he cancelled an evening out with you and his friends, to meet up with an ex.*

Ouch. When she put it that way, I could see the problem. I could tell Matt that I was pulling out of Kiran's birthday to meet up with an old friend, certainly. But, with his lawyer's persistence, he was bound to ask questions about who exactly this friend was. And I would probably end up admitting to him that Andrew wasn't just an old friend, but a much more significant figure in my past. It sounded fine in principle, but if I imagined Matt doing the same to me, then yes, I could see the problem.

I opened up my Hotmail again and wrote a quick reply to Andrew, determined to rip the plaster off before I had a chance to regret it.

*That's fantastic about the competition*, I wrote. *Congratulations. I am so sorry that I can't make it that evening – I am going to a friend's birthday, and I really can't miss it. I am so sorry that I'll miss you, after all this time. I'll be thinking of you. Good luck. Nx*

The regret that engulfed me as I sent the message was much worse than I had anticipated. My immediate impulse was to send another message telling him I had changed my mind, that I would be there after all. But I had made my decision now, and it was time to move on. I decided to go shopping for nice underwear that evening after work, to give myself a boost and to remind myself that I wanted to commit to my relationship with Matt and give up the fantasy of anything ever happening with Andrew.

And things were going really well with Matt; we had been together over a year now. True, we were very different. Matt was focused on his career, having just been made an associate at his firm, while I was still spinning my wheels with temping and singing. He wasn't into my kind of music, or any music at all aside from techno tracks that he listened to while running. But he had made an effort to learn about jazz and he helped me with my website and went loyally to my gigs whenever he could. We both liked reading about history, though I tended towards biographies of medieval queens, and he was obsessed with the Second World War. I also loved spending time at the flat in Camden that he shared with two other guys his age; I didn't know anyone else who lived so centrally, except for Joe. We went for picnics on Primrose Hill, and for Sunday lunches at the Princess Victoria, and the locations made it feel like I was in a rom com.

Most importantly, Matt had substance. When I asked him why he had chosen to be a lawyer, he said, 'It sounds cheesy but . . . I really value the idea of justice. The idea that everyone should get what they deserve, no more and no less.' His parents were divorced too, in a much messier split than mine, and it didn't seem much of a reach to imagine that he had been drawn to study law as a way of bringing order on to the chaos of everyday life. As I flipped through racks of underwear after work, I decided that I had done the right thing, saving myself the emotional upheaval that would come of seeing Andrew. Even if I did meet him that evening, what would happen afterwards? He would go straight back to Berlin, and I would be left with all my old feelings in turmoil again. It had been hard enough to say goodbye the first time: a second time could be even worse.

A week later, I was heading to the restaurant in Soho where Kiran was having her birthday. It was an Italian place, but not an old-school Italian with red and white checked tablecloths and candles stuck in Chianti bottles; this was the new type of Italian place, with Venetian bar snacks, filament bulbs and salvaged furniture. It wasn't possible to reserve smaller tables, but Kiran had reserved a big table downstairs since there were nine of us. Joe and his girlfriend Julie were the first ones there when I arrived, lounging around at the end of the table, both dressed in black. That is, Joe was lounging, while Julie was surveying the room like an MI6 agent on a covert mission. I didn't have a great rapport with Julie – she made efforts to be friendly, but they always seemed odd and stilted, as if she was copying some alien's guide to human behaviour. But Caroline and I loved speculating about her and Joe, who was as laid-back and scatty as she was rigid and precise. Maybe that was it? Differences were good, I reminded myself.

'Hi guys,' I said. 'Ooh, what are those?' They both had bright orange drinks in front of them in huge goblet-type glasses.

'Aperol spritz,' Julie said, looking puzzled. 'You've never had one?'

'No – can I try yours, Joe?' I asked. He slid his towards me, and I sipped it before I clocked Julie's appalled expression. 'Mm, that's actually quite tasty,' I said, feeling mildly provoked by her reaction. I remembered Joe saying that she was extremely germophobic. But she was also into bungee jumping and skydiving; how could tasting someone's drink be riskier than that?

'Is that your boyfriend?' Julie asked.

I turned to see Matt, festooned with cycling gear – he always seemed to arrive brandishing an arsenal of helmets, locks and wheels and dressed in high-vis gear. It seemed a bit unnecessary, seeing as he had only come from Holborn, but he always dressed for extreme conditions. Soon, though, he had shed all his accessories and was his handsome, well-dressed self again.

Everyone arrived together shortly after that: Paul, Javier, Caroline, Kiran and her new boyfriend Ben. I was almost blinded by the glare of Caroline and Kiran's statement necklaces, which were very big that season in both senses. (I had one on as well.) Kiran had also had her hair straightened with a Brazilian blow-dry; Ben couldn't take his eyes off her. A recent arrival, Ben was clearly going to be a keeper. Having declared her intention of writing down a list of her most important criteria in a man and only dating guys who met at least twenty-five out of the thirty of those, Kiran had met him on a night bus, and they'd been inseparable ever since. Caroline was the only one of us who was single, but she didn't seem to care; she was doing really well at work and having fun going on random dates.

I was sitting between Matt and Javier, Paul's boyfriend, a softly spoken guy who was visiting from Barcelona. They had met eight months earlier, while Paul was there for a stag weekend, and now they travelled back and forth every two months. I had only met Javier twice before but I had heard all about him: the eldest of six, raised by a single mum, he was slightly deaf in one ear after a bout of childhood measles, which had inspired him to take up a career as a paediatric nurse. All very perfect, but I was worried about Paul being in yet another long-distance relationship. We had both been burned, in different ways, by romance at a distance, and I couldn't see things with Javier working out long-term. But I knew better than to say anything to Paul about that.

'Hey, did you tell everyone about your new job?' Julie asked Joe, once we had all ordered. It was little plates to share, though Julie had ordered her own meal.

'No – what new job?'

'I've got a job as a character animator,' Joe said. 'In Brown Bear Studios. They make the World of Warcraft games.'

Cue mad excitement from all the men, who obviously played this, while the rest of us were thrilled for Joe; I knew this was something he'd wanted to do for ages.

'They're also working on a film . . . so that's exciting,' Joe said. 'Anyway – enough about me. Happy Birthday, K-dawg.' He raised his glass in a toast to Kiran, and we all followed suit.

'Yes, Happy birthday,' I said. 'The big two-five.'

'I know – so old,' said Kiran. 'I'm in my mid-twenties now. Where will it all end?'

'Well, we die,' said Julie. 'That's where it will all end.'

I was the only one who heard her other than Joe, and I caught his eye; we both laughed. She really did have a dark side. Caroline and I had speculated all kinds of lurid things about her and Joe's sex life; surely there was some upside to her being so intense?

On my other side, Paul was talking to Matt about work. His conversion course was over, and he was a trainee in a solicitor's firm, near Matt's; they even knew some people in common.

'You know, I keep saying to Norah that she should do a conversion course,' I heard Matt say to Paul. 'She has the right kind of head for the law.'

'Really?' Paul said, politely sceptical. 'I didn't think she'd be into that.'

'Well, obviously she won't want to be temping for ever,' said Matt.

I pretended not to hear them but I couldn't help being slightly annoyed that he was giving Paul his views on my career. He had mentioned this idea to me several times, and each time I had told him I wasn't interested. It had become a bit of a bone of contention, to the point where I felt like telling him I already had a dad. To distract myself, I started talking to Javier. He and Paul were addicted to some new show about dragons – they watched it together, in their different countries, while messaging each other a running commentary.

'The dragons are not a big part of it,' Javier assured me, when I expressed doubts about it. 'You would love it, Norah, it's full of great characters, the female parts are so good. Danaerys Stormborn . . .'

'Oh, that sounds like Joe,' said Kiran. 'Stormborn.'

'How so?' Julie said.

Kiran said, 'His birthday – you know, 15 October 1987. The Great Storm?'

Julie shrugged her shoulders; this was obviously news to her. What did she and Joe talk about? Perhaps they didn't do much talking.

'Were you talking about *Game of Thrones*? I started watching it but I had to turn it off,' said Caroline. 'It's just too gruesome.'

Now everyone started talking about films and TV they had hated or walked out on.

'I walked out of *The Day After Tomorrow*,' Paul

admitted. 'I was very, very stressed with A-levels, and the prospect of having to do all my exams, and then deal with an ecological apocalypse and a new Ice Age, was just too much.'

'I walked out of *Castaway*,' Matt said. 'Most boring film ever. Nothing happens – he just sits on an island for three hours.'

'Thank you!' said Julie. 'So boring, right? And when he makes friends with the football – what was that about?'

I caught Joe's eye, again: he knew that was one of my favourite films.

'Wilson!' Joe said, under his breath.

'Wilson,' I replied, grinning.

Luckily, the food started arriving then, so nobody took much notice of this, or the ghost of a wink that Joe gave me, or the way I widened my eyes at him to tell him to stop.

'I think I'd do really well on a desert island,' said Joe.

'Sure you would,' I said indulgently. Joe would be no use at all on a desert island – he would just lie around sunbathing and sketching. Whereas Matt would be excellent at tracking down coconuts and signalling for help; I was fairly sure he knew Morse code.

Now the others were all talking about school sports and what they still played.

'I'm trying to persuade Norah to get into sport – or at least come running with me,' Matt says, putting an arm around me. 'She doesn't seem to have played any sport at school.'

'No, none of us did. That's how we all met – hiding in the PE hut while the rest of the class did cross-country running,' Kiran said.

'And yet you now run three times a week on the treadmill,' said Ben. He was a nice guy with an air of quiet amusement, who seemed content to be an audience for Kiran's stories and performances.

'That's different,' said Kiran.

'It *is* different actually, you're right,' said Matt, and he started explaining the distinctions between running on a treadmill and outside. Julie seemed extremely interested and soon the pair of them were talking away about heart rates and shoes and different terrains. I ignored them and focused on the food, which was divine; a fennel salad with slivers of almond, little plates of linguine with clams, thinly sliced steak with white truffle cream, and mini pizzas with leeks and Taleggio cheese. I glanced at my watch and realized that Andrew's piece would probably be playing right now. I didn't even know if it was for chamber orchestra, piano or what. Andrew had replied to my email with a very nice message, saying he completely understood and hoped to see me next time. But he hadn't suggested an alternative time to meet during his stay, and I hadn't felt brave enough to do so either.

'Your hair looks beautiful, Kiki,' I told her, trying to stay present.

'Thanks!' she said, flipping her blue-black mane. 'It took an hour and a half . . . I had the stylist's whole life story by the time she finished.'

I was just thinking that that sounded like hell on earth to me – I hated going to the hairdresser, especially having my hair blow-dried – when Matt said to me, 'Your hair would look really good like that. You should try it some time.'

'Mm,' I said. That was a compliment, right? That must be how he meant it. Just like it was a compliment when he wanted me to go running with him, or when he suggested that I do a law conversion course. But little by little, it was starting to feel as though he had had enough of going out with a curly-haired, singing temp, and wanted to upgrade to a straight-haired, running lawyer. It might seem like a rom com when we met on Primrose Hill, but what about the casting?

I had always thought that Matt and I had lots in common, but suddenly I was having doubts. I thought of a recent occasion where I'd been sitting in a bar while I waited for Matt to arrive, glued to my book, a biography of Isabella of Castile. I remembered thinking that if only he'd been ten minutes late, I could have finished my chapter. That wasn't a great sign, was it? Even Matt's books on the Second World War, which I had held on to as a sign of our shared interests, tended to gather dust on his bedside until his cleaner moved them without him noticing. Matt was a nice guy; that wasn't in doubt. But tonight, for the first time, I was realizing that might not be enough, for either of us. There was a distance between us that would remain no matter how fast Matt ran – or cycled.

I was distracted from my thoughts by some general exclamation: Paul had just announced something.

'That's wonderful, Javier! Are you guys going to live together?' Caroline was asking.

'I have got a job in London, at Great Ormond Street Hospital,' Javier explained to me. 'So I'm moving here next month. I'm going to stay with Paul while I look for a place of my own to rent.'

'That's amazing! Congratulations, guys!' I glanced over at Paul, who was beaming. I was so happy for him. So why was I feeling wistful?

Maybe it was the fact that here were two people who had maintained a relationship in spite of the distance. It made me wonder whether, had I been more positive about things with Andrew, it would have been different. Or even tonight – why hadn't I just accepted his invitation, purely to catch up with him as a friend? There wasn't any romantic overtone to his email, after all. I could have just gone for old times' sake, without betraying Matt in any way.

In fact – maybe I still could? I looked surreptitiously at my watch. It was 9.30 now. The concert would be ending around ten; I could just about make it to the South Bank, if I hustled. I felt bad about leaving Kiran's birthday, but I thought she would understand – or even if she didn't, it was something I had to do, or I would always regret it.

'I'm really sorry everyone,' I said quietly. 'I'm not feeling very well . . . I think I'm going to go home.'

'Really? I'll walk you out,' Matt said.

'No, no, please stay and have your pudding. I'm fine. I'll get a taxi home. Will you let me know how much it is for my share of the bill?'

He said, 'Are you sure? I could put you in a taxi.'

I felt worse that he was being so nice, but I just said, 'Yes, of course – don't worry.' After giving Kiran a big hug and my apologies, I hugged Caroline. Her smile said 'Busted' but also 'Good luck'; I telegraphed back at her 'Thank you – I have to try.'

I got the Northern Line right away, though it seemed to take me as long to emerge from Waterloo station as it did to get there from Leicester Square; I always forgot how huge that station was. Soon, though, I was on the South Bank, hurrying along towards the concert venue. Seeing all of London, lit up in the spring evening, the river with its illuminated boats and the strings of lights in the trees, I dared to feel optimistic. Surely I would make it in time to see him even if I missed the performance? He would have to stay afterwards for a drink. Wouldn't he?

I found the Queen Elizabeth Hall, raced inside and hurled myself into a lift for the sixth floor, where the performance was taking place in a temporary auditorium. It was only 10.10. I had expected to see a few stragglers, maybe Andrew himself having a drink nearby, but the place was completely empty aside from a lone usher, slowly clearing up empty glasses and discarded leaflets. The stage, with its black backdrop, was empty except for a grand piano. Everything else was gone. The performance must have been shorter than I'd thought – or perhaps they were just having drinks somewhere else.

I walked to the back of the room and found a pile of programme leaflets. There he was: Andrew Power. His piece was a sonata for violin and piano in E major. The programme listed his studies at Trinity and Juilliard, his work as a composer's assistant and now his job with the string quartet in Berlin. He was also composer in residence for a student chamber orchestra – fancy. But it didn't say where he was staying or where he was going for a post-concert drink – both things I should have asked, but it was too late now.

I walked around all the bars in the Queen Elizabeth Hall, but of course he wasn't there, and nor was anyone else who looked as though they had been performing. I kicked myself for not checking where he was staying; I could have gone along and met him for breakfast. Why hadn't I just said yes when he asked to meet me?

I decided to go home at once before I plunged into total dejection. On the way back, I received a text from Matt. *Hope you're feeling better? It was £38.50 for the bill, but no rush to pay me back x.* Sighing, I remembered what Matt had said about justice – the idea that 'Everyone gets what they deserve, no more and no less.' Well, I was getting what I deserved. I had been indecisive and wishy-washy and had ended up lying to Matt after all. And I had ignored my doubts about him, instead of following my heart. But I wouldn't make the same mistake again. The next time I saw Matt, I would have a talk with him, pay him his £38.50 and release him back into the wild, so that he could meet someone he didn't have to improve or upgrade. And I wouldn't settle again for someone who didn't make me feel the way Andrew had. Life was too short to do otherwise.

# 16. On Raglan Road

I've spent so long getting changed, and ruminating over the evening of Andrew's concert, that I am running seriously late, and Joe has to knock on my door, yet again, when it's time to leave for the supper club.

'Are you – oh.' His eyes widen as he takes in my appearance. 'Hey, Norah – you could have made an effort,' he quips.

'God, can't you be serious ever?' I step back to look again at my many efforts in the mirror. I can't create Veronica Lake waves by myself but I've done a kind of side braid and a lot of eye make-up. 'It's my new dress. Is it too much?'

'No, it's not too much,' he says. 'You look great. Honestly.'

'Thank you. So do you,' I add, clocking his slim grey jacket, dark trousers and black shirt. The man packs like a Tardis; I don't know how he fitted all that in his wheelie.

'Don't sound so surprised. Come on, let's go.'

I slip on my mohair coat, and we walk down the steps to the main lobby, me holding up my skirt so I don't trip, and Joe waves me ahead of him through the revolving doors. Seeing Stephen's Green all lit up in the light of the Shelbourne's lamps, with a horse-drawn carriage clattering by, it almost feels as if we've stepped back in time.

I tell Joe, 'There's something about winter in the city, with everyone all dressed up, that makes me think of *War and Peace*.'

'What?' he says, looking out for a taxi; the rank outside the hotel is empty for once.

'You know – *Metropolitan*.' It's a quote from one of my favourite films. 'Don't you feel like we're in a nineteenth-century novel?'

'Sure . . . Ahoy, milady!' he says. 'Look, here's one.'

I'm still laughing at his attempt at nineteenth-century conversation as we step into the taxi. We give the address and soon we're crossing the Liffey, driving towards Mountjoy Square, where the supper club is being held. The traffic is terrible; we're clearly going to be late. The street we're on now looks somewhat less upmarket than the area around the Shelbourne: there are lots of sad-looking hostels but also Santa Stop Here signs and Christmas decorations. We pass a church with people coming out, presumably from a late Mass. I have no idea what tonight will be like, but at least it will be an adventure. Or maybe a scam to defraud us dumb tourists of our euro dollars? But then I remember that Helena's niece runs it. Also the shop assistant's friend: presumably the same person.

'Do you know this place – have you been here before?' I ask the taxi driver, just to double-check.

'Oh yes, the supper club near the Joy. I do indeed.'

'So we're not going to be kidnapped?'

He laughs. 'Well, you might have sore heads in the morning, but I'd say you'll get out in one piece.'

'What's the Joy?' Joe asks.

'Mountjoy Prison,' says the driver.

The place itself, when we arrive, is in darkness, and I'm wondering if we have the right address before I see a candle shining in the window. The taxi drives off, and we get out and look around. It's another Georgian square, like a mirror image of Stephen's Green, but smaller and less manicured looking. The houses on either side have been lovingly restored, but this building is more dilapidated, its stone steps worn down and cracked.

'So you think they're definitely not going to murder us?' I ask Joe.

'Well, if they do, let's hope they give us dinner first.' He lifts the brass knocker, which is in the shape of a dolphin, and knocks three times. I get a strange shiver, like a feeling that something odd is about to happen, but I attribute it to the cold night air and my thin silk dress and stand a bit closer to Joe while we wait for his knock to be answered.

The door is opened by a girl in a nineteenth-century-style maid's outfit. I'm completely thrown; is it supposed to be fancy dress? If it is, we didn't get the memo.

'Good evening! Welcome! I'm Lily, the caretaker's daughter . . . I've been completely rushed off my feet this evening.' She looks at us both, as if to check for a reaction, then continues, 'Norah and Joe? That's great. I'd offer to take your coats, but it's pretty freezing obviously, so you may want to hold on to them until we get upstairs . . .' We walk up a grand staircase, and I get a general impression of a bare-bones building in a very run-down state, softened by candelight everywhere and even a stained-glass window on the first-floor landing.

'So you're from London, great stuff! Are you visiting friends or family?'

'It's kind of a long story,' I tell her.

'Plenty of time for stories tonight! I'll just give you a bit of history: this is Mountjoy Square . . . we are the only true Georgian square in the city, each side of exactly the same length. The square used to be one of the most prestigious addresses in Dublin, but the north side of the city fell out of favour when the Duke of Leinster built his house on Kildare Street, and all the fashionable people flocked there instead. And this side of the city never really recovered.'

'When was that?' I ask, thinking she'll say 1900 or thereabouts.

'In 1748, I think. Now, sit yourselves down! We have a table plan, so you can find your names and make yourselves at home, there's wine on the table. Everyone, this is Joe and Norah.'

She ushers us into a grand, high-ceilinged room with six windows on one side, overlooking the square. A huge log fire lights up one end, burning in a marble fireplace beneath a tall gilt mirror. The only other light is provided by the great branches of candelabras all down the table, reflecting off the white tablecloths and forests of glassware. The other guests are all seated already, including Pat and Helena – luckily nobody else appears to be in period costume. We exchange general smiles and hellos as we file around looking for our place names. I'm delighted to see that I'm sitting beside Pat, but I'm taken aback when I realize Joe is at the other end of the table.

'That's good, they're observing Joe's rule – we can compare notes later,' he says.

'Sorry we're late,' I say, sitting down beside Pat, who is on my right.

'You're grand, don't worry. You look absolutely stunning, Norah!' says Pat.

I thank her sincerely and introduce myself to my left-hand neighbour, Damian. He's civil but is obviously getting to know the dark-haired girl on his left and returns to his conversation with her at the earliest opportunity. Opposite us are three friendly women called Miriam, Theresa and Sorcha, and their husbands, whose names I instantly forget. Across the table from me, Joe is beside a fragile-looking blonde girl in plunging black. She perks up decidedly when Joe sits down beside her. I'm very confused; he's obviously at the singles end of the table while I'm in couples central. But it doesn't matter; I'm not on man-meeting duty and I'm also really happy to have the chance to talk further to Pat.

'Thank you,' I say as Theresa, across the table, pours me a glass of champagne.

In my limited experience of these things, the food often takes a good hour or two to appear and is pretty exiguous when it does. But Lily, despite her lackadaisical air, seems to have a military grasp of things. Flanked by two helpers, she brings out an array of dishes: a fat, brown roast goose, spiced beef and a roast ham, as well as a glossy mushroom pie for the vegetarians. There are further dishes set down, of blancmange, jelly, a dish of figs, almonds and raisins, small bowls of chocolates and sweets, and a pyramid of oranges and apples. The whole thing seems very old-fashioned, down to the cut-glass decanters of port and dark sherry on the white tablecloth, but I decide it must be a reference to something, maybe a Georgian feast to reflect the age of the house. One of the men carves the goose, while Lily brings a dish of floury roast potatoes around the table.

'So what have you seen so far, in Dublin?' asks Theresa.

I mention Trinity and Bewley's but admit that we haven't seen much else, as we've been too busy hanging around enjoying ourselves. Everyone laughs.

'Now, that's the way to do it when you're visiting a city,' says one of the husbands. 'If I go to Madrid, I want to see Madrid – I don't want to be trapped inside the Prado for six hours, looking at pictures of beheaded saints.'

'Ignore him, he's a philistine,' says Theresa.

'I would recommend one museum here, though: the Dead Zoo.'

'He means the Natural History Museum,' Theresa clarifies. 'It's great all right. It's completely old-school, just a load of stuffed animals in cases.'

'The best things, though, are the giant Irish deer,' he says. 'You go inside, and the first things you see are these three skeletons of prehistoric deer, each the size of a small elephant, with antlers three metres across . . . they weighed a thousand kilos. They're absolutely magical. That's the best thing in Dublin, to my mind.'

Everyone laughs at this, but he remains adamant; the best thing in Dublin is not the Book of Kells, or Brian Boru's harp, or the Tara Brooch, or the Ha'penny Bridge, or a freshly poured pint in the Guinness Brewery, but the Giant Irish Deer in the Dead Zoo.

'Is it true that everything in Dublin has two names?' I ask. 'The Dead Zoo, the Joy . . .'

Nobody seems to have heard this, and they all shake their heads before reeling off dozens of examples of pubs and hotels still known by their old names, plus lots of ribald nicknames for the city's statues.

'I tell you what does have two names in Dublin – hipsters,' says another man. 'First rule of hipster club: change your name to the Irish.' There's a chorus of protests and laughter, but he continues, 'Come on. Dave Murphy will fix the plumbing – but Daithí O Murchú can set you up with a beehive or a fixie bike.'

'That's not true! People use the Irish version of their

names for love of the language,' says Sorcha. 'Not because they're hipsters.'

'There's an overlap,' says the husband.

'Where do you and Helena live, Pat?' I ask her as soon as the conversation's moved on.

'Westport, County Mayo. We run a small bookshop there, though we both used to work in TV.' She tells me a little more about their work in film and TV design, and how the bookshop is kitted out with memorabilia from sets they've worked on over the years. They haven't left it at Christmas for years, and they're trying to resist phoning to enquire about sales or stock level every hour. I tell her I'd love to visit it someday.

'Joe would love it too, I'm sure. He works as an animator – a character modeller, I mean,' I add.

Pat glances over at Joe, who's still deep in conversation with the blonde girl, and back at me. 'But you're here for a reunion with an old friend – that's not him, is it?'

'Oh, no. It's a long story, as I said.'

She gestures with her glass, and I end up telling her the whole story: meeting Andrew, keeping in touch, and the plan for Christmas Eve, which he might or might not remember.

When I'm finished, Pat says, 'That is a great story.'

'Do you think it's crazy? It does sound crazy, I know.'

'Far, far stranger things have happened. If he turns up, you never know what it could lead to.' She smiles. 'And if he doesn't, you won't regret giving it a go, will you?'

'Yes. Joe thinks I've gone completely mad. But I think it's worth a try.'

Joe, maybe picking out his name, looks up at this and smiles over at me questioningly. I smile back, hoping he hasn't heard me, my record still unchanged since last night.

'How long have you and Joe been friends?' says Pat.

'Oh, since we were teenagers.'

'He's a handsome man, isn't he?'

I look sideways at Joe again, who is still deep in conversation with his neighbour. He does look very handsome, his cheekbones lit up by the flickering light, his dimples coming and going as he smiles. The blonde girl is still hanging on his every word, laughing frequently at their conversation.

'Yes, he is,' I say, wondering why everyone keeps saying this – Maria, now Pat; I'm surprised the taxi driver didn't have a view. 'We're just friends though. Anyway . . . I don't mean to bore you with my love life. What about you and Helena? How did you meet?'

'She came to look at our house. I say our house, because I was married at the time. I married a bit too young, to the handsome young doctor who seemed to be the answer to all my dreams. And then I realized that actually you can be far lonelier inside a marriage than single.'

I take that on board, nodding.

'And then Helena arrived on my doorstep, to see if she could use our house for filming. She was a locations manager, before she moved into set design. We got to know each other during the making of the programme. And then . . . we fell in love, while I was still married. It was quite a mess for a while. But we got through it, and we've been together over twenty years now.' She smiles again, and I wonder again if I could ever radiate that kind of peace and contentment. Unlikely, even if I joined an ashram or a nunnery or managed to get my email inbox to zero. That's just the way she is, and that's not the way I am. Maybe that self-acceptance in itself is the first step to Being More Pat?

Sorcha leans across and says, 'Norah, I know where you should go tomorrow, if you don't have any plans. Go and see the sea. Dalkey is a beautiful little village – you can get the train there and then walk up Killiney Hill and walk down to the beach.'

'Howth is even nicer, though. And it has the best fish and chips, and the best view,' says her husband.

'Yes, it has a good view of the Southside,' says someone else. This obviously refers to the Northside–Southside divide which, clearly, is like the Cripps and the Bloods for Dublin, except with joshing instead of guns.

There's even more joshing, interrupted by Lily, who, it turns out, is really called Laoise, clapping her hands to get our attention.

'Ladies and gentlemen. Please retire to the drawing room, and we'll have some tea, coffee and maybe even some music.'

I tell Pat I'm going to the bathroom and go out in

search of it, eventually finding it downstairs on the first landing. Pushing the door open, I catch the tail end of a conversation between two girls who are using the hand dryer.

'No, they're just friends, he told me.'

It's the blonde girl who's been sitting beside Joe, and from the startled look she gives me I can guess what else she's been saying. I slip into the cubicle, feeling oddly unsettled. Obviously, it's totally up to him if he wants to hook up with this girl. I'm sure he won't just abandon me to find my own way back to the hotel – or even if he does, I know how to get a taxi.

I wash my hands and press a damp paper towel on my face, wishing I'd brought something with which to tidy up my smudged eyeshadow. I find some Vaseline and make do with that. Suddenly I'm picturing Joe's face, as he sat across the table from me, talking to that girl. It's something I've seen dozens of times before, so why am I bothered by it tonight? I decide that it must be because I'm far from home and feeling vulnerable about the whole Andrew thing.

As I go upstairs, I can hear singing coming from the drawing room: one of the husbands is singing a capella. I give Joe, who's on the other side of the room, a quick smile and sit down on a sofa beside Pat and Helena. We don't talk because everyone is listening to the music, a traditional air I don't know. At first I'm just astonished that this group of strangers, who have only met tonight, are now sitting around listening to someone singing so unselfconsciously. Then I'm struck by the beauty of the melody – and by the words, which describe a couple meeting on Raglan Road – and on Grafton Street – before going their separate ways. It makes me think of Andrew again, and a shiver goes down my spine.

'What was that song called?' I ask when it's finished.

'That was "Raglan Road",' Helena says. 'A great song. It was meant to be a different song, but nobody knew it.'

'What do you mean – it was meant to be a different song?' I'm confused.

Helena sighs. 'It was all supposed to be inspired by "The Dead".'

'What dead?' I'm getting completely freaked out now.

'The short story by James Joyce,' Pat says, reassuringly. 'Have you not read it, Norah? It's about a dinner, at Christmas time – a wonderful story.'

'In it, someone sings this song, "The Lass of Aughrim", which reminds the narrator's wife of her old love,' says Helena.

'Michael Furey. He died when they were young – of TB, wasn't it?' Pat asks Helena, for all the world as if they're talking about real people.

'Yes. Anyway, the whole evening was supposed to be like the dinner in "The Dead". I told Laoise she should have scripted and cast it properly but she wanted it to "unfold organically",' laments Helena. 'Sometimes people need things spelled out.' She shakes her head while Pat tuts reassuringly: it's clear who the worrier is in this relationship.

I feel another shiver. With all these songs and stories of dead or long-lost loves, the whole thing is starting to feel a little creepy. Now Joe is saying goodbye to the blonde girl, and he crosses the room to sit beside me as another traditional song starts up. I introduce him to my new friends, and they start chatting while I watch her putting on her coat. I find myself trying to see her expression, but she has her back turned so I can't tell whether she's looking devastated or blissfully happy. Probably neither, I remind myself.

I'm wondering if Joe's settled in for the evening but instead he nods towards the door, once, discreetly.

'Wouldn't that be rude?' I say, quietly.

He shrugs eloquently, and I remind myself that we're not under any obligations. I'm sure the singsong here would be fun, but I suddenly want to be back in my hotel bed, away from this place. Anyway, it's late. I can remember my mum telling me that nothing good happens at parties after 2 a.m.; I think the time zone shifts as you get older, so that means midnight for me now.

As soon as the song ends, we say goodbye to Pat and Helena, and I ask if I can get their details or see them before they leave. Pat gives me the business card for their bookshop, which has her mobile number and Helena's.

'Or you can just phone our room – room 212. We're there 'til Stephen's Day.'

'What's Stephen's Day?' I wonder briefly if it's some national holiday in honour of a famous Irish Stephen – Stephen Gately from Boyzone?

'That's the 26th,' Helena explains.

Again with the two names! Joe comes back with our coats, and to my relief we get a taxi fairly quickly. We don't talk much beyond exchanging a few notes on our dining companions, and I make a conscious effort to keep my distance as we both sit in the back of the taxi. I try not to look at his face, lit by the sliding amber street lights, or his long legs stretched sideways in the back of the taxi. Or his hand lying on the seat between us. What is wrong with me tonight?

'Are you OK, Norah?' Joe says, as we turn the corner towards Stephen's Green and our hotel. 'You're very quiet. Did you have a good time?'

'Oh, yeah! I'm just tired.' I consider jokingly asking him about the blonde girl but I decide not to. It's none of my business, and anyway, if I'm here to seek out Andrew, he's allowed to have some fun too.

## 17. How Long Has This Been Going On?

*Monday, 23 December 2019*

Over the years I've learned that a few of my mum's sayings are actually true. Some are quite mad (e.g. always salute if you see a lone magpie; never trust a man who wears red, or a trench coat) but some are sensible, factual and correct (e.g. things always look different in the morning).

This turns out to be the case this morning. When I wake up, it feels as though last night was a dream, from Laoise/Lily answering the door to the singing and everything in between. In the cold light of day – and it does look extremely cold, with a leaden grey sky – it's clear that my weird feelings of possessiveness over Joe were due to champagne and the odd atmosphere of the dinner. If it weren't for the string of emails I've already received asking me to review it, I would think I'd imagined it all. I snooze the email, meaning to review it later, though I know I probably won't. I know I should support creative endeavours, but if I reviewed everything that I bought, ate or wore, I'd never have time to do anything else. My phone buzzes as soon as I put it down: Joe.

*How's the head? See you at breakfast in thirty mins?*

I send him a thumbs-up emoji and take a long shower, luxuriating in the hot water and rainforest showerhead, as well as the posh geranium-scented gel. I must remember to ask Joe to give me his if he's not taking it home. No doubt the half-finished containers will knock around the bottom of my toiletries bag for years to come, but the heart wants what it wants.

He's there before me when I appear, wearing a chunky black polo-neck – he's one of the few men I know who can carry one off.

'I just ordered another full Irish breakfast. Want me to make it two?' I nod, and he waves at the waitress and makes sign language to say 'Same again.' He knows I always need to grease my wheels when I've had too much to drink. The normality of it is all very reassuring. As he told that girl: we're just friends.

'So, for today,' Joe says. 'I have a suggestion.'

'What's that?'

'Get out of town for a little adventure. Lazareena recommended this place called Killiney Hill . . .'

'Oh, I got told about that too. Wait, who or what is Lazareena?'

'The girl I was sitting next to. Guess how you spell it.' I refuse to guess, so he shows me her Instagram profile: Lasairfhiona99. I'm surprised there were ninety-eight more of them.

'That's wild. What's with all the letters? Was there a national letter surplus or something when they gave out names?'

'Dunno. It's pretty, though, isn't it? It means flame of wine.'

Damn. That *is* very pretty. How typical of Joe to ask what someone's name means. And how smug she must have felt telling him 'flame of wine'.

'So she's followed you on Instagram?'

'Yes. She's an artist, so we were chatting about that. She does these pen-and-ink illustrations. She's got an Etsy shop as well. I'll show you –'

'That's OK, thanks. So – are you going to meet up again soon?' I say this in a joking way, and I'm unexpectedly thrown at his reply.

'Maybe, if I'm at a loose end tomorrow – Christmas Eve.' He smiles at me. 'She said she'd be at a pub in town with a few friends. I might go and meet them, if you're busy.'

'Oh!' I'm about to ask, busy with what, but then I remember: with Andrew, of course. 'Great. So she recommended Killiney Hill, did she?'

'Yes, and a village called Dalkey. Killiney rhymes with whiney, and Dalkey rhymes with Walkie, which seems appropriate. We can get the Dart there, apparently.'

'OK, then.' I'm less keen on the idea now, but I realize I'm being somewhat irrational; all these recommendations must mean it's a nice day trip. And some fresh air might do us good today, to blow away any remaining crazy from last night.

*

An hour later, we're on the Dart train, whistling out of Pearse station. The concierge at the hotel was firmly in agreement that this was a good use of our time, though she was a bit concerned about the weather.

'There's actually snow forecast,' she tells us. 'But I don't think it will happen, it hasn't snowed in Dublin for over ten years. It never snows at Christmas anyway, much as we'd all love it, so I'd say you'll be fine.'

'I don't think the weather knows it's Christmas,' Joe says afterwards, but we decide to wear all our layers just in case, because it really is freezing. It's probably a stupid day to go for a walk, but we're committed now.

The automated announcements regularly tell us where we are, but they're in Irish, so it's a mystery. But the Dart only goes two ways, so we can't get that lost, and both ways end by the sea. Joe and I sit side by side, both facing forwards so we can see the view. The train passes by a football stadium, a cricket pitch and the backs of various red-brick terraced houses – and then, with a whoosh, it's out of the city and running alongside the beach. We're headed south with the low winter sun slanting into our eyes, the navy-blue sea and the ochre strand to the left of us, a peninsula sleeping on the horizon. The right-hand window shows the city unfolding beside us, with blue mountains in the distance. Two red-and-white striped towers loom over a building beyond the strand – an old power station, probably.

I turn to smile at Joe, and he smiles back; we don't

need to say anything. He takes out his camera and snaps a few pictures of the view. The train is so quiet and peaceful, presumably because it's leaving the city centre for the suburbs at 10 a.m. Even the seats are a tranquil green colour, and the faces of the people, gazing out at the sea, look peaceful. I know it's probably just me projecting my holiday feelings on to them, but I do think people seem more relaxed here than in London.

'Everywhere has its problems, though,' Joe says, when I tell him this. 'Rents are really high here, because of all the tech companies pushing up prices . . . and it's not like anything else is cheap.'

'Did Lasairfhiona tell you that?' I ask, trying not to sound too arch.

'Yeah. She said rents were "desperate" – that was the word she used.' He chuckles . . . affectionately? Was that an *affectionate* chuckle? I am tempted to comment on the Lasairfhiona of it all but I decide not to.

The stations go by in a peaceful parade: Booterstown, Blackrock, then Dun Laoghaire, which is a proper harbour, with ships and a pier, and some beautiful Georgian terraces overlooking the water. Then the window starts to fog up, maybe because we're breathing on it too much or because the temperature is dropping. I'm about to wipe it with my sleeve when Joe says, 'Wait.' He leans across me and, with his fingertip, draws the outline of our reflections on the window – it's just a dozen lines but it perfectly shows his face and mine, side by side. I know that Joe sketches all the time and it doesn't mean anything, but I'm oddly disappointed when our station approaches and he wipes it out.

Dalkey turns out to be a pretty little village, with doll-sized houses painted in sweetshop colours, all decked out for the season with tinsel and lights. We duck into a tiny bookshop called The Gutter Bookshop, glad of the warmth, because it is freezing, with a whistling wind straight off the Irish Sea. I buy a book of Irish poetry, not because I particularly need it but because I'm incapable of going into a bookshop and leaving empty-handed. Especially a small independent one with a kindly owner wearing a 'Yes for Equality' rainbow badge.

As we start climbing the winding road towards Killiney Hill, Joe asks me about Pat and Helena. I tell him about her offer to try and connect me with some relatives.

'It's just strange – having a grandparent from here, but I don't know the place at all.'

'I can imagine,' Joe says mildly.

'I know,' I say, thinking how trivial this is in comparison to his experiences.

'I'm cool about it now, though,' he says. 'You know when we were younger, I felt like a fraud because I didn't have any Chinese friends or speak Chinese ... That was when I started doing all that reading about

Chinese history. But it doesn't bother me any more. I'm learning Cantonese because I want to – not because I have anything to prove. I am who I am.'

He sounds so confident and self-assured; I'm struck by the contrast with how he used to be, when we were younger. I think he was a people-pleaser then, but now I'm realizing how much he's changed – and how strong he is, under his jokey exterior. The fact that he didn't tell our friends he was coming to Dublin with me – I thought that was him being evasive, but maybe he just didn't feel he had to. I'm still pondering this when he turns back to help me up a final few steps towards a high platform where we can see more.

We straighten up to look back down at the winding road. High granite walls edge the wooded path, with the occasional gated doorways showing glimpses of houses and sea views. Each is beautiful in its own way; ivy-clad, slate-roofed, with bay windows overlooking the sea, turrets or widow's walks.

'Apparently a lot of these belong to celebrities,' Joe says. 'Van the Man lives in one. Have you heard him called that before?'

'Van Morrison? Um – yes, I have, Joe.' I am not even going to ask where he got this from; Joe has a painful case of mentionitis.

A woman walks by with a golden retriever, clad in Lycra with a padded gilet: a Fulham lifejacket, as Kiran calls them.

'Did you hear Met Eireann have issued a red weather

warning?' she calls in cheery fashion, as if she knows us already. 'We're getting a blizzard!'

'Hm,' Joe says when she's gone. 'She's the first walker we've seen. A bad sign maybe?'

'Let's just get to the view – it can't be that much further.'

We've turned from Sorrento Road on to Vico Road, and a stunning vista has opened before us, with three mountain peaks crowning a further bay to the far south. Fir and cedar trees meet over the narrow road, the grey sea roaring behind them. It's like Cornwall, or like a colder and windier Italy. I get out my phone to take a few photos, and just as I'm stepping back to try and get a better angle, I hear Joe shout, 'Norah!' His arm whips out to pull me back, just as a car roars past, having shot out past a blind corner seconds earlier.

'Are you OK?' he's asking. I stare in terror at the departing car, my knees suddenly buckling under me. Joe grabs me and holds me, and I cling on to him and bury my face in his shoulder.

'It's all right,' he murmurs. 'You're OK.' He's still holding me, so I detach myself slowly and back away.

'I'll be fine. Let's just get to the top of the hill,' I say, my teeth chattering.

A steep climb up a wooded path takes us into a park, where it's a little bit more sheltered. We soon see the fabled Killiney Hill obelisk, and start to climb up towards it, heads into the wind. I've mostly recovered from my shock now and I'm almost enjoying the feeling of being buffeted and blown, completely at the mercy of the elements. It feels as though just one more gust would be enough to blow me off my feet and into another world. We reach the top, and I turn to Joe and smile. 'We made it.'

'Come here,' he says. He pulls me in beside him, cheek to cheek, for a selfie, but my hair has other ideas, whipping across both our faces. He pulls the stray strands away from my face and tucks it into my collar. I put my cheek back beside his and he takes the picture. *Click.* I hear it and I also feel it. Oh, God. What is happening here?

'Let's get you inside somewhere. You're going to freeze,' he says, decisively.

I nod. The sky has completely clouded over, the wind is going through me, and I can feel a few flakes, though it's too soon to know if it will stick. He goes to take my hand as we clamber down, but I pretend not to notice and leap on ahead like a startled goat.

# 18. Going Back

We're still quite a hike from the village and we seem to have come down the hill the wrong way, since we're in a car park. 'Excuse me – is there a café or anything open around here?' I yell to a woman who's bundling two dogs into the back of a jeep.

'Try Fitzpatrick's Hotel,' she calls back over the wind. 'It's two minutes up the road that way.'

'Two minutes,' I pant. 'We can make it. Oh, God, why did we ever think this was a good day for a walk?'

It's so windy that I can barely make out the outside of the hotel except that it looks like some kind of miniature castle, with grey battlements and turrets. The relief of coming inside and feeling the swing door close behind us is indescribable. Through my squinting eyes I see red carpets and cosy alcoves, and a fire burning in the hallway, but it also seems unusually busy, with some kind of function or reception.

'I'm afraid we're closed for a wedding,' says a man in uniform, coming up to us. I'm so cold I can barely get the words 'Oh no' out, but Joe says, 'It's blowing a gale outside – could we just have a cup of tea, somewhere out of the way? We won't stay long. We're tourists,' he adds.

'Well – all right. Come in,' says our saviour, and we exchange relieved glances. Soon we're seated at a table in the hall, beside the fire, facing the front window and tucked away so we can't be seen by the rest of the room. Dusk is descending over the bay, and miles below I imagine all the Christmas trees being switched on, candles lit, fires being kindled, while the wind rages outside. At our table, there's a little tealight candle, and a waiter who I'm guessing is a sixth-former or the equivalent, strikes a match and lights it for us, after taking our order for two cups of tea. Joe edges the candle towards me, and our hands touch briefly before I draw mine away. I get busy stirring my drink and start playing with a sugar packet before ripping it awkwardly and spilling sugar everywhere.

'Since when do you take sugar?' Joe asks me, sweeping it off the table into his hand. I'm trying to think of a plausible excuse when he says, 'Look at that.'

I look up. The light in the room has changed; it's suddenly dark outside though it's only three-thirty, and a sighing, gusting noise is rising steadily over the background chatter. There are big arrangements of poinsettias against the windows, now looking even richer and redder as the windowpanes grow whiter and whiter at an incredible pace. It's snowing properly now – not just a few flakes but an absolute whiteout, sent from nowhere to remind us that the elements are in charge.

'A freak snowstorm,' says an older man standing nearby, looking awestruck but also rather thrilled, as well he might; I've heard of these but never seen one. We made it not a moment too soon.

'The Micra won't be able for that. I'll have to get Dermot to put chains on the Subaru,' says a woman beside him.

The hotel manager from earlier – Gareth, according to his name badge – comes over to ask if we want anything else. 'Also to let you know the situation outside . . . They're closing the roads everywhere – even the Dart's stopped running. Will you be able to get back to where you're staying?'

'Not by the sounds of it. Do you have any rooms?' Joe asks, obviously thinking the same as me: they will be booked solid with wedding guests.

'I'm not sure. The storm hit earlier up in the mountains, so there's people booked in who are stuck in Wicklow. But some other guests who weren't staying are booking in now, because they don't want to travel, so I'd go and check with my colleague at reception soon, if you are interested.'

'I'll go now,' Joe says to me, and he races off to the desk almost before the guy has left us. I sip my tea and watch him talk to the woman at reception, feeling bewildered by this rapid turn of events. I can see Joe talking away and gesturing towards me, and I try and look extra forlorn and shivery, which isn't hard. This seems a very long conversation for what should just take five minutes, and I'm getting increasingly worried – until I see him take out his credit card: phew. But then, long after they should be finished, there's even more chat. Is he ... flirting with her? Yes, he is. God, he's impossible. But I'm actually relieved to see it. Maybe I have been feeling something towards him, but it doesn't mean anything: it's just because we've been spending all this time together. Hormones, no doubt. I'm sure the same thing happens in prisons.

'Do you want the good news or the bad news?' Joe says, returning to the table.

'Bad news, please,' I say, without even having to think about it.

'The bad news is, they only had one room left. Is that OK? I do realize it means we're now in a 1940s farce.'

'Fine,' I say, relieved that he's making a joke of it. 'You'll probably have to hide under the bed when my husband comes in, but that's OK. What's the good news?'

'The good news is that we got a room. You're welcome!'

'Thank you.' Looking at the blizzard outside, I can see that this is a good thing. As for the whole sharing a room thing: it would be too ridiculous to start worrying about it. We're grown-ups after all; and I can sleep in all my clothes.

'It was meant to be the wedding singer's room, apparently,' Joe says. 'She is snowed in, up in Roundwood – she's broken-hearted not to make it, by all accounts.' He grins, obviously repeating verbatim what he's just heard, and then waits expectantly for my answer.

I gaze at him silently. 'And you're telling me all this because . . .'

'No reason,' he says. 'I just thought it was interesting. The bride is going to be very disappointed. They haven't told the couple yet. They're still serving the meal.'

'Joe,' I say. 'Just come out with it. Do you think I should spring out of a cake and volunteer to sing? I don't even know what kind of thing they're doing.' I bet the first dance will be something by Ed Sheeran or John Legend, which is not something I can really carry off.

'Well, Orla – on reception – says they're a rock'n'roll band,' says Joe. 'They're called the Blue Notes. That sounds more like jazz, though, doesn't it?'

I start to laugh – this is just too ridiculous. And then I can't stop; the laughter keeps bubbling up and out of me. I'm also hopeful now that he wasn't flirting: he was sounding out the situation for me.

'Did you set this up?' I ask.

'Nope,' he says. 'You're right. It would be a crazy idea. You're probably a bit rusty, anyway, aren't you? And you don't do well with no rehearsal.' He's looking straight at me, daring me to react.

'I actually do fine with no rehearsal,' I say, aware that I'm walking right into his trap. 'I did it at Finnegan's, didn't I? Remember that?'

'Was that you?' he says. 'I thought it was Kiran who got up and sang.'

'Shut up! OK, fine.' I shake my head at him, laughing again despite myself. 'Fine! If it makes you happy. I'll tell them I'm available, and they can decide.' I'm sure the band will have no intention of letting some unknown, who they've never played with before or even heard, get up and sing with them.

Half an hour later, I'm in a back room with piles of crockery and folded uniforms, meeting the band. There is Ronan on lead guitar, Sinead on keyboard, Kevin on drums, Paul on saxophone and Johnno on bass guitar. I've had my mini-audition, and now we're running through the set list with a backing track on Ronan's phone, making sure I know all the songs, which it turns out I do. I almost laughed out loud when I saw what the first song was. I can't wait to tell Joe about it; that is a sign if ever there was. Not to mention that there's been heavy moral pressure applied to me by all the band, plus Gareth and the two bridesmaids, once they got wind that I was here. No one has *said* that if I don't sing we don't get the room after all, but I feel there's definitely some kind of karmic bargain in play.

I don't need any pressure, though. I don't know if it's being in a new place, or having Joe with me, or the general unreality of being here in this castle in the storm, but I know that I can do it. I want to do it. I've been wasting time for far too long, and tonight I'm going to sing. For one thing, there are no sad songs; it's a wedding, after all.

'But what will you do?' I ask Joe, when I go to get the room key from him so I can change. 'I mean, I don't want to leave you down here while I'm up there singing – all lonely and bored.'

'Oh, I won't be bored,' says Joe, with a glint in his eye. 'And if I *do* get bored, I'll just go upstairs and wait for you in our room. Don't worry – you'll be great.'

I shiver at the phrase 'our room' but I dismiss the thought for now. I have more pressing worries. Like the fact that I'm about to get onstage to sing, for the first time in six years, with a group I've never even met before, let alone performed with. And it's for a wedding! This isn't some lounge bar full of drunken businessmen, where I can fudge and muddle through something even if I forget the words or miss my cues. The stakes couldn't be higher.

'Oh, God, Joe, I'm really not sure about that,' I say suddenly. 'I think I was being a bit arrogant, thinking I could hop up and just sing like this. I am completely unprepared. What if I balls it up? I could ruin this wedding!'

'No you won't. You will be great,' he says again. 'You've done it before and you can do it again.'

'You really think so?'

'I know so.' He smiles down at me. 'What do you tell your students, when they're nervous about doing their choir solos and whatnot?'

'Oh, I tell them to focus on one person in the audience and sing to them . . .' My pearl of wisdom now seems like the lamest advice ever. *I'm sorry, Ashanti*, I tell her silently. I didn't get it.

'Great – do that.' He cups my face with one hand – something he's never done before – but I don't even have time to worry about how right it feels. 'This is long overdue. Just get up there and enjoy it. What are you wearing, by the way?' He looks doubtfully at my jumper and jeans. 'Can you perform like that?'

'No – I have to go and get changed right now! We're on at five.' It's 4.35 already, though it feels like midnight. 'Aisling, one of the bridesmaids, is basically a genius and brought a spare black dress complete with tights and pumps. They're a size too big for me but I won't be walking much.'

'You fill those shoes,' Joe says, squeezing my shoulder.

I'm still gripped by the worst pre-stage nerves I've ever felt as I get ready. My knees are trembling, I feel nauseous, and my hands are ice-cold. But the minutes march on, until it's time to get onstage with the other performers. When five o'clock comes, I step out in my borrowed dress and beam at the crowd, while Ronan takes the mike.

'Good evening, folks – we're the Blue Notes and we're very happy to be with you this evening for this very special occasion, the wedding of Astrid and Stephen!' There's mad applause, and I relax a little as I remember two great things about weddings. Yes, the stakes are high, but there's also a lot of goodwill, and above all, the focus is really not on you. Ronan introduces the band and then adds, 'We're also very happy to have a special guest singer for you tonight . . . all the way from London town, the very lovely Norah Baker!' More applause. Tapping my mike, I say, 'Good evening, and a big congratulations to Astrid and Stephen: I hope every Christmas is as special for you as this one.' I smile at the couple, who are coming up to the floor for their first dance, and then nod to Sinead, who plays the opening chords while I sing that wonderful intro, Motown-style, just like I did on the sticky stage at Finnegan's. And then a whoop goes up in the crowd as they watch Astrid and Stephen start their first dance: a jive to 'All I Want for Christmas Is You'. Everyone is clapping, lots of phones are being held aloft for filming. As I discovered on that Christmas Eve all those years ago, a bit of adrenaline is sometimes no harm at all. I find one person in the room and think of him while I'm singing. And as I sing the final 'You, baby,' I point in his direction. He doesn't move or react in any way but I see him smile.

There are more huge cheers as the couple finish their jive, and then we go straight into 'Rocking around the Christmas Tree,' which is the signal for more people to join them on the dance floor, with the older relatives showing everyone how it's done. Then it's 'Frosty the Snowman', then a rock'n'roll version of 'Santa Claus Is Coming to Town', which gets all the under-tens up, and they all stay on for 'Jingle Bell Rock'. I have a few hairy moments with the lyrics of 'The Man with the Bag' but I manage to get through it OK. I've never been so grateful for the weekly vocal exercises with all my choral students, which means my voice is still in a condition to sing at all. It's so high-energy I would be exhausted if it wasn't for the buzz in the room, which keeps me flying through the next forty-five minutes, when we then take a five-minute break.

'That was fantastic! Thank you so much!' To my amazement, it's the bride herself, Astrid, who's come over to thank and hug me and bring me a glass of water – completely unprecedented in my limited wedding experience.

'Oh, no, thank *you*,' I reply. 'It's been brilliant – this is such a lovely wedding, such a perfect time of year for it. And that first dance! It was fantastic.'

Astrid, who's the most relaxed bride I've ever met, seems thrilled to hear it and starts telling me about their search for the right summer wedding date, and then realizing that Christmas would be ideal because all their friends living abroad would be back in town, so nobody would have to travel.

'I mean, a Monday wedding is ordinarily something you wouldn't do to your worst enemy, let alone your friends and family – but everyone has tomorrow off anyway, so it worked out perfectly. These things always do! Anyway, lovely to meet you – thanks again!' And she's off in a cloud of bridal glamour, leaving me even more determined to do a good job for the remainder of this gig. I want to go and find Joe and make sure he's OK, but Ronan is waving at me from the band stage, and I see that Joe's already in conversation with a pretty wedding guest in a pink dress. Averting my eyes, I jump back onstage and focus on the music.

The second half of our set goes by even quicker; it's only thirty minutes – as Aisling the bridesmaid said disarmingly, we're only on for a short while to give the old people something. Everyone is still happily dancing, and I manage to keep up to the unaccustomed pace, though I get a bit tangled up in the words of our finale, 'Must Be Santa'. There's wild cheering and applause as we finish and take our bow, and I'm pouring with sweat and wishing I'd brought a tissue onstage – I really hope Aisling won't mind if the dress comes back looking as if it's been in a sauna. We're taking what I think is our final bow, when I notice a woman coming up and asking Ronan for a request.

'What does she want?' asks Sinead, when she's gone.

'I told her you might not know it, Norah. Do you? "Going Back" by Dusty Springfield. I ordinarily wouldn't do requests, but that's the bride's mother.'

What are the chances? I smile and shake my head, reassuring Ronan that, yes, against all the odds, I do know it.

'Isn't it a bit downbeat though?'

'It's only an encore – it'll be grand. We'll give it socks. OK, folks!' he says to the others. "Going Back".'

Sinead starts on keyboards, and I come in softly, thanking my lucky stars I can remember all the words. I didn't really understand the song when Andrew first played it for me in Italy. But now I do, or I understand what it means to me at least. It's about going back to the confidence of youth but also having the wisdom of age. And knowing that heartbreak might lie ahead, but also that I'm stronger than I thought I was, and braver too. I've lost illusions but I've gained in other ways. I was right that it wouldn't have sounded much good with just me and Andrew's guitar. It needed a fuller sound, the resonance and the richness you only get with many musicians, all bringing something to it, building a crescendo together. And I can hear the same resonance in my voice – it hasn't degraded as I feared, it's got richer. The song wouldn't have been right for me then; it's right now. By the time I get to the lines about living your days instead of counting your years, the tears are gathering, but they're happy tears. I find Joe's face in the crowd, and the pride in his eyes pushes me over the edge, until the tears are sliding down past my smile. I'm crying *and* singing in public and I don't even care.

But I'm not the only one who's been overcome with emotion. Everyone is clapping; there are tears in a few eyes, and a few people are on their feet. I know for sure that it's the song they're responding to, rather than our performance, but I have no idea why it's struck such a chord.

'How does everyone know that song?' I ask Ronan, mystified.

'It was on an old ad here, a Christmas ad. Years ago,' he says, beaming at me as we all take our final bows. 'About a young man going home for Christmas – and his mammy switches on the immersion – oh God, I'm going to cry myself. Thank you, Norah, that was great.'

'Hah.' I start to laugh at the absurdity of it all, wiping away my last tears. 'Please don't thank me, honestly. I should be thanking you. And Mairead.' Poor Mairead, snowed up in Roundwood. She missed a great night.

'Do you take cash, or would you like a bank transfer?' Ronan asks me, on the money like a true musician. I don't even consider it; I know that taking money would be against the spirit of this particular night. They've given me much more than money.

'Oh, honestly, I don't want it. Please give it to Mairead, and she can give it to charity if she doesn't want it. Thanks again, everyone. You were brilliant.'

After a final quick goodbye to my new friends, I jump off the stage and run straight into Joe's arms. He tightens them around me, smiling at me without saying a word. I hold him even tighter, so glad that he was there to persuade me – and share it with me.

'You were fantastic, Norah. Were you happy with how it went?' he asks, and I nod, beaming wordlessly.

The DJ has set up now and starts playing an Ed Sheeran song. I knew Ed would make an appearance at some point, and I'm only too happy to let him take over. Joe and I start dancing together, my arms hooked behind his head. It doesn't matter that I'm in borrowed shoes two sizes too big, or that he's incongruously in his jeans and shirt among all the dinner jackets – I can't stop smiling, or leaning my cheek against him.

'We've never actually danced together before, have we?' I murmur into his shoulder, my voice hoarse from singing. 'Not even at Kiran's wedding . . . or Paul and Javier's.'

'Yes, we have – Gangnam style,' Joe says. I snort with laughter, and he dips me, Hollywood style. Then – just as I'm wondering if I have the nerve to kiss him – he pulls my face towards his and he kisses me. It's a completely magical kiss, and I'm powerless to do anything but kiss him back, regardless of the part of me that's screaming: Joe! You're kissing Joe! We resume dancing, his chin resting on top of my head. He clears his throat to speak, and I expect he'll be saying something about how this isn't a good idea. But instead he says, 'So are you back? Is the Fabulous Norah Baker back?'

'I hope so.' I feel fabulous – and fearless. So I reach up and kiss him again, soaking up the feel of his lips, his hair under my fingers, the scent of him. It feels so right. Even that part of me that was sounding an alarm a few minutes earlier is getting into it.

'So . . .' he starts to say and trails off. 'Wow.'

There's nothing to say, so we smile at each other, wordlessly and awkwardly, and just resume dancing.

'So did you make a new friend? The one in the pink dress?' I ask, trying to aim for normal joshing.

'Who? Oh yeah. Just chit-chat.' He grins. 'I told her I did animation, and she said, "Manga?"'

'What? Oh.' Obviously, seeing his face, she decided any animation he did had to be Japanese. 'Sorry about that.'

'I've had worse.' His arm tightens around me. 'I wasn't paying much attention anyway.'

Suddenly Ed gives way to Lady Gaga, and Astrid storms the floor, flanked with her bridesmaids and all her female friends. This would normally be right up my street, but not tonight. We both stop dancing, lean back and look at each other.

'What do you want to do next?' Joe says. 'Do you want to get a drink, or . . . ?'

Another fork in the road. I know that the answer is go to bed – as in, make him sleep on the floor or me go to bed in all my clothes, after improvising some ear-plugs and eye mask (my retainer, alas, is back in the other hotel). But I don't want to do that. I want to go to bed and do everything to him that I've been longing to do ever since we climbed that hill together – ever since this morning, even. Things we shouldn't do if we want to stay friends, but who cares about friends when a man looks at you the way Joe's looking at me?

So I take his hand and lead him off the dance floor. It's probably not a sensible decision, but I'm tired of being sensible. I am tired of overthinking everything and being pessimistic as a default; I want to feel care-free and take risks again, the way I used to. Outside the ballroom, a quick glance at the window tells us the storm is still blowing, but we don't stop to look; we walk up the stairs without a thought of what might happen tomorrow, which, in case I've forgotten, will be Christmas Eve.

# 19. Coffee Cold

### *Christmas Eve, 2019*

In Dublin in December, the sun doesn't come up until around 8.30 a.m. I know this because it's 8.45, and I've been awake for some time, curled into Joe's arm and watching the window gather light behind it. The room is beautiful: a gold two-poster canopied bed, yellow antique wallpaper and a seventeenth-century oil painting smiling down from the wall opposite.

I'm still wearing my top, which I retrieved from my bag, and my pants, but Joe's stripped off to the waist, giving me the opportunity to admire the muscular arm wrapped around me and, if I wriggle around, his bare torso. He's sleeping peacefully, dark eyelashes fanned out on his cheek and mouth relaxed. I'm torn between admiring him – it is a beautiful sight – and thinking: this is Joe. I'm in bed with Joe. *Joe.*

It was wonderful. But it's still, obviously, something we can't ever undo. As long as we're here, in this bubble, it's OK, but what about later today? Where on earth do we go from here? What am I going to tell the girls, and what do I do about Andrew?

'Hey.' He stirs and pulls me towards him. 'Are you

awake? Come here.' He kisses me, slowly, eyes still closed, and hooks his leg over mine.

It feels so good that for a while I just go with it. I can't believe we've wasted any time sightseeing here, while we've had our hotel rooms back at the Shelbourne. Right now, I would trade all the seven wonders of the world in for a complete, no-holds-barred VIP tour of Joe. But I'm not coping well with the uncertainty of it all, and I can't understand why he seems so relaxed.

'Shouldn't we talk about this first?' I ask, feeling suddenly agitated.

'Sure,' he says, rubbing his eyes. 'What do you want to talk about?'

'Well ... everything.' I don't know how to express my frustration; I just want him to acknowledge that it's not that simple. 'Where do we go from here?'

'Where do you want to go?' he asks, sitting up.

'No – where do you want it to go?' I ask. I almost laugh, this is so absurd.

'OK,' Joe says. 'I suppose we just continue being friends, but with – this.' He gestures at the space between us.

'What?' I inch away from him. 'Do you mean, like, *friends with benefits*?' I inject every last possible bit of scorn into the phrase.

'No. I mean – be together. See each other. See how it goes.'

'See how it goes?' I stare at him. 'Just like that? As if we've just met on Tinder? What about our friendship?'

'Well, sure. But . . .' He tails off, and I'm expecting him to say, 'We can still be friends.' Instead he says, 'I do have feelings for you, you know.'

'Do you? How long have you had these feelings?' I'm half-hoping he'll say he's been madly in love with me since the night we met, so his reply is oddly disappointing.

'I suppose I first felt it when you said you were coming here, to meet Andrew. I hated the thought of him not showing up, and you feeling disappointed. But then I started to realize that I hated the thought of him showing up even more. I don't want to lose you to another guy, Norah.'

'So was this just about beating the competition?' I say. This is harsh, I know. But I'm feeling confused, and desperate for some clarity, even if it's just a confirmation that this won't work out.

'Of course not! I have always cared about you – I just didn't know how much, until you came up with this idea.' He pauses. 'I can remember really wanting to kiss you before. But it was bad timing, both times.'

'When?'

'Well, the first time was the night we all went to Finnegan's.' He almost smiles. 'I was just working up my courage to ask you out, when the girls dragged you onstage. But then I was glad afterwards, because I realized that I didn't want to just go on a few awkward dates with you and then lose touch with you.'

'Well, exactly! What if we go out on a few awkward dates and lose our friendship now?'

'We won't,' he says, which is the most ridiculous answer ever. He obviously doesn't have a clue what getting involved with each other would really mean in terms of our friendship, or else he does know and he doesn't care; I don't know which is worse.

'What was the other time?' I ask.

'What other time?'

'The other time you supposedly wanted to kiss me.'

He sighs. 'The year when – when I came to your place, on Christmas Eve. But that obviously was bad timing.'

'Yes, it was,' I agree, feeling stung at the memory. 'And so is this! You know I came here to meet Andrew – and yet you drag me up here.'

I know this is totally uncalled for, but he responds with an even lower blow. 'I didn't drag you up here! I remember you leading me off the dance floor, not the other way around.'

This makes me gasp aloud. But then his next words make me feel like slapping him.

'As for Andrew, he won't be there. He's had ten years, Norah. If he really wanted to be with you, he could have before now. If he wanted to find you badly enough, he would have.' He frowns, an unwelcome idea obviously dawning on him. 'Are you still going to meet him? Even after what just happened between us?'

'Yes! I mean, no. I don't know!' This is the truth. 'It's Christmas Eve, and I'm supposed to be meeting him in nine hours. And this has just happened, and it's messy, and I don't understand how you don't see that!' I take a breath. 'Joe, we're not like these two strangers who can just hook up and see where it goes . . . Imagine if we went out for a few weeks, then broke up. How could we ever be friends again?'

'We could.'

'No, we couldn't!'

'Well.' He pauses. 'It's a bit late to worry about that now, anyway, isn't it? I mean we've already . . . crossed a line. So why not see where this goes?'

I shake my head. I don't have a reply for this question, because the real message is in his tone: he sounds *unconcerned*. He obviously doesn't see the stakes being as high as I do. And that hurts almost more than anything else – that he's prepared to roll the dice and lose me as a friend, just to have some fun.

There's a long pause while we look at each other. 'It will still be awkward regardless, won't it?' he says.

'Yes, but that can't be helped.'

'Maybe it can. I've been offered a job. In Japan.'

'What?'

'Yeah. I got approached by a studio there, last month. They got in touch, I sent them some work . . . and they've offered me a job.' He raises his eyebrows briefly. 'Based in Tokyo. So if you don't want to be with me, I can make your life easier by going to Japan.'

'*Japan?* What about this flat you're supposedly buying?'

'I'd rent it out,' Joe says.

'But what do you mean, be with you? Do you

261

mean – go on dates? Like, be a couple – just like that?' I don't understand how he thinks it could be that simple.

'Yes,' he says, and the simplicity of it catches at my heart. 'Go on dates. Be a couple. Just like that.'

For a minute, I allow myself to think that it could be that simple – that we could just seamlessly turn our relationship into something completely different, without worrying about what the future holds.

'But if you don't want to, I can take the job. Which means no awkwardness for you. I'll move to Japan, and that will be that.'

'Oh, my God.' I clasp my fingers to my temples. 'Are you giving me an ultimatum? Honestly, Joe. Is that the choice you're giving me? Go out with me, or I'll move to Japan?'

'No! I don't mean it like that. I mean . . .' He trails off, as he obviously realizes that's exactly what he's just said.

This is like a nightmare. This time yesterday, Joe was one of my best friends; now we've slept together, and he's going to move abroad unless – what? Unless I go out with him and we fall in love? I always have loved him, in a way. I just didn't think I could love him in that way, and now I feel like I could if only he would acknowledge that this is a big deal and not just act as if we're talking about taking up some new evening class together.

'I can't deal with this,' I tell him. 'Joe, I can't talk about this with you right now. I need some space, I need to clear my head.' I start pulling my clothes out of my bag and pick up my borrowed dress. It was on the floor, where I threw it earlier – when we sank into each other's arms. It wasn't awkward then; it felt like heaven. But now it's turned into a waking nightmare, one of those ones where you're speeding in a car without a steering wheel, or falling down an endless lift shaft. I bundle myself back into all my winter clothes and sling my coat over my arm. Normally, at this point, when leaving a hotel room, I would do a final sweep and look under the bed and in all the drawers, to make sure I haven't left anything else behind. But there's nothing left for me here. Only a glimpse of Joe's face as I walk out the door, looking stricken, as if the scale of what we've just lost is beginning to sink in.

# 20. I Get Along Without You Very Well

Downstairs, the hotel is like the *Mary Celeste*: I imagine all the staff who were meant to come in this morning are still snowed in. And I'm really not sure how I'm going to get back to the Shelbourne, if everything is still shut down. I've found a bag to put Aisling's dress in and I ring the bell at reception, half-expecting nobody to answer. There's the sound of a hoover in the distance, though, which cuts off after a minute when I ring a second time. A girl makes her way over and takes Aisling's dress and my note, without looking too surprised by my lengthy explanation.

'No, the Dart is running again,' she says, when I enquire. 'I came in myself from Bray.'

Thank goodness for that; we're eight miles from the Shelbourne, and I was picturing a very long, freezing trudge back to the city centre, with Joe fifty paces behind me throughout.

'I don't know if we paid for the room either,' I say, realizing that Joe may have just given his card details to secure the booking. 'Can I pay for half of it?'

'No, it was paid in full last night,' she says, after checking. *Damn you, Joe,* I think, though it's true that I would have been equally annoyed with him had he not paid for it.

Outside, the snow is lying deep and undisturbed, sparkling white crystals catching the light under a near-cloudless blue sky. My sunglasses – thank God – are still in my bag from our first morning sightseeing. The air is fresh and crystal-clear as well, and I take a deep breath before setting off down the hill towards the Dart station. Retracing the way I came with Joe, I find the station and go out to wait on the freezing platform, huddled in my coat on a bench – there are no seats inside, which seems a missed opportunity in a place with weather like this. Eight minutes to wait for the next train; I hope Joe doesn't catch me up.

I'm still processing everything that's happened in the past twenty-four hours. But of all the things that are nagging at me, I keep thinking of the year Joe referred to – when he came around to my house at Christmas. I had started a postgraduate diploma in vocal studies at the Guildhall, in September, and I had never been busier or more exhausted. So when my dad phoned me, one evening at the beginning of October, I just sent it to voicemail. I wanted to run into Sainsbury's before catching the bus home to Peckham, where I was now living in another flatshare.

Dad's voice message was nothing unusual. 'Just ringing to say hello, love. Any news? Oh, and I got two tickets for Ronnie Scott's in a couple of weeks – it's the Mingus Big Band, should be fantastic. Phone me back.'

I phoned him as soon as I'd got home and made myself some dinner, but he didn't reply, which was unusual – normally he kept his phone charging on the hall table whenever he was home, even though I had tried to explain to him that this wasted the battery. When I phoned him again the next day, there was no reply, and by that evening, twenty-four hours after his first call, I felt concerned enough to call my mum.

'What do you want me to do, darling?' she said. 'He's probably just lost his phone or his charger.'

'He's never done that before,' I said. 'And he hasn't sent me an email or anything either. It's not like him.'

She sighed, and I felt bad for involving her in my worries; she and my dad got on fine these days, but she didn't go out of her way to spend time with him. But I didn't want to phone any of his friends over something which might be nothing, and Miles was living in Nottingham by then. Mum had been divorced from Dad for more than five years, but when you had kids together, as she had said herself, you were connected for life.

'He's probably at some jazz thing, you know. But if you like, I'll go and knock on his door tomorrow morning. I can bring him some of my chutney, I've just made a batch.'

'Thanks, Mum.' I hung up the phone, still feeling oddly uneasy. True, it had only been twenty-four hours, but it was so completely unlike Dad not to phone me back; normally he phoned me several times a week. It was 7 p.m. now. Without letting myself think too much about what I was doing, I got my spare key to his house and started on the long and awkward journey from Peckham over to Ealing. When I finally got there, I rang the bell and waited for Dad to appear to upbraid me for making such a fuss – shortly he'd be making us both cups of tea. There would be a new episode of *Doctor Who*, which he loved but saved for the times when we were together. I didn't love it myself but I watched it with him anyway.

No answer; I was properly worried now. I let myself in, noticing that all the lights were off even though it was dark. Then I heard the record scratching on the turntable and I knew. I knew even before I came around the corner and saw his legs, fully clothed, lying on the ground, and then the rest of him.

I have very little memory of the rest of that night; I definitely fainted, and came around to find myself sitting on the ground near Dad's body. I remember trying uselessly to revive him using my dimly remembered lifesaving skills. I didn't know if I was supposed to ring an ambulance, or what, so I rang Mum, after several fumbled attempts. She came around straight away and was like a superhero – phoning an ambulance and the police, then sitting with me while I screamed and sobbed, late into the night. I stayed at Mum's that night, but it wouldn't be right to say that I slept there; I felt like I would never sleep again.

Since that night, I had been in a state of shock. As Dad's next of kin, I had mountains of admin to do but

I didn't mind, because keeping busy seemed the best way of surviving things. Mum helped me with some of it – dealing with the coroner and the autopsy; phoning his friends; phoning the Guildhall to ask for leave for me. But there were certain things that I had to do, since neither Miles nor Mum wanted to. I got the death certificate. I planned the funeral service. I chose the music – Aretha Franklin singing 'Amazing Grace'. I had meetings with solicitors and accountants and started the long process of probate. And the worst task of all: I cleared out his flat. Miles came down from Nottingham to help me for a week, but it was so obviously going to take longer than that, so I left the flatshare in Peckham and moved back into Dad's flat to do it. I didn't want to – I wanted to keep it all exactly as it was, in his memory – but it had to be done, so that we could sell it. Mum helped me as much as she could, until we had an almighty row over Dad's record collection, which he had left solely to me in his will.

'I put an ad on Gumtree,' she said. 'I've had three replies already. I've given them your number.'

I completely lost it, crying and sobbing, for the first time since that first night. 'Norah,' she said as soon as I'd stopped. 'I didn't mean to upset you. But think about it. Yes, the records are yours, but they're worth a lot of money, which you need. You're getting into even more debt with your diploma. And it will take at least a year for you and Miles to see anything from the sale of the flat.'

I stopped listening, because I was now wondering if I was being unfair to Miles. Dad had left him his car, which was so obviously nothing compared to the records, which were probably worth five figures. 'Do you mind me keeping them?' I asked him later. 'I know I could sell them and we could split the proceeds. Just tell me if you think I should do that, because I don't want us falling out over it.'

'No, don't do that,' Miles said. 'It was your thing. I get it. I'd like just one to keep though, to remember him by.' He chose 'Kind of Blue', by Miles Davis, and we were both weeping by the time he left.

Since then, I had stopped asking Mum for any help with the admin, and I also hadn't cried once. I kept expecting the horror of it all to hit me at some point and pin me to the ground in agony, but I felt completely numb – not sad, not depressed, just strangely exhausted, no matter how much or how little I slept. I had taken a break from my gigs, partly because I had enough on my plate, but mostly because I just felt that I had no singing in me. But in December Ernie, my pianist friend, phoned me up.

'I've been asked to perform at a private event, a party at a member's club,' he said. 'They want a singer. Can you do it? If you can't, I can ask someone else – Buki maybe.'

'No, I'll do it,' I said. I put it in my diary and set several reminders in my phone, as I was in such a state I was bound to forget. The evening came around, and I almost did forget until I came out of the Guildhall campus and remembered, just in time to rush across to Soho.

'Are you all right, sweetheart?' Ernie asked me, as I came out from the changing room and took up my position beside him. He had known Dad through the jazz circuit and had been among the small gathering at the funeral. I nodded and even mustered up a smile. He brought out the set list and put it on top of the piano, and we started off with 'Bewitched, Bothered and Bewildered.'

From the moment I started singing I knew it wasn't going to be a brilliant gig. The song, which had always been one of my favourites, seemed stale and over-familiar, and instead of thinking of the words I let my eyes rove around the club. It was a beautiful place, raffish yet elegant, with red panelled walls and a roaring fire in the front room. Upstairs was an exquisite dining room, with half a dozen chandeliers and every spare inch of wall covered with an eclectic collection of paintings. I would normally have been over the moon to be singing here, but tonight it felt flat and pointless. But I was experienced enough, by now, that I could trudge through the songs without anything going wrong. We would perform until 11 p.m., when I would get the Tube home to the empty flat in Ealing.

The song ended, and I waited to hear the intro for the next one, not remembering what it was supposed to be. The sprinkling of familiar notes rose up, and I actually started singing before I realized what it was. It was 'I

Get Along Without You Very Well'. Suddenly my throat closed up and my eyes pricked with tears. I was drowning in memories. Dad, in the kitchen on Christmas Eve, playing this while he was cooking – asking me if I'd like to hear Chet Baker's version. I would never let him choose a record for me again, never laugh at one of his silly jokes, never talk to him again. I opened my mouth for the second verse, but nothing came out. 'I've forgotten you –' I sang, or rather whispered, and then I had to stop because I was crying properly. Several heads were turning. I knew if I didn't leave the room right away I would be even more disruptive so I slipped back out, towards the changing room, where all my things were.

A minute later there was a tentative knock on the door. I thought it might be the manager, but it was Ernie, looking concerned.

'I'm sorry, love,' he said. 'Things on your mind, I'm sure.'

He sounded so much like my dad in that moment that I started again; positively weeping and sobbing in a way I hadn't at all, or not since the first week, burying my face in my coat to muffle the sound.

Ernie patted me tentatively on the shoulder.

'I'm so sorry, Ernie,' I said as soon as I could speak. 'I can come back out and finish the set, if you just give me five minutes.'

'I wouldn't hear of it, love,' he said. 'You go home and get a good night's rest. I know what it's like to lose somebody. It's an awful load to carry.'

I sighed because that was what it felt like: a terrible load, and one that was invisible to anyone but me. I felt so completely alone in my grief, because Mum didn't miss Dad in the way that I did; not even Miles seemed to feel the same way. I had been his daughter but I had also lived with him for those three years after university, and I was his next of kin, dealing with solicitors and probate – a strange position that I couldn't expect any of my friends to understand. Caroline had been very kind, but her dad had left when she was eight, so I felt guilty talking to her about it too much. And Kiran, much as I loved her, wasn't great with this kind of thing: she sent flowers, and took me out for dinner, but after a few chats I could feel her sympathy but also her unspoken hope that soon I would be moving on.

On Christmas Eve, I got myself and my suitcase to Mum's flat. I don't know what I had expected – the place covered in dark cloths, or all of us just to eat rice – but she was in full Christmas preparation mode, with Radio 4 on and every kitchen surface covered. We sat down together, and soon I was peeling potatoes and cutting up parsnips and brushing the glaze on the home-made mince pies, just as we had last year, and just like we would next year and the year after that.

'You're not going out to meet your friends, love?' Mum asked, when we had finally finished. 'Miles is out at the Drayton.'

'Not tonight. I'm just going to have an early night,' I said.

'Do you want to watch TV with me? I was going to watch *Victoria Wood's Mid-Life Christmas*.'

Once again, I felt the guilt, that every time I was leaving one of my parents alone I was somehow betraying them. But I was tired of carrying it around with me; it hadn't done Dad any good.

'No thanks . . . sorry, Mum, I'm just going to read in my room.'

I went to my room, but I couldn't read. I just stared at the wall, which was painted a generic magnolia with a few abstract prints Mum had bought from a friend who ran a gallery. I was just about to put on my pyjamas when there was a knock on my door. I looked at my watch, startled to see that half an hour had gone by.

'Norah, it's me again.' Mum. 'There's a friend of yours here to see you.'

A friend? It was probably Caroline, but why didn't Mum just say so? 'Who, Mum?'

'Joe,' she hissed through the door.

'Oh.' I sat up, looking around the room. I crawled out of the bed, to put on my giant, most unflattering mohair cardigan. 'OK, I'll come.'

Joe was at the door, holding a package.

'Hey,' he said when he saw me. 'I didn't want to disturb you . . . I just wanted to drop off your Christmas present.'

'Oh, God, I completely forgot we were doing Secret Santa – I don't even know who I had,' I said.

'You had Paul. He's fine about it,' Joe said. 'Are you busy, or can I come in?'

'Come in,' I said. I couldn't be bothered to take him through to the living room to Mum; I brought him back to my bedroom. Or rather, the spare room. Miles's room here had much more of his stamp on it, with all his posters and his old CD collection, plus all his textbooks and school reports going back to 1999. Not that I minded. My stuff was all at my dad's; that was how our family divided, me and Dad on one side, and Mum and Miles down the other. Except now the symmetry was gone; it was me versus Mum and Miles. They didn't mean to exclude me, but I felt the oddness and imbalance all the time.

Back in my room, I got back into bed. 'Sorry, you don't mind, do you? I'm just cold. I'm cold all the time.'

'No, that's fine . . . here you go,' said Joe, handing me his package, beautifully wrapped with brown paper and stamped with a holly-leaf pattern.

It was two DVDs: *Castaway* and *Rocky*. I smiled for the first time in ages, as I remembered how baffled I had been when Joe had greeted me with 'Adrian!' after my first gig.

'I know you love *Castaway*,' Joe said. 'And *Rocky* is a good one too. It's about surviving.' A doubtful expression crossed his face. 'I mean maybe *Rocky* isn't really going to be much help to you right now. I like it anyway. I don't know. I don't really know what to say to you right now, if I'm being honest – this is all I've got, Norah. But I'm here whenever you need me.'

The kindness was too much for me, and I started to cry. Joe looked alarmed but then he came over to me and put his arm around me. I leaned into his woollen shoulder and cried harder than I had before in my life, while he stroked my hair and told me it was going to be all right.

'I'm sorry,' I said, when I'd recovered. 'I'm just a bit down.'

'Don't be sorry,' he said. 'It's really awful, Norah. I know how much you loved your dad.'

'Did you know I found him, Joe?' I asked. I hadn't actually told any of my friends that yet; the funeral had been small and private and nobody had asked me any details, understandably.

'No, I didn't. I'm really sorry.'

'It's the worst thing that's ever happened to me,' I said dully.

Joe nodded, and we sat there in silence for a while.

'I'm thinking of doing something different with my life,' I said after a minute. 'I was thinking of doing teacher training. Do you think that's a crazy idea?'

'No, not at all. I think you'd be an amazing teacher,' Joe says. 'What would you teach – history?'

'No. I'd rather teach music,' I said, feeling the first glimmers of energy in months. 'I don't know if I can, without a music degree. But maybe, with this diploma . . .

I don't know.' I felt myself slipping back into inertia. 'Do you want to watch this?' I said. '*Rocky*, I mean – I don't know about *Castaway* right now.'

He put the DVD into my laptop, and within minutes I was distracted by the story of the lovable lunker trying to make it as a boxer. I even laughed at one point, when Rocky said, 'To you it's Thanksgiving, to me it's Thursday.'

'That's how I feel,' I said. 'To you it's Christmas Eve, to me it's Tuesday.'

As the story went on, I felt my eyes closing, and without thinking anything of it I leaned on Joe's shoulder and let myself relax for the first time in weeks – months.

When I woke up it was close to midnight, and he was gone. I found a Christmas card and opened it to read the message. 'Don't be a stinker, be a thinker. Or something. Call me if you want to hang out – we don't have to talk about anything in particular if you don't want to. Merry Christmas. J x'

The next morning, I woke before 10 a.m. for the first time in ages. I felt crushed by sadness, but it was better than the horrible numb feeling that had dogged me for months. I was in a new world now, and I didn't like it but I could survive there.

'What did Joe want?' Mum asked me the next morning. I knew it was just a turn of phrase – she meant to ask what brought him here – but it annoyed me nevertheless.

'He didn't want anything,' I said. 'He was giving me something.'

The train pulls into the station, and I settle into a window seat. Soon I'm watching the sea go by, thinking of the last time I saw it, sitting beside Joe. I find myself remembering how he showed up for me for the rest of that year after Dad died – not with any deep conversations, but just consistently; going to the cinema with me, taking me for lunch or forwarding me articles he thought I'd enjoy. I still have those DVDs he gave me, and the card he gave me, with his distinctive spiky black handwriting. That's the thing about old friends. You know certain things about them that you might not know about newer friends: like what their handwriting looks like, their middle name (his is James), their childhood address and their parents' first names. I even know his mobile number by heart. He's always been there, part of the backing track of my life. If I lost that friendship, because of some ill-advised fling between us, it would be so awful.

And yet Joe doesn't see any of this difficulty, and his solution to any awkwardness is for him to move to Japan. As if putting an ocean between two people has ever changed anything.

The train is pulling into Pearse station, which I know is my stop to get back to the hotel, so I stand up and make my way out. I'm sure to my fellow passengers I look more or less like the rest of them; just another last-minute hungover shopper, dashing into town for a last present or a few rolls of wrapping paper. I can't quite believe, myself, how much has happened since we caught this train in the other direction. But I decide not to waste any more time ruminating on Joe and get myself calm and centred for what tonight was meant to be all along; my reunion – I hope – with Andrew.

## 21. I Say A Little Prayer

Back in my room, I take a shower and lie down for a quick power nap, and wake up two hours later. I'm actually glad of it; I didn't get much sleep last night. I have a mad thought of going out to try and do some last-minute shopping or sightseeing, but I can't face it. Instead, I order a toasted ham and cheese sandwich and a Coke and consume both while still in my hotel bathrobe. I am feeling much better now, and I'm able to contemplate this evening more calmly than I ever have before. I'll go to Bewley's at 6 p.m., and I'll wait ten minutes and maybe, just maybe, Andrew will show up. If he does, then great. But if he doesn't – I'll still be alive. I'll still have my job, and my flat. I'll be Miss Jones, and I'll be totally fine with that. I'm enough, by myself.

I might be enough by myself, but I am getting cabin fever now. It's 3 p.m., and I don't know where Joe is. Not that I want to see him right now, but I hope he's OK – and I would like to talk to someone. So I'm delighted to receive a WhatsApp from Pat, asking me to join her in the 1848 Bar.

The hotel is, as they say here, jammers; it is Christmas Eve after all. The roar of conversation would be deafening if it wasn't for the deep, plush carpets, and it's so packed and so hot I'm melting in my woollen jumper. I slip into the 1848 Bar, which is a little quieter, and find Pat sitting at the bar.

'Well, how is it going?' she asks. 'Helena has stepped off to BT's to get some Clinique for the mammy, but I'm taking a breather. If it's not done by now, it's not getting done, that's my philosophy.'

'Wise words. Would you like a drink?' I ask her. 'Hello, Gerry. What do you recommend tonight? I mean this afternoon.' It's Christmas, so time has ceased to have any meaning.

'Tonight I have a mull of Smoking Bishop,' says Gerry, which makes Pat dissolve into giggles. 'Smoking Hot Bishop? Is that the fella from *Fleabag*? I'm only codding you, Gerry – it smells delicious whatever it is.'

'Hot port, red wine and orange, and a few other secret ingredients,' says Gerry, pouring us both a glass. 'Here you go, ladies, here's to your health.'

'And yours, Gerry. Have you everything ready for tomorrow? Have you the last bits bought?'

I sip the Smoking Bishop, which tastes as delicious as it smells, and as I listen to them chat, I realize I'm going to miss Dublin – more than I thought I could after a few days, anyway. I would like to come back, and I am also going to look into tracking down my dad's side of the family. Even if they can't be found or have no interest in me, I'd like to know about them, just for myself.

'So,' Pat says, when Gerry is serving someone else. 'I have news for you. I've heard back from Marita Byrne, who was my neighbour back in Drimnagh.'

'Oh yes?' I ask. I had almost forgotten this, as it seemed so incredibly tenuous.

'Marita's mother was Margaret Byrne, whose sister Cora left for Manchester in 1955. Of course, you'll have to check it all out and do your own research. But there can't have been that many Cora Byrnes, from the Liberties, who moved to Manchester in 1955. By all accounts, Cora was a difficult character, and once they left, they didn't keep in touch much, bar the occasional Christmas card. But Marita is a dote. She asked me to give you her number, so you can call if you'd like to. But you're under no obligation, of course.'

I'm stunned.

'I'm sorry. Say all that again. I need to write this down.'

Pat patiently repeats all the information and adds, I'm afraid Cora and er husband died a few years back. Margaret is still with us. And Marita married a very nice fellow who works at the Mater Hospital. She has two children, who are about your age I think – Emer and John. You'll have to check with Marita, of course. But it sounds to me as though you have cousins.'

'Cousins,' I repeat blankly.

I'm so overwhelmed that I start crying for the second time in twenty-four hours – which itself was the first time after I don't know how many years. I don't know what's more emotional: the idea that I have unknown relatives, or the fact that I can never tell my dad about them.

Pat listens to me as I try and explain all this. I hadn't told her that my parents were divorced, and she asks me to back up and explain the sequence of events a little more.

'You've been through an awful lot,' she remarks. 'Have you ever had any help, Norah, any counselling or the like?'

'Not really. I mean, not at all.' I think back to the year after Dad's death. I poured myself into all the business of admin, finished my singing diploma and then immediately signed myself up for a postgraduate teaching degree. The training was gruelling, but I welcomed it, because it meant I didn't have to think about what had happened.

'But do you think I need to? I mean, everybody loses a parent.'

'I don't know what you need to or don't. But you lost your family unit at a young age, and then your father – plus you were his next of kin, so you were responsible in a way most daughters wouldn't be. I'd say you could do with something.'

'Do you think I was young?' I have a sudden memory of what a temporary staff member said to me years ago. We were talking about parents' evenings, and I mentioned that I'd lost my father at a young age. She asked how young, and when I said twenty-six she said, 'That's not so young.'

I tell Pat about this, and she shakes her head. 'What a silly remark,' she says. 'Presumably, she meant not young compared to school-age children. But it's still young to lose a parent. And it doesn't matter what age you are, really. I was fifty-five when I lost my mother, and it devastated me. And you had even more to contend with. That's why I suggested help.'

'So, therapy?' I ask.

'Maybe. I don't know if that's a magic bullet, but you could look into it.' What she says next takes me by surprise. 'In the meantime, why don't you light a candle for him? It is Christmas Eve.'

I'm so addled by everything that initially I assume she means this in some metaphorical sense, but she means it quite literally and suggests two nearby churches that would be open. 'I don't know if it's your usual thing,' she adds. 'But there's a great comfort sometimes in lighting a penny candle.'

Just as I'm trying to absorb this suggestion, Pat asks, 'Where is Joe?'

I wasn't planning on telling her, but it all comes out: the walk, the snowstorm, the wedding, the kiss.

'What an adventure,' says Pat. 'I'm glad you weren't swept off to sea with a gale; that was some storm. But what's happened with Joe? Was the chemistry not there?'

'Oh, no, quite the reverse. It was – the best ever,' I say, realizing how true this is. 'But . . . he seems to think we can just go out together and see what happens. And I think it's more complicated than that.'

Pat looks puzzled, and I can tell that to her ears this sounds like an utterly lame excuse.

'I suppose I'm scared,' I admit. 'I'm scared that it wouldn't work out and that I'll lose him. And I don't want to lose him the way I lost my dad.'

Oh, no. Now that I've started the crying habit again, I can't stop. Pat passes me a tissue, and I pat frantically under my eyes.

'Sorry . . . oh God, what a mess. And I'm supposed to be meeting Andrew this evening!'

'Well, go and meet Andrew,' Pat says. 'And that will help clarify things with Joe. But regarding losing him . . .'

'Yes?'

'Well, that's always the risk you take. When you fall in love with someone.'

'But that's just it. What if we're not in love and we lose each other over something that's just a fling?'

'If the friendship is strong enough, you should survive it. And anyway . . . isn't it worth the risk?'

'But it's the fact that Joe doesn't seem to see any risk. That's what worries me. Plus, it's the timing. What about Andrew?' I add, weakly, feeling as though I should stick up for him somehow, even if Pat has forgotten all about him. 'I'm planning to go and meet him – I don't think he'll show up, but what if he does? What should I do?'

'I don't know. You'd have to see if he's as appealing on Grafton Street as he was in Italy. I mean, was it the man or the moonlight? It's easy to fall in love in Italy, with the wine and the roses and all. Someone who can spark a flame up on Killiney Hill – in a snowstorm – well, that's the real deal, if you ask me.'

I don't have an answer for that.

'Maybe there's something else going on with Andrew,' Pat says thoughtfully. 'When did you say you lost touch with him?'

'Oh, around six years ago.'

'Six years ago? Wasn't that when your father died?'

'Yes. It was the same year.' I can't believe this has never occurred to me. 'I would have emailed him, to tell him what had happened, but he hadn't replied to my last email so – I never did.'

'So there's unfinished business there,' says Pat. 'You haven't told him about your dad, and until you do maybe it's hard to accept that your dad really is gone.'

I stare at her for the longest time. 'Pat, are you sure you should be running a bookshop?' I ask. 'Shouldn't you be a psychotherapist or a priest or something? Or an oracle?'

Pat looks pleased. 'No, I love bookselling. Though I wouldn't mind having a Christmas holiday more often – this week has been delightful.'

We finish our drinks, and then Pat goes off to meet Helena. I go back to my room, unable to settle to anything. I pick up my phone a dozen times intending to text Joe, but I don't know what to say to him so I put it down again. Soon, it's almost time to dress to 'meet'

Andrew – assuming that's what I'm going to do. I'm wondering what to wear when I hear my phone ringing. It's Mum. I answer right away.

'Merry Christmas, Mum,' I say, sitting down at the end of the bed. 'How's the retreat?'

'It's very good, darling. It's been very helpful.' She pauses, and I can hear something in her voice, an unfamiliar note of uncertainty. 'We've been discussing our loved ones . . . and, well, I realized I shouldn't have cancelled our plans together. I am really sorry about that.'

'Oh, Mum.' More tears! When will it end? I blink them back and gaze out the window, trying to stay calm. 'It's OK,' I tell her. 'I know you were keen on the retreat.'

'Yes, but I should have had my priorities straight. I had made a commitment to you and I should have honoured that.' She sighs. 'You've always been so self-sufficient, Norah. I never felt as though you needed me that much, even when you were little. And you idolized your dad so much, I sometimes felt as though you didn't even want me.'

'Hang on a second, Mum,' I say. 'Were you calling to apologize – or to have a go at me?' I'm slightly joking, but also not.

'To apologize! I suppose we should have spoken about all this before. I know I wasn't a great support to you after Mike died.'

'No, you were, Mum,' I say, remembering all her help with the lawyers, the accountants and the estate agents.

'I mean emotional support,' she says. 'It hurt that he

was so obviously your favourite parent. You two had so much in common, and I was the baddie who was always saying no to things . . .' She sighs again. 'Anyway. I really was ringing to apologize. I am sorry we're not together this Christmas and I hope you'll let me make it up to you.'

'You can make it up to me, actually,' I tell her. 'I would like us to talk about Dad more. Just tell me all the things you remember that I never knew. Even if they seem silly.'

'There were so many things,' Mum says. 'Let's make a date when you come back, and I can tell you all about them. Oh, darling, don't cry. Tell me, what else has been happening?'

I go over to the chair beside the window, overlooking Stephen's Green. 'How long have you got?'

Half an hour later, I put the phone down reflecting on the fact that Mum and I just communicated more in that conversation than we have in what feels like years. She was surprisingly positive when I told her 'something happened' with Joe, though she dismisses my concern about it ruining our friendship. 'Well, the friendship's already sunk, isn't it? So you might as well go for it with him.'

'Thanks, Mum, but I don't think it's going to work out.' I explain my doubts and add, 'Plus, it's the timing – right when I'm supposed to be going to find Andrew.'

'What, are you still doing that?' Mum asks, as if she's talking about some long-abandoned fad like dry-body brushing.

'Yes! I've come this far, so of course I am. Even it's just to know where he is or what happened to him – or why I can't find him.'

'Well, I hope he's not dead or anything,' she said. 'That would be a real shame.'

It wasn't very well phrased, but it's a possibility I still can't ignore. I flop back on top of my bed and try to think. I wish I'd asked those people at the supper club if any of them knew a musician of his age and description. If Dublin is a village, then some of them must know him, or of him. Something is tugging at the edges of my consciousness, something that might be the clue I need. What is it? Something someone said, about how everything in Dublin has two names. We were discussing the Dead Zoo . . . I shiver again. Wait. What was it that guy said about people changing their name?

'First rule of hipster club: change your name to the Irish.'

I roll over and type frantically into the internet. My initial searches don't yield anything, because I don't know exactly what to look for, but after a few goes I type, 'Translate surname Power in Irish' and literally seconds later I've found him. Here he is. After six long years, he's unscrolling before me like Lazarus rising from the dead.

I shake my head, unable to believe that he's been here all along under a different name. Andrew de Paor, contemporary composer. Teaches at the DIT Conservatory of Music and Drama. He's written music for film and TV; he's won competitions . . . I find his website and eagerly click on the bio page to see his photo. He looks a little older, and a bit softer around the edges, but it's *him*. It's the boy I met in Italy, but grown-up and eminent. I feel a rush of nostalgia mixed with gratitude that I found him: after all these years, it's definitely him. I'm so relieved that nothing did happen to him; he's alive, and he's flourishing.

'Andrew!' I say out loud. 'You pretentious git! You could have told me you were changing your name!' I feel a bit miffed that he never thought to mention this. But, I realize now, it's possible that he did tell me. I was in such a state after Dad died, I could well have missed an email, even one from him. Or maybe he wrote to my old address by mistake – or maybe I mistyped when I told him what my new email was . . . I'll probably never know.

I scan the bio page and take in all his prizes and credits – there are so many I have to scroll down through several pages. Compositions for RTE, the BBC and German TV; composer residencies at the Banff Centre and the Helene Wurlitzer Foundation, New Mexico. No mention of wife or kids, but it's not that kind of website, I suppose – and how would he have time with all these awards and accolades? Then I go on YouTube and listen to one of his pieces: *Eternity in C, for string quartet.* It's really beautiful; a simple melody, stated by the cello and then repeated by the violins and viola, full of sadness but also hope and consolation, repeated over and over. I remember him telling me that he loved canons and wanted to compose one for strings.

'Why?' I asked.

'Because they sound like life, I suppose,' he said. 'We repeat days, seasons, the year's events, over and over – just with a little variation, but we're always coming back to the same things. No matter how bad or good a day is, there's another one to follow it and another one, ad infinitum . . . which is sad or hopeful, depending on how you look at it.'

I shake my head. After all my years of wondering and searching, he's been here under my nose the whole time. I know now that he's alive, I know he lives in Dublin, and I'm going to go to Bewley's at six, just to see.

It's 4.20 now. I check my phone briefly to see if Joe has been in touch, but there's nothing. What is he playing at? Is he planning to avoid me for the rest of our trip – and what on earth is the journey home going to be like, if so? I hesitate, wondering if I should just knock on his hotel room door so that we could talk things through. But I still don't know what I would say, so I put my phone away, deciding to focus on Andrew instead. As my mum used to tell me years ago, when I was dithering over multiple options: it's always best to just stick to the original plan.

## 22. I'm Beginning to See the Light

Before I go to Bewley's there's one last thing I want to do. Pat had suggested two different churches; St Ann's on Dawson Street, or St Theresa's – also known, of course, as the Carmelite Church – off Grafton Street. Saint Ann's has a carol service taking place, so I make my way to St Theresa's instead. It's on Johnson's Court, a small alley that runs down one side of Bewley's and seems to house mainly jewellery shops. It's very pretty: beneath my feet the lane seems sunken in the middle, with snow collecting at the sides, and above my head there's a web of thousands of miniature little lights, strung up all down the length of the alley like a fishnet full of stars. The church's entrance is halfway down, a high arch with a black gold-embossed gate, which is open just wide enough to squeeze through.

I can't remember the last time I went into a church if not for music or a wedding. The quiet darkness is lit only by banks of candles and a low light coming from the stained-glass windows above the altar. There's a handful of people, scattered here and there throughout the pews, some kneeling, most seated. In a side chapel, I find a little offertory stand full of flickering white candles and reach into the stand, take an unlit one out and light it up, as instructed. Sitting down on a pew opposite, I watch the little flame gathering height. I thought maybe some magical feeling of peace would descend on me but I just feel awkward. Is this it? Or is there more I should be doing, some particular prayer I should be saying? I don't really know, but it's rare for me to sit with my thoughts like this without rushing on to the next thing – maybe I have more in common with Mum than I had thought. Even when Dad was alive, I was always rushing around, often at the expense of time with him. I think of that Christmas Eve when I fell out with Kiran at the Drayton – I wish I had stayed behind and listened to music with him, or watched a film or made dinner together.

But it's not as though we didn't do that other nights. I was a good daughter to Dad; that's what Mum said earlier on the phone, which I found reassuring in a way I hadn't expected. After he died, I reproached myself bitterly for not taking better care of him. He did give up smoking, but I should have made him exercise, drink less, join clubs.

'But that wasn't on you, Norah. He lived his life exactly how he wanted to, and he was never, ever going to change. You did nothing wrong,' Mum said. 'And neither did he, really. He could have done this or that, but who's to say if that would have made any difference? He was unlucky.'

Poor Dad. He was unlucky, and so was I. I've always been quick to minimize what happened, to say that 'he had a good life' or reassure people that I'm fully over it, but maybe I'll never be completely over it. I think about a game I once played with Paul and Joe, Never Will I Ever, which Paul said was a much more interesting game than Never Have I Ever: you had to name things you would never do in life. There are so many nevers with my Dad. I will never be able to tell him that I've stopped singing, or that I love teaching. Never introduce him to my future husband, if there is such a person. The thought 'though he did meet Joe' floats into my head, before I whoosh it straight back out again. I'll never have him walk me down the aisle. Never have him hold his grandchild.

And it will never not be sad. Still, acknowledging what happened, and that it's OK to still feel sad about it, seems like a start. *I miss you, Dad*, I think, trying to send my thoughts his way. *I wish you could see what I'm doing now and where I am — I wish we could talk or be together just one more time. But I'll never forget you.*

I put a coin in the offertory box, as Pat instructed me, and step back to see my candle among all the others. I lit mine from somebody else's, and someone will light theirs from mine, so that even when I've gone and my candle's burned out, the flame will keep going, through Christmas and beyond. I think of what each candle must represent, each loss or hope or prayer, and gather a little comfort from the thought.

A sound makes me turn my head; it's a tuning fork. There's a small group standing at the altar, and the conductor is giving them each their note; it must be a chamber choir rehearsing for tonight's service. Emerging from my side chapel I see all the other worshippers have slipped out, and it's the conductor and her choir. I can't resist sitting down for a while to listen. They sing 'The Lamb' by John Taverner, and 'What Sweeter Music' by John Rutter. And then, just as I'm expecting another modern piece, they start singing 'O Little Town of Bethlehem' in four-part harmony so lush and beautiful that you hardly notice the lack of instruments. I let my mind drift, thinking how beautiful it is, this magical alchemy of words and music that's kept it passed on for generations, so that countless voices are singing it this evening. *The hopes and fears of all the years are met in thee tonight.*

Tonight. With a shock, I realize it's already 5.35 – I have less than half an hour until I meet Andrew. I slip out of the church quietly, thinking I should just about have time to go back to the hotel to change.

The side entrance, the one I came in through, is locked, so I end up going out of the front porch, emerging on to a completely different street. I get totally turned around and end up walking the wrong way for a good ten minutes before I figure out what's happened. Now I'm worried that I no longer have time to go back to the hotel – in fact, soon I'm wondering whether I will even be able to make it to Bewley's on time. I try and figure out the map on my phone before finally, to my relief, I locate the way back to Grafton Street. As I pace along, I feel a memory tugging at me. Something about the dark slush and the reflections of the colourful windows on the wet reminds me of the damp evening when I spoke to my mum and found myself walking through the streets of Soho. All the way to Joe's place.

I stop short, frozen to the pavement as passers-by hurry past me. I can almost feel a shaft of illumination descending on me out of the darkness, as something strikes me. I didn't have to think about walking to Joe's that time; I just followed my feet and arrived there, because that was where my instinct brought me, when I was cold and sad and confused. And there and then, standing on the damp pavement in Dublin, I realize what I think I've always known: that Joe is my home. He's where I will always want to be. Whether Andrew turns up, at this point, is sort of immaterial. Andrew is the faded photograph on my wall; Joe is my foundation, the walls that hold me up and keep me safe. Andrew is the summer dress that I've outgrown; Joe is the winter coat that I will want to wear for ever. I just hope he still feels the same way about me.

I take out my phone, suddenly desperate to get in touch with him. But it rings out. I know he never listens to voicemails, so I tap out a message for him.

*I'm sorry about earlier. Please call me.* After a minute, I write another message: *Going to meet Andrew — if he's there, I'll tell him goodbye.*

It's not great, but it'll have to do. Ten minutes later,

there's still no reply, and he hasn't read it either. I'm halfway down Grafton Street now. By the time I see Bewley's, the clock is already at a minute to six. There are plenty of people around, but none of them is Andrew – I can't say I'm surprised.

I walk towards the café, suddenly unsure if I should be here at all. What if Joe feels I've rejected him and he's packing his bags to leave? Shouldn't I be running back to try and find him, instead of waiting here for someone who won't show up? But just as I'm wavering, I spot a familiar face among the crowd. He's leaning on the wall of Bewley's beside the clock, his hands shoved in his pockets. I stand rooted to the spot for a moment: I can't believe he came. He sees me, and a smile breaks out across his face – qualified at first but then a full grin, a smile I'll never get tired of seeing. I hurry towards him.

'I thought, if showing up here is the way to your heart . . . I'd better give it a go,' Joe says.

'Oh, I'm so glad.' And I fall into his arms, before kissing the life out of him. 'I am *so* glad you're here. Did you get my message? I'm sorry about before. It was just new to me, and I was scared.'

'Shh. It's OK, Norah.' He kisses me back. 'I did get your message. You didn't need to apologize. I'm sorry too. You were right. It is scary – it's terrifying, and I should have admitted it earlier. But I'm willing to take the risk.'

'I feel the same way.' I'm beaming at him.

'Thank God. Norah . . . I want to be the one who

meets you under clocks. I want to be in this with you, properly.'

'Me too.'

'Good. Let's do it.'

The crowds, the noise and the sound of distant carol-singers, all fade away as we lose ourselves in each other again. It's hard to imagine that I could be so lucky, that my best friend could become the love of my life like this, but I think, against all the odds, I am going to be that lucky. I couldn't ask for more. I reach down, and hold his bare hand in my gloved one. I've just realized I completely forgot to pack a Christmas present for him, but I know he won't care.

'So . . .' he says, after a few more minutes have gone by. He glances up at the clock and he doesn't have to say anything, because we're both thinking the same thing.

'So,' I say.

'It's nearly ten past six.'

'I know.'

He bites his lip, but I think I know exactly what he's thinking: how predictable. I'm surprised by his next words, nonetheless.

'Are you disappointed?' And I see the concern in his eyes and I know that he genuinely doesn't want me to be disappointed, and not just for selfish reasons.

'No, I'm not,' I say truthfully. 'I found him actually – I found him earlier online. He changed his name. And so at least I know what happened to him. The rest of it doesn't matter.'

'Are you sure?' Joe says, and I nod emphatically. I got what I came for: I resolved things with Andrew. It turns out you can do closure all by yourself. He's not dead and he's probably right now tucking a kid into bed or having a drink with his wife. And the thought doesn't lacerate me, as it would have even a week ago. I hope he's as happy as I am.

'Some people accuse me of being "a late person",' Joe says, looking at the sky. 'And yet . . .' His smile grows in response to mine, and I decide to let him gloat just a little bit; he deserves it.

'Well, you are a late person, Joe. Just not tonight.'

'No. Not tonight. Tonight I wanted to be on time.'

Suddenly I think of something. 'Joe. What about this job in Japan? I can't even remember the details, I was in such a state when you mentioned it. Is it something you really want to do?'

I'm dreading that he will say 'Yes' and I'm not totally reassured when he says, 'Maybe? But there are other things I want more.'

'But shouldn't you – shouldn't we talk about it?'

'It's fine. Let's talk about it later – not tonight.' He reaches for my hand again. 'What do you want to do now?'

I smile up at him, thinking that I really don't mind what we do, as long as we're together. And that it would be a shame to waste our hotel rooms – both or either of them.

I'm just about to suggest that we go back to the hotel

and immediately start making up for all the time we've wasted, when a voice behind me makes me almost jump out of my skin.

'Norah?'

I freeze to the spot, almost too scared to turn around. It's a voice I haven't heard in a decade, but I recognize it anyway. He sounds a little older now, and he's breathless, as if he's been running or rushing. But it's him, nonetheless. He's closer now.

'Norah? Is that you?'

I don't even need to turn around; I know it's Andrew.

## 23. Old Flames

*Christmas Eve, 2019, 6.10 p.m.*

I've had to perform some awkward introductions in my life, but this one is a keeper. I literally don't know what to say to either of them or how to explain one to the other, especially while I'm reintroducing myself to this new Andrew: older, quite a bit softer around the edges – and with, yes, a beard. A beard! I know we joked about it, but somehow I really didn't expect that.

'Um – Andrew, this is Joe. Joe, Andrew.'

Joe is the first to react, putting out a hand. 'Good to meet you,' he says.

He sounds so smooth and confident that I'm not surprised to see Andrew do a slight double take, evidently on the back foot at finding a gatecrasher at our reunion. 'Good to meet you too, Joe. Happy Christmas to you.'

'Merry Christmas,' Joe says.

I'm just wondering whether we're all about to embark on the world's most awkward three-way blind date, when Joe solves the dilemma for me.

'Norah,' he says, 'why don't I let the two of you catch up? I'll see you back at the hotel.'

'Are you sure, Joe?' I ask, suddenly reluctant to let him go. But he smiles at me, with that new smile I already love, and says, 'I'm sure. Have fun – I'll see you soon.' He bends down to kiss me on the cheek and then with a final, friendly nod to Andrew, he's gone, walking back up Grafton Street. God, that was smooth, I think, watching him go. When did he get to be so smooth?

'I can't believe you showed up!' Andrew is saying. 'So – how are you? It's *been* a while!'

'It sure has,' I agree, smiling. 'How have you –'

Andrew speaks at the same time: 'So is he your –'

'Sorry!' Andrew says. 'Let's start again. Welcome to Dublin!'

'Thank you!' I say, wondering if we're ever going to move beyond these niceties. Or go inside: I'm absolutely freezing. 'It's lovely here!'

But just as I'm about to suggest that we go inside, . we're both startled by the sound of a new voice.

'Andrew? Andrew Power! Come here to me!' It's a beautiful blonde woman, even taller than me, advancing towards us in a high-collared fake fur coat. 'How are you? It's been ages!'

'Ah – Grainne! How's it going!' Andrew sounds a bit flustered, but Grainne seems thrilled to see him, and I'm reeling from a new idea: is it possible that Andrew has arranged to meet multiple women on Grafton Street on Christmas Eve? Did he go around Europe collecting email addresses and laying breadcrumb trails to bring credulous women to Bewley's, just to see who would turn up?

'So are you in Dublin now, or still in Berlin?' Grainne asks.

'No, no, I'm back in Dublin. And you?' he says.

'Australia!' says Grainne. 'I'm in Sydney. Working for an auction house. Work in the morning, beach in the afternoon, it's the best!'

'Fantastic!' Andrew introduces me, and then, just as I'm wondering whether I should call Joe back for a double date, Grainne says how nice it was to meet me and dashes inside to meet her friends.

'Whew. Small world!' says Andrew, looking down at me with a comical expression. 'What did I tell you? Walk down Grafton Street on Christmas Eve, and you'll meet the world and his wife.'

That wasn't exactly what he said – he phrased it more poetically at the time, didn't he? But I know what he means, so I just smile and say, 'Small world indeed.'

'Well, listen, let's go somewhere. Have you time for a drink and a catch-up? How about . . . Let's see. Everywhere will be jammers. I know – let's head this way.'

'What about Bewley's?' I ask, confused, but letting him lead me away. We're walking back up Johnson's Court.

'They were full – I poked my nose in to check. And I don't know about you, but I could do with a pint. I want to know exactly where you've been and what you've been doing for the past – I can't believe it's really been ten years?'

He leads me through a few more streets, a few more left and rights, around the same network of little streets Joe and I explored the other day. 'Ah,' I say knowledgably. 'The Purple Flag District.'

'Hah, I know! What's that all about? Notions.' He holds open a door, and we go inside. 'It's sort of Dublin's worst kept secret. I love a hotel bar, don't you?'

'I do, actually.' I let him lead me upstairs, past some glass-panelled door into a cute, hidden little spot. It has that drawing-room atmosphere that I noticed in a few other places here; grand but a bit faded around the edges, with green wallpaper and glass-fronted bookcases. It is very busy, but we manage to find a seat at the bar, where we order a champagne cocktail for me and a pint of Heineken for him.

'This seems to call for a celebration, doesn't it? I can't believe you actually turned up,' he says.

'I can't believe you turned up!' I say. 'I mean, what are the odds? Especially when you didn't reply to my last email.' This is how I know my feelings for him have done a 360-degree turn – I could never have imagined admitting to him that I had been keeping a tally of who emailed who last.

'Wait,' he says. 'You never replied to me, surely? You gave me your new email address, I mailed you back, and I never heard anything. I'm fairly sure of it.'

'No! You never did. I would remember!' We argue

about it for a few more minutes before our drinks arrive and we decide to chalk it up to a miscommunication. It was a long time ago, after all.

'Anyway – cheers,' he says, and we clink glasses. 'You look beautiful, Norah. You haven't changed a bit.'

I laugh, suddenly realizing how unkempt I must look, in my woollen jumper and jeans without a scrap of make-up – it's a very different look for our reunion than the one I would have aspired to earlier. At least I've had a shower; or was that yesterday? 'You haven't changed either,' I tell him, going for politeness over sincerity, because truthfully he does look older, with a few grey hairs and a little bit more 'moss on the rock' as Kiran would say. 'Though, Andrew, I have to tell you, at one point I thought you were dead. You disappeared online,' I tell him. I love this new honest me; I can't imagine admitting this to him previously, either.

'Oh yes, the name!' He looks a little self-conscious. 'It's a bit pretentious, I know. But there was another Andrew Power, a fellow who plays the flute; we kept getting mixed up. And I thought it would be good to have a stage persona. You know, to keep the paparazzi at bay.' He grins.

'You have done very well though,' I tell him. 'I just listened to your canon for string quartet. It's beautiful, really.'

'Thank you,' he says sincerely. 'But what about you? You disappeared as well! I googled you too, you know . . . What are you up to now?'

It sounds such small potatoes compared to him, with his fellowships and scholarships and film compositions. But I'm proud and happy to tell him what I do, because I love it.

'So that's why I couldn't find you – I was looking for a singer, not a teacher. But it sounds like you have a lot of music in your life,' Andrew says. 'That's a beautiful thing.'

'Yes – I do.' I smile at him, wondering if he always used that type of hippy-ish phrase. I can't decide if he seems more like an old friend or a pleasant stranger – or both; it's almost as if he is one of my long-lost cousins. Which, I realize now, he could easily have been. I have to bite my lip so as not to laugh.

'And are you still singing?' Andrew asks.

'Well, not really. But I'm going to start again.' I explain about my hiatus, which leads me on to telling him about my dad.

'I'm so sorry to hear that,' he says. He reaches out a hand and pats me briefly on the arm. 'That's a terrible thing. I remember you talking about him – he sounded like a great man. The two of you were close.'

'We were. But Andrew, I know you lost your dad too and I was thinking recently, I never asked you about that . . . I didn't understand at the time what it was like.'

'I probably wouldn't have told you much,' Andrew says. 'I think I sort of packed it away. There's a certain shame about losing a parent that young. You feel different, and nobody wants to at that age. It's hard at any age. But I can tell you it gets better. The load doesn't get any lighter, but you get stronger, better at carrying it, is all I can say really.'

I nod, finding this comforting somehow.

'But I wouldn't have been able to tell you that at the time . . . I was very closed off about the whole topic, or anything like it, and it caused me problems for years really, in my relationships . . . I'm getting better, though some would say that's debatable.' He smiles at me ruefully and sips his pint.

Some instinct, or inkling, leads me to ask him, 'So are you seeing anyone at the moment?'

'I am, yeah.' He nods. 'She's a singer, as it happens. A mezzo soprano, called Zuzana – Zu. She's Czech. So she's on tour a lot, and I travel too. But we're making it work.'

I nod and think how just a few weeks – a few days! – ago this scenario would have filled me with jealousy: Andrew as a successful composer, dating a no doubt beautiful Czech opera singer. But now I think: good for her, not for me. 'Making it work', with all its compromises and phone calls and stolen weekends, Skypes and calendar summits – it sounds tiring and stressful and ultimately unsatisfactory. Though I hope they're happy; he deserves it.

'Does she know we're meeting up tonight?' I ask, suddenly.

'Oh yes, she does.'

'And she doesn't mind? How did you explain it?' I ask, dying to know.

'I told her the truth ... that we met on holiday and had a romance, back in the day, when we were very young. That we busked together and then we kept in touch as friends. And we lost touch, but I had made this commitment to turning up – so even if I hadn't wanted to, which I obviously did, I felt like I should.' He raises his shoulders. 'She's fairly superstitious – like a lot of singers, in my experience. She has the whole thing with the lucky necklace and all the rituals before each performance. So she said I should keep my promise – sort of karma, I suppose.'

I nod but I'm thinking: *as friends*? Then I realize that I can actually ask him. 'Is that how you thought of me, Andrew? As a friend?'

'Well ...' He makes a face. 'Somewhat? Maybe not entirely? Yeah, maybe I massaged the truth a bit there. Am I a terrible person? But I knew you would have moved on with your life, like I have.'

I nod, not feeling terribly inclined to be honest, at this point, about how very close I came to not moving on at all. I take a moment to feel solidarity for that other Norah, who would have turned up and had her expectations totally dashed. Especially when he continues, 'I wasn't expecting to rekindle anything. How could we? You remember what you said – about jazz being all about the moment.'

'No, you said that!' I protest. 'It was about wine. You said wine was about the moment.'

'Did I? I don't remember that.' He frowns, then

laughs. 'Which I suppose proves my point. We shared a special season, but maybe it wasn't meant to continue beyond that.'

'Fate without destiny,' I say, remembering Joe's words.

'Ah,' says Andrew. 'That's great. That's it exactly – fate without destiny. I was completely wrapped up in my work, you know, when we met. I didn't have the maturity for a serious relationship or any interest in one, really. I loved emailing you, but to be honest I wasn't in that head space. I do remember feeling sad when you got your boyfriend – Mark, was it?'

'Matt.'

'Yes. But that time that you couldn't come to my concert . . .'

'Yes! I remember that. I wish I had made it.'

'It's OK, Norah. I was disappointed when I read your email – but I was also slightly relieved. Because even if you didn't have a boyfriend, I didn't see how we could go back to how things were – or continue them, once I was back in Berlin.'

'It would have been hard,' I agree. This is rather sad to hear, but I suppose it confirms my instinct, at the time, that it would be too hard to say goodbye to him all over again. And Kiran's pragmatic instinct that he just wasn't into the idea of rekindling anything. If he had wanted to continue seeing me, of course I would have. I probably would have moved to Berlin, had he asked me. But that didn't happen, and it's OK.

'Anyway – here we are now,' Andrew says, as if he's

311

reading my thoughts. 'Isn't that the miracle? The fact that you and I turned up tonight, after ten years, for old times' sake – that's a beautiful thing. And I still remember the music you taught me, and maybe you've remembered a few of the tunes I inflicted on you.'

'Oh! That reminds me! You'll never believe what happened the other night – I mean yesterday.' I tell him about my impromptu gig at the wedding, and singing 'Going Back'.

'No way! I'd say you brought the house down. And singing Dusty! Fair play.' He shakes his head in admiration. 'I wish I'd been there to hear it. Wasn't it lucky for them you showed up?'

'It was lucky you taught me that song.'

'I suppose so. It's funny, isn't it? How we can just be in one another's company, for however short a time, but we leave our mark on each other. It's a bit like your dad, you know, with the music.' He smiles at me. 'He taught you all those songs, didn't he? So when you sing, you're bringing that part of him back. And then you'll teach the music to other folk, and on it goes.'

'A canon,' I say.

'Exactly. Did he play an instrument? I can't remember if you said.'

'No, he never did. He was a quantity surveyor. He never played a note in his life – he was just a fan.'

'No music without an audience. He must have been so proud of you,' says Andrew.

'Thanks. I think he was.' Oh, why does everything

make me cry these days? I clear my throat and gesture towards the barman, who obliges with another round, which Andrew accepts with a silent thumbs-up.

'You had such a beautiful voice,' Andrew continues. 'Still do, I'm sure. Why did you give it up, really? I'm sure it wasn't just losing him?'

I sigh. 'Probably not. If I'm being honest, I think I also wasn't hungry enough. I just wasn't prepared to make singing my whole entire life and try and market myself and promote myself to be saleable or try and be the next Joss Stone or whatever . . . I hated all that. I just wanted to sing.'

'So just sing,' says Andrew. 'That's the secret, Norah. I've done reasonably well; I'm not Arvo Pärt or Hans Zimmer – but it doesn't matter. I learned a long time ago that no matter whatever so-called heights I reach, there's always going to be some score I didn't get asked to write, or some prize that somebody else wins, or someone else who gets a better review . . . so now I try to just do my thing. The work is its own reward.' He breaks off and laughs. 'Sorry, I didn't mean to give you a philosophy lecture.'

We chat a bit more: about music, and our work and our lives in London and Dublin – Andrew says he has a place in Portobello, which causes me to do a double-take until he explains that this is also the name of an area of Dublin.

'It's a little terraced cottage,' he says. 'It had three teeny-tiny bedrooms upstairs but I knocked them all together to make one massive master bedroom with a free-standing bath – I love it.'

There was a time when I would have thought that sounded marvellous and had all kinds of fantasies about visiting him there and experiencing both the bed and the bath ... Now I think it sounds like a terrible idea in terms of resale or rental value, not to mention the strong bachelor vibes it's giving out. It proves my theory that you can date someone and still continue to be very much a bachelor. I wonder if Zuzana has views on it and the lack of a room for any kind of future Czech-Irish baby; but no doubt she knows what she's doing.

As if following my train of thought, Andrew asks, 'So how long have you been with – sorry, I'm desperate with names. John?'

'Joe.' I smile at the 'desperate', remembering this was the same word Lasairfhiona used. 'That's a tricky question. I've known him for ever, but ... it's new, between us.'

'That's great. He's a lucky man,' says Andrew. 'What does he do?'

As I explain, it occurs to me that Andrew and Joe have a few things in common – aside from me. They're both creative, obviously, and talented and charming. And they're both down-to-earth, easy-going and unpretentious. But I think Joe is a tougher character somehow – he's stronger. I could lean and lean on Joe, and he would never budge; he would be like a rock.

Whereas I could imagine Andrew, without meaning to, sliding away at the first hint of pressure. Partly I'm basing this on what he said about not being ready for a relationship – which I think isn't fully resolved – and partly I remember him not really acknowledging my music going badly when I told him in my emails.

Or maybe it's just a question of their priorities. With Andrew, I think his music would always come first, and he would put the best of himself into it, and I'd have to make do with what was left over. It was that way from the start, after all. He had his career to consider, but it wasn't as if he couldn't have tried to base himself in London or at least visit. I blamed myself for not replying to his offer to meet up, but wasn't it a bit too little too late? Even the fact that he's turned up ten minutes late this evening is quite revealing, I think.

For a moment I can imagine a parallel life, where I did follow Andrew to New York ten years ago, and then to California and Berlin, eking out some kind of living on the fringes of his existence, helping him fill in forms for grants or waiting patiently while he scribbled in composition notebooks. Joe is dedicated to his art, but I know that won't stop him placing me front and centre of everything he does. Like with his job offer in Japan. It would probably be a great opportunity for him, but it seems like he's planning to turn it down, to stay in London.

'And we stayed in these amazing tents, in the desert in New Mexico. You got up, when the sun was rising . . .'

Andrew is telling some story about his residency with the Wurlitzer Foundation, which is interesting, but it's gone on for a while, leaving me time to ponder something. I don't even know how interested Joe is in this Japan job. But if he is, he might be giving away a great opportunity that he would consider if he was single. What did he say? *There are other things I want more.* And I haven't given it a second's thought. And I've been sitting at this hotel bar, chatting to an old flame, for – I check my watch – well over an hour and a half. In fact, it's been two hours.

'Do you need to beat feet?' Andrew asks.

'I do.' I stand up and start pulling on my coat. 'Sorry, Andrew – I didn't see the time.'

'Well.' Andrew gets to his feet. 'It's been such a pleasure to see you, Norah. Let's not leave it another ten years. Here, let me give you my email address – and you can give me yours. Your real one. When I'm next in London I'll come and talk to your students, if you'd like. And I'll take you and Joe out to dinner.'

'Would you really? That would be great. I'd love to meet Zuzana too.' I lean forward to give him a hug, and I'm deeply relieved to find that I feel nothing, except affection for an old friend.

'I almost forgot,' Andrew says, as we're waiting for the bill. 'I have something for you . . .' He reaches into his satchel and takes out a photograph which has been sandwiched in a hardback diary. 'Remember her?'

It's the photo that he took of me while we were waiting for the ferry at Lake Garda. I'm smiling at the camera, hand shading my squinting eyes, wearing my black dress. It's like meeting an old friend. I stare at the girl in the picture, and think: yes, I remember you.

'I found it while I was clearing out my old room at home . . . My mother has been after me for years to sort it out. I found this in a drawer. And I felt a bit funny keeping it – you know, with Zu.'

I'm a little surprised to hear this – isn't that a bit of an overreaction? But then I imagine how I'd feel about Joe keeping a photo of an old girlfriend and I get it. Andrew continues, 'So I brought it along tonight just in case you showed up. I still can't believe you actually did . . . But anyway, there you go. A little something to remember our trip.'

I don't need the photo to do that, but I thank Andrew anyway and tuck it into my bag. I feel so lucky that these two men, who have been circling in my head for so long, have settled into their rightful places: Andrew is a pleasant old pal, and Joe is the one who – well, the one.

It takes ages to pay the bill, but eventually we're outside. I reach for my phone to text Joe, to tell him that I'm on my way back to the hotel, but it's dead. It's somehow 8.30 already.

'You'll have to listen out for the bells, at midnight,' Andrew says. 'They ring out all over the city, you should hear them very well from the Shelbourne.'

He smiles down at me, and for a second I do feel something close to a pang, for what never was. But it's only for a minute, and then it's gone. With a final good-bye, we go our separate ways – him to his mum's place in Bray, while I start racing in the direction of the Shelbourne, without a backward glance.

## 24. What a Difference a Day Makes

*Christmas Eve, 2019, 8.45 p.m.*

As I walk briskly towards the hotel, I'm a little worried that Joe might not have expected me to stay quite so long, or to go somewhere that wasn't Bewley's – what if he came back and looked for me? Hopefully he'll understand that we had a lot to catch up on.

More seriously, I'm thinking again about the job offer in Japan. I'm still not clear on the details, but it surely represents a big opportunity as well as a great adventure. I wonder where in Japan. Presumably Tokyo or another big city. My knowledge of the country is fairly hazy, but I've seen pictures: lots of beautiful forested countryside as well as big cities. Caroline went, and she said the food was the best she'd ever had. And I remember my dad telling me that there was a big jazz scene there, particularly in Tokyo.

Would I be completely mad to even suggest to Joe that I'd consider going there with him, if he moved? I do love my job, but wasn't I worrying, at the end of term, about blinking and finding myself still there in thirty years? As I approach the Shelbourne, I decide that I'd better talk to him properly about it. I'm obviously leaping many stages ahead but I want Joe to know that I'm open to anything he really wants, because I am madly in love with him.

I stop short, on the slushy pavement, as it hits me. I'm madly in love with Joe!

I run inside up the red carpet, smiling at the uniformed doorman, and hurtle into the lobby. I take a quick look among the crowds in the downstairs bar, to check that he's not waiting there with a book, but I don't expect him to be. I'm too impatient to wait for the lift, so I run up both flights of stairs until I arrive, breathless, at his door and knock.

There's no answer. I give it five minutes and knock again, but still nothing. Getting worried now, I let myself into my room and without bothering to switch on the lights, I jam my phone into my charger, to see if he's sent me a message. It's completely dead so it won't do anything at all at first. As I wait for it to charge, I gaze out the window at Stephen's Green with its Christmas lights and wonder if he decided to – what? To do some last-minute shopping? Suddenly I remember Lasairfhiona and her invitation to Christmas Eve drinks. But I'm sure he wouldn't have gone out with her after everything that happened between us. Would he?

My phone has one per cent battery by now, but there's nothing from Joe. I send him a message – *I'm back in my room. Where are you?* But there's no reply. I give it five long minutes. Nothing at all; no blue tick, even. Then I go out to his room and knock again; silence, so

I go back to my room. Maybe he decided that I was out for the night with Andrew, so he has gone for drinks with Lasairfhiona as he originally planned. I suppose that's fair enough, but I feel upset – and worried. Suddenly I feel a horrible, uncanny shiver. Could something have happened to him – some horrible misadventure on the way back to the hotel? If he's run into some kind of trouble, of what kind I don't know, I'll never forgive myself.

To distract myself, I open my bag and take out the photo Andrew gave me. I hardly recognize myself, I look such a baby – and I'm so slim, too, though I couldn't see it at the time. I remember feeling self-conscious in my bikini on that holiday, but now I think: why didn't I just wear bikinis all day long? As I gaze at the picture, I realize something else. I came here looking for Andrew – but maybe the person I really needed to find was that younger me. The Norah who took risks, sang in bars, travelled around Italy and went on holiday with a man she barely knew. I'm not that girl any more, and I wouldn't want to be. But maybe I can find some way of recapturing that sense of adventure, and fearlessness.

But these life lessons, as I know by now, are never one and done, because it doesn't stop me fretting about Joe. Of course, it's harder to be fearless when you have so much more to lose. What my experiences have taught me, though, is that, whatever happens next, whatever life throws at me, I will survive. Even if I lose

Joe somehow, I will be OK. More than OK. Though I still wish I knew where on earth he was.

There's a knock on the door. 'Norah?'

I've never moved so fast; within less than two seconds I'm scrabbling to open the door and then hurling myself into his arms. 'Joe! Where were you? I thought you were dead! Or with Lasairfhiona!' Which would be better than being dead, of course, but I wouldn't want to have to choose. I kiss him deeply, then pull him into the room and start to kiss him again.

'Wow,' he says after a minute. 'I'm not going to lie: if this is what happens when I fall asleep by mistake, I'm going to do it more often.'

'Oh God, you fell asleep? How *could* you?' I can't believe he's been peacefully snoozing while I've been going out of my mind.

'Well, you were on your date. So I did a bit of pacing back in my room, but it's been a busy few days, and I don't know about you, but I haven't been sleeping at all well. I just thought I'd close my eyes for five minutes – and then I just woke up and saw your text, twenty seconds ago.' He pauses. 'So – how was your reunion with Andrew? Still crazy after all those years?'

'It was fine. It was nice.' I have to think for a minute to recall how exactly it was. I'll tell Joe later about Pat's perceptive comments about my 'closure' with Andrew.

'"Fine" and "nice" sound like exactly what I was hoping for. I have to admit, I did wonder if I was completely crazy, letting you go off for a drink with your old flame . . . But I also wanted you to lay the ghost, so to speak. So that there's no more unfinished business.'

'There isn't . . . or rather, there is, but it's between you and me. Come here.' And I pull him back down on to the bed, and he takes my face in his hands and kisses me, and then we stop talking for a while.

Some time later, we're tangled in each other's arms, contemplating whether we're hungry enough to order room service or whether we should just run a bath. I'm leaning towards the bath option, but Joe says he doesn't want me getting hungry and angry later, so we order two cheeseburgers and a bottle of red wine.

'The perfect Christmas Eve meal,' Joe says, after it's arrived.

'Isn't it?' I start on mine, while he pours me a glass of red wine. 'Oh, that's better . . . I'm not sure if I've actually eaten anything today, have you? Or wait, I had a toasted sandwich earlier.' I shake my head; this whole holiday business has not been great for my cholesterol. 'But, Joe, there's something I want to talk to you about.'

He looks wary. 'OK . . . What is it? Andrew wants to be in a thrupple with us?'

'A what? Oh – no. Though he does want us to meet his girlfriend, Zu. She's an opera singer apparently.' I start digging into the fries, which are every bit as salty and greasy as they should be. 'No, I wanted to talk to you about Japan. Or ask you about Japan.' I make the ultimate sacrifice and pause my chip inhalation, so that

I can talk properly. 'Is it a big opportunity for you? Because I don't want you to miss out.'

'Really?' He holds my gaze for a long moment, and I feel momentarily dizzy from the look in his eyes.

'Really. Are you keen to go? Because . . . I'd consider it,' I say.

'Consider what – going long-distance?'

'Ugh,' is my uncensored answer. 'I suppose. But honestly, the thought of having to Skype you and deal with time differences and get on a plane in order to see you – when I've only just found you, so to speak – sounds awful. If we're going to do it, I'd rather just do it.'

'So you'd come with me?' he asks, with that dizzying look again. 'What about work?'

'I'd probably ask for a sabbatical,' I admit. 'And I would definitely have to be able to work there, so we'd have to look into visas. But what about you? How do you feel about it?'

'Well . . .' he pushes away his empty plate and wipes his fingers on the linen napkin. 'Honestly? I don't want to go. I mentioned it as a kind of emergency ripcord – but I didn't want to pull it, particularly.'

'Really?' I feel confused now as my hazy visions of temples and forests and skyscrapers and sushi fade from view.

'No. I am doing pretty well where I am, you know. Taking on bigger roles, doing new things – I'm not eager to change it. The money is pretty good, but the hours would be very intense, more so than here. But . . .

it's very nice to know that you're open to it.' He pauses. 'Nice isn't even close to being the right word. It's wonderful. To know that you would even consider it. So that was why I asked you all those questions. Sorry, that was a bit self-indulgent.'

'It's OK.'

He raises an eyebrow. 'It's not that I'm not thrilled. But what caused the change of heart about me – I mean, about us? This morning you weren't so sure.'

'It was no one particular thing – it was everything.' I hesitate, trying to put in words how I'm feeling. 'I suppose I've spent so long chasing shadows and carrying a lot of baggage around with me. And today I started to see how I can let it go, if that makes any kind of sense.'

He nods. 'I'm really glad. For your sake, as well.'

'I was scared too, honestly, Joe. I was scared of losing you completely . . .' I remember my conversation with Pat. 'I still am,' I admit.

'I know. But I'm not going anywhere,' says Joe. He pushes aside the tray and puts his arm around me so that we're both leaning back against the bed's padded headboard. 'By the way, on a less important note – your phone has been hopping. Do you want to take a look? Or not – it can wait.'

'Really?' I pick up my phone, which does indeed have lots of notifications. I check 'Yass Queens' first. The first message, sent at 6 p.m., is from Kiran and says, *BUSTED! My mum's been messaging with your mum – she tells me that you are on a sneaky romantic break with JOE?! As in our old friend JOSEPH LEE? WTF? When were you going to tell us?*

Caroline's message, sent immediately afterwards, says, *Norah, is this true? I've always thought the two of you would be great together* ♥ *Pls tell all, am dying to hear?!*

I feel very relieved. It's not that I thought she would object, but there's a difference between not objecting to something and being wholeheartedly happy. I wouldn't have let it stop me, if she wasn't – but I'm awfully glad that she is.

Then Kiran, two minutes later, *YES – UPDATE PLEASE?*

I show Joe. 'This is what I've got. What about you?'

'Similar . . . Kiran's not very discreet, is she?'

'No. But she must be surprised. They never saw us together, did they?'

'They do now.' He shows me a message on the boys' chat. Paul: *Rumours are reaching us that you might have ditched our Friendmas for a reason – a reason with long curly hair. Can you confirm or deny?*

'We don't have to reply,' Joe says, flinging his phone back on the bed. 'Let them work themselves up into a frenzy, it will be fun.'

'Really, Joe?' I would have thought that he would be even more anxious than me to be on-message and explain ourselves to them. But he's far more interested in a lock of my hair, which he's twirling around his fingers.

'Yes, really.' He grins at me. 'I honestly don't care what they think. If you're happy I'm happy.'

'Me too. But look, let's throw them a crumb, since it's Christmas. We could send a picture?'

Joe raises one eyebrow.

'Not like that, you twerp . . . I'll put on my dressing gown.' I reach for my hotel bathrobe, and slip into it, freeing all my hair from under the collar with some difficulty. 'Lean in beside me and we'll take one together.'

We smile at the camera together; then at the last minute I turn to kiss his cheek, just before the phone clicks. Next minute, the picture is winging its way to London and to our friends on the main group chat. It's like waiting for the sound of thunder after lightning; within less than five seconds, both of our phones start fizzing and hopping with emojis and messages ranging from the affectionate and sentimental to the sarcastic and downright indecent.

'Uh-oh.' Joe holds his at arms' length. 'We've done it now.'

'Yes, we have.' I beam at him. 'Good, now let's put those away. Oh, I just thought of something. You know those five weddings I was invited to next year?'

'I certainly do. Pains in the arse – how dare they invite you to a lovely wedding, when you could be sitting at home counting your flights-and-tights money.'

This makes me laugh, and suddenly I can't stop. All the tension and emotion of the last few days is fizzing up inside me, and I spend a good few minutes laughing helplessly, while Joe looks at me in puzzlement, before I manage to calm myself down. 'Well, maybe I'll go after all – and you could come with me, as my plus one? And, Joe, I'm going to start singing again. Maria's putting together a gig in February and she's asked me to sing . . . would you come and see us? It's in Walthamstow, though. Bit far, I know.'

'I don't know, this is all sounding very onerous. Weddings *and* a gig?' He leans down and kisses me. 'Yes, Norah. I would go to the ends of the earth for you – I'll certainly go to Walthamstow.'

As we kiss again, I hear the sound of bells starting to peal out all over the city, just as Andrew predicted. Nothing on this trip has turned out remotely the way I thought it would, and I'll be eternally thankful for it. This is turning out to be the best Christmas I could ever have hoped for – and if the signs are right, next year will be even better.

# Epilogue: You Make Loving Fun

## *Christmas Eve, 2020*

'Well, it's fair to say that this year hasn't been exactly what we expected,' Joe says. 'But I'm grateful that I had you to help me get me through it . . . Merry Christmas.'

'Me too. Merry Christmas, Joe.' I clink my flute against his and watch the bubbles rise and twinkle in the candlelight.

We're in Joe's flat in Bloomsbury. The purchase of his new flat in Acton fell through over the summer, as did the new building for his company. So he's held off his search for now – partly because neither of us want him to live so far west while I'm still in North London, and partly because we have very tentatively discussed the idea of buying a place together. So we're back in the same room where we were last December. Except that this time, instead of my former perch beside the fireplace, we're both on his couch, my feet in his lap, and in our soft clothes – in fact, I'm wearing the flannel shirt he had on last time, having annexed it quite early on this winter. And there's a lot more evidence of me around the place – not just the drawer of things I keep in his bedroom, and my laptop and teaching materials, but also my trumpet and music stand. Joe's place is a lot more soundproofed than mine, and the flat downstairs is empty. Obviously, my singing has had to take a back seat this year. The gig in February, at the Greyhound in Walthamstow, was my first and last appearance, and I don't know when I'll be able to sing in public, with other people, again.

'Are you sad about not seeing your mum tomorrow?' Joe asks.

I shake my head. 'Not really – she'll be with Miles and Amanda so she won't be alone; that's the main thing. And you're not seeing your family either. So we're both in the same boat. And anyway – I am really happy to be able to do it just the two of us. I'm not such a fan of family Christmases, I've decided.'

'Not even if Emer or John invited you over?' Joe asks.

I smile and say, 'Maybe. I think I might let them meet me in real life before committing to a Christmas together, though.' One of the minor disappointments of last year was a cancelled trip in May to meet my Irish cousins. Marita and I made contact before we left Dublin – Joe insisted that I call her, and she came to meet us in the Shelbourne on Stephen's Day, as I now call Boxing Day, and we had a very pleasant and surprisingly emotional chat. She was also able to explain to me the difference between a first cousin once removed (which is what she is, as my dad's cousin) and second cousins, which are her children. I've since made friends with Emer and John, all online; Emer, astonishingly enough, is a music teacher, and John plays the tenor saxophone when he's not working in an accountancy firm. I've even managed to join them on Zoom for a couple of family quizzes. And I have a standing invitation to come back and visit them in Dublin as soon as that's possible – maybe on the way to visiting Pat and Helena in Westport, County Mayo. I follow the bookshop on Instagram, and the huge skies and bleak beauty of the landscape have become a kind of tantalizing dream which Joe and I keep promising ourselves we'll reach one day.

The oven beeps, and Joe goes to take out a tray of sausage rolls – Mum's speciality, which she now sells locally, though these were a freebie. She is in the process of building up a mini catering business, Dinners by Deborah: she's filling the freezers of all the time-poor and cash-rich denizens of Ealing and Chiswick and now has her sights set on Barnes.

'I never want to have another boss again,' she told me. 'I should have done this years ago. But it's never too late, is it? I think I've got at least another two career changes in me before I keel over.'

Mum's new business – and the huge success of Joe's film, released at exactly the right moment to millions of desperate parents – are among the few bright spots in a year that has otherwise been so awful for so many people. Even we, who are so outrageously lucky, have found it hard. I've lost count of the sleepless nights

I've spent worrying about my students for various reasons, and teaching online has been gruelling: twice the effort for half the effect. But throughout the trials and challenges, the one shining light has been Joe – the rainbow at the end of my storm. Loving him, and being loved by him, is something I can't describe in words, and barely even in music; just an endless delight. I was right about him being a rock, because I've leaned on him more this year than I could ever have imagined leaning on anyone, and he hasn't faltered once. There is nothing I don't like about him.

'Nothing?' Kiran teased me once on our weekly Zoom session.

'Nothing?' Caroline asked, her new engagement ring flashing as she adjusted her screen.

I thought carefully. 'Well, he still has terrible taste in music. But we're discovering a bit of common ground. I played him Miles Davis's "Kind of Blue" again, and he said he could just about stand it, as background music. And we both like Fleetwood Mac. It's a start.'

Interrupting my thoughts, Joe says, 'Do you remember this time last year, Norah? When you came over, and I made you a cocktail, and you strong-armed me into going to Dublin with you?'

'I strong-armed you? That is not the way it happened!' I protest. 'You were all over it. You and your ulterior motives.'.

'Of course I had ulterior motives,' Joe says. 'I didn't think he would show up, and I wanted to be there to pick up the pieces. I was amazed when he did rock up. Even though he was ten minutes late.'

Joe still teases me about Andrew's timekeeping, and on the one occasion I've been in touch with Andrew this year – when he spoke to my students over Zoom, about composing – Joe told me to make sure to tell him a time that was ten minutes earlier.

'OK, OK,' I say, nudging him with my foot. 'You know, I think you should be grateful to Andrew really. Because if he hadn't arranged to meet me in Dublin, you and I never would have gone there together. And then – who knows what would have happened? Laugh at fate all you like; I think that was fate at work.'

'Actually, I'm more grateful to your mum,' Joe says. 'Had she not changed her plans at Christmas, you wouldn't have gone haring off to meet Andrew. And if you hadn't decided to do that, I might not have woken up to how I felt about you.'

'Don't,' I say, horrified at the thought. Because without our trip together I might not have realized how I felt about Joe either – and I could have let the love of my life slip through my fingers.

'It didn't happen,' Joe says, just like he did right after saving me from the speeding car on Killiney Hill. 'Look, I know it's not Christmas yet but . . . I have something for you.'

'A present? I thought we weren't doing presents until tomorrow!' Joe is so wonderful at buying presents, and I'm terrible. I got him some smart-touch gloves, but I know he's going to outdo me like he did last year, when he gave me the emerald pendant necklace I had admired in the vintage shop in Dublin. He went back there after I left, showed the assistant my picture and asked her what I'd been looking at.

'Just a little stocking-filler. I do have something else for tomorrow but I thought this could be fun for this evening . . .' He produces a giant package, wrapped in brown paper with his signature ink stamp on it.

'You didn't have to! Is it a hamster cage?' I start tearing at one end of it.

'What? No, it's not a hamster cage!' I forgot that this is one thing I would change about Joe: I thought it would be fun to get a pet hamster, but he's vetoed it until he – or we – get a bigger place. 'Open it up.'

'Oh – wow.' I finish tearing off the paper and sit back on my heels. It's a karaoke machine. 'Joe! This is so cool! Thank you so much. I love it. And I love you.'

'I know you miss singing,' Joe says. 'And I know this isn't the same, but maybe it can keep you going until you can do it properly. Here – pour us both another drink and I'll set it up.' I'm still hanging around his neck kissing him, but I break off just for long enough to make us a Poinsettia cocktail: champagne, cranberry juice and a dash of Grand Marnier.

I've barely sipped at mine when he stands up. 'That should do for now. Why don't we try . . .' He presses a few buttons, and some familiar chords start playing. It's 'Baby, It's Cold Outside'. 'Remember this? I had it playing when you came inside, that night, back in December last year . . . You explained to me that it was all wrong.'

'I did indeed.'

'Aha, yes, but – there are some runarounds. John Legend has done new lyrics. Or – and I like this one – you can also swap the parts around so it's less, ah, problematic. Like this. I sing the first part . . .' I let him start and then, laughing, I join in and sing the male part. I've never sung with Joe before, and, as I expected, he sounds absolutely terrible. But he's great fun, he brings a lot of character to it, and you can't fault his commitment – which is exactly what you want in a karaoke partner.

'That was great! I love this – thank you, Joe,' I say, when we're finished.

'You sounded great. Me, not so much. Have you thought any more about your stage name, by the way?' he asks casually. 'Norah Baker still works. Or what about . . . Norah Lee? Or Norah Lee Jones? I like the sound of that . . .'

I turn around from queuing up songs and look him full in the face to see if this is just a joke, or if he means what I think he means. Seeing as his surname is Lee.

'Are you . . .'

He nods, looking the same combination of terrified and ecstatic that I feel. 'I am, if you are. I know you'd prefer to have a measured discussion first, with a list of pros and cons. But I just had to ask. Norah, you know I love you. Will you marry me?'

'Joe! Oh my God – of course I will! Hang on.' I turn around and type into the search bar with shaking hands, until the song I want starts playing: 'Signed, Sealed, Delivered'. I have got more into Motown lately; it's so joyful and fun, and it can't be *all* jazz all the time.

'So is that a yes?' he asks, and a smile breaks out over his face as I nod and kiss him. Then he continues, 'Is this it now? Are you only going to communicate through the medium of songs, like in a musical?'

'No. Well, maybe!' I definitely feel like singing now – in a way I haven't in years. As Joe pulls me closer and kisses me again, I wonder how on earth we're going to plan a wedding with the way things are; but then I decide not to worry about it. If this past year has taught me anything at all, it's that there is no point in reliving the past or fretting about what's in store. From now on I'm going to try taking things one step at a time, hopeful about the future but also living fully in each moment, while I still have them.

# Acknowledgements

I'm so grateful to everyone who helped me during the writing of *Baby It's Cold Outside* or who worked their magic behind the scenes. Firstly, to everyone at Michael Joseph: thank you Rebecca Hilsdon for commissioning the story, and to Rebecca and Clare Bowron for the fantastic edits which lifted the book to a whole new level. Thanks also to Zana Chaka, Hanifa Frederick, Sriya Varadharajan and Katie Williams, and to Nick Lowndes and David Watson. Huge and heartfelt thanks also to my agent Rowan Lawton for her faith in me, without which this book would not exist.

I couldn't have written this book, either, without those who took time out of their busy lives to share their expertise with me. Thank you to Rosie Breckon and Ed Watkins, who advised me on what it's like to teach music in a secondary school. Thank you to Christina Kenny, who put me in touch with Ed and also provided the low-down on the teen scene for girls in early noughties Ealing (including her description of a raid that I have stolen almost word for word). Thank you to Edmund Joliffe, who was so generous with his time, and so much fun, for talking to me about life as a composer. Thank you also to Hermione Ruck-Keene, surely one of my best-connected friends! Thank you to

Ian Steplowski for taking time to share his expertise on character modelling. Yang Chi Ying was of invaluable help in filling in some details of Joe's background, not all of which are shown here: thank you Yang, I learned a lot. And thank you to the wonderful author Lijia Zhang, who advised me on *yuan fen*. All of these people have accumulated a lifetime's knowledge, of which only the tiniest tip of the iceberg is showing in this story – any mistakes are all my own. Thanks to my sister-in-law Anne and my niece Marianne for advising on Mountjoy Square and hipster Irish jokes. Also thank you to my friend and fellow writer Deirdre Mask, who encouraged me when I was wondering if it was crazy to think I could write an entire novel during a pandemic . . .

Last but not least, thanks to Alex: for supporting me in so many ways over the years, including weekends when I bashed at the keyboard. In the words of Fleetwood Mac: you make loving fun.

# A Note on Locations

The supper club in Mountjoy Square is fictional, but was inspired by a pop-up supper at Dublin's tenement museum in Henrietta St (14henriettast.ie). Pat and Helena's bookshop in Westport is also fictional but was inspired by the wonderful bookshop Tertualia, the Quay, Westport, Co. Mayo. The youth hostel in Verona exists and is still open, at 10 Via Santa Chiara (ostello-verona.it).

At the time of writing, Bewley's Café is open for takeaway only – which is a sad state of affairs. I can only hope that it will open its doors again soon, and that I'll make it there before too long, to order tea and a sticky bun.

# He just wanted a decent book to read ...

Not too much to ask, is it? It was in 1935 when Allen Lane, Managing Director of Bodley Head Publishers, stood on a platform at Exeter railway station looking for something good to read on his journey back to London. His choice was limited to popular magazines and poor-quality paperbacks – the same choice faced every day by the vast majority of readers, few of whom could afford hardbacks. Lane's disappointment and subsequent anger at the range of books generally available led him to found a company – and change the world.

*'We believed in the existence in this country of a vast reading public for intelligent books at a low price, and staked everything on it'*
**Sir Allen Lane, 1902–1970, founder of Penguin Books**

The quality paperback had arrived – and not just in bookshops. Lane was adamant that his Penguins should appear in chain stores and tobacconists, and should cost no more than a packet of cigarettes.

Reading habits (and cigarette prices) have changed since 1935, but Penguin still believes in publishing the best books for everybody to enjoy. We still believe that good design costs no more than bad design, and we still believe that quality books published passionately and responsibly make the world a better place.

So wherever you see the little bird – whether it's on a piece of prize-winning literary fiction or a celebrity autobiography, political tour de force or historical masterpiece, a serial-killer thriller, reference book, world classic or a piece of pure escapism – you can bet that it represents the very best that the genre has to offer.

## Whatever you like to read – trust Penguin.